Maxine Barry lives in Oxford. She is a full-time author and also practises calligraphy.

MAXINE BARRY

ISLAND DAZE

Complete and Unabridged

ULVERSCROFT
Leicester

First published in Great Britain in 2008 by
Robert Hale Limited
London

First Large Print Edition
published 2009
by arrangement with
Robert Hale Limited
London

British Library CIP Data

Barry, Maxine
  Island daze.—Large print ed.—
  Ulverscroft large print series: general fiction
  1. Kidnapping—Barbados—Fiction
  2. Stepmothers—Fiction 3. Romantic suspense novels
  4. Large type books
  I. Title
  823.9'14 [F]

  ISBN 978–1–84782–512–4

Published by
F. A. Thorpe (Publishing)
Anstey, Leicestershire

Set by Words & Graphics Ltd.
Anstey, Leicestershire
Printed and bound in Great Britain by
T. J. International Ltd., Padstow, Cornwall

This book is printed on acid-free paper

1

Florida, USA

Tahnee Sawyer parked her low-slung, classic Porsche in the first available parking lot she could find, and fairly leapt out, almost forgetting to lock it behind her. It was nearly noon, and the fierce Miami sun beat down on her head mercilessly as she ran across the crowded parking lot.

Ahead of her, the six-storey, brilliant-white building that was St Mark's Hospital sparkled cheerfully, looking like a newly made giant wedding cake, but Tahnee could only feel a dragging sense of dread as she dashed through its smoked-glass revolving door and into the cool lobby. Banks of ferns and a trickling fountain centrepiece went unnoticed as she headed straight for the low, walnut-veneered reception desk. St Mark's, a relatively new hospital with a first-rate reputation, catered mainly to the city's richest and choosiest citizens, so it was hardly surprising that her father's personal assistant had ordered him to be taken here when he'd collapsed at his desk less than half an hour ago.

'Calvin Sawyer, please?' Tahnee said breathlessly, almost afraid to say her father's name out loud in case the receptionist's face should fall, indicating the worst possible news. But the woman, in her fifties and with firmly waved, dark brown hair, simply tapped the keys on her console, read the information on her screen then smiled briefly up at her and said, 'Take the elevator to the third floor, and follow the dark blue line to the Breverman Wing. You need to speak to the nurse manning the desk there.'

Tahnee took a deep, calming breath and thanked her, then moved off on legs that felt distinctly wobbly beneath her. Frustrating, when everything in her screamed at her to hurry. She'd been working at her gallery, The Spindlewood Tree, when she'd got the call from Marisa, her father's PA, telling her that he'd been taken ill, and it had taken her a heart-rending half-hour or so to negotiate the city's fierce traffic. But her mobile phone had remained reassuringly silent throughout the journey, and now that she was here at last, she reminded herself once more that no news was good news.

She pressed the button to call the elevator with a finger that shook as she lifted it. A woman holding a bunch of flowers and a man clutching a teddy bear both glanced at her as they joined her in the wait for the next car. The woman noted her white face and the fine trembling that shook her small, five-foot, five-inch frame and smiled in sympathy, sensing a soul in turmoil. And hoped that the pretty little thing wasn't heading for bad news.

The man, a forty-something executive with a major radio station, noticed only her slender body, which wore a tailor-made pants suit in mint green as if she'd been born on a catwalk. He was still eyeing her delightfully rounded derriere as the elevator opened and they all piled in. Only then did he notice her face, and his eyes rounded. The most striking thing about her was, perhaps, her hair — a blonde so white it was almost silver, and cut in a style that reminded him of some weird sci-fi series. Her fringe was dead straight at either end, but dipped into a razor-sharp V in the middle of her forehead, the middle point of which reached to the bridge of her nose. Cut high on the back of her neck, leaving her nape fully exposed, two silver wings then swung down across her cheeks, to end with two equally sharp Vs, pointing exactly to each corner of her mouth, which was wide and generous. The shape of her geometric hair only highlighted her striking triangular-shaped face, and big, violet-coloured eyes.

Those stunning eyes barely met his as the doors closed behind them, and she reached out impatiently to press the number three button on the elevator panel.

As she stepped forward to do so, her scent, light and floral, wafted gently in the enclosed space, and the man, noticing the older woman eyeing him with an amused look, quickly glanced away.

Tahnee was oblivious to the male interest focused on her as she willed the car to ascend the few floors more quickly. Once it slid open, she shot out and glanced around, picking out the dark blue line that led off towards the east. In a matter of moments she'd found the relevant desk, and the nurse in attendance again tapped her details into the computer. 'He's in room 42, Doctor Galsworthy is with him. I'll just let him know you're here. You're the patient's daughter, you said?'

Tahnee swallowed hard and nodded, too relieved to speak. Her father wasn't dead. *He wasn't dead. He wasn't dead.* The words ricocheted around her head, making her feel dizzy with relief, and she wobbled a few steps towards the nearest chair and abruptly sat down. She had to wait for a few more agonizing minutes, before the nurse came back.

'You can go in now. Take the next corridor on your right, and it's about halfway down.'

Tahnee nodded and set off, aware of her heart tripping quickly in her breast. The corridors were white, cool and elegant, with photographs of Miami's native flora and fauna decorating the wall spaces at frequent intervals. The all-pervading scent of disinfectant and air freshener, however, reminded her of where she was. The last time she'd been in a hospital was when her mother had died when she was only ten. The memory of that made her hands and feet go suddenly cold, and when she tapped on the door to number 42, she felt a sudden rush of nausea.

When she walked in the room, however, the first person she saw was her father, Calvin Sawyer, sitting up in a bed, and looking pale but undeniably alive and as take-charge as ever. He was talking to a tall, grey-haired man who didn't look impressed, while Mike Greening, a senior vice-president of Sawyer Enterprises, leaned against a wall, shaking his head in exasperation.

Tahnee understood why as she realized what her father was saying. ' . . . and then I can come back tomorrow, maybe in the afternoon, and you can do the tests then.'

'No!' The word exploded from her and made everyone jump, since none of the men had noticed her come in. Mike Greening, her favourite among her father's right-hand company men, grinned with relief at seeing her, and the tall grey-haired man, who could only be the doctor, stepped back, making room for her at the patient's bedside.

Calvin Sawyer scowled as his daughter came and perched on the edge of his bed, then smiled as she reached for his hand and kissed the back of his knuckles.

'There's no need for you to be here, sweetheart. Who called you?' Calvin muttered gruffly. 'Don't tell me — that fusspot, interfering, no-good secretary of mine. This time I'll fire her for sure.'

Tahnee half-laughed, half-sobbed to see her father so like his normal self. On the drive over she'd been fearing the worst — a massive heart attack, maybe, or a stroke. But apart from the fact that his voice seemed weaker than usual, he didn't seem much different from the last time she'd seen him — which had been for Sunday lunch. 'Dad, you fire Marisa at least once a month. You'd be shocked silly if she actually upped and went.'

Calvin grunted. Like his daughter, he wasn't tall, and his hair had long since gone white and wispy; but for all that he had a frame that was almost stick-thin, Calvin

6

Sawyer had always had 'presence'. And it radiated from him still, an almost electrical energy which fired a fierce determination to succeed. It was what had helped a Wichita farm boy to build one of the greatest privately owned manufacturing companies in the US of A. Not even going to college, he'd started with a small factory producing farming machinery when he was only nineteen, but had quickly expanded to producing washing machines, lawnmowers, power tools, plumbing and heating products, right down to hairdryers and curling tongs. In his twenties, he'd opened offices and factories on the east coast, then the west, and every state in between until, it seemed, virtually every household in America boasted at least one piece of machinery that bore the Sawyer trademark.

It had made him a billionaire before he was forty, and, less fortunately, as stubborn as a mule when it came to getting his own way.

'Daddy, what's going on?' Tahnee demanded sharply. 'Marisa said she found you slumped over your desk. What happened. Was it a heart attack?' She turned to look over her shoulder as she said this, spearing the doctor with her violet eyes.

The medical man hastened to reassure her. 'No, Miss Sawyer, we don't think so. We've

7

run an ECG and several other tests, but apart from a murmur that he's had for some time now, your father's heart seems to be pretty sound. But it's been under some stress, I think.'

Tahnee nodded, turning to look at her father again. 'It's those stomach pains again, isn't it? Daddy, you insisted it was just indigestion!'

Calvin Sawyer, who wasn't intimidated by presidents, monarchy, or even patent lawyers, shuffled a little on his bed under his daughter's accusing eyes, and mumbled something.

'What?' Tahnee said sharply. 'And don't lie, Daddy.'

'Probably was only indigestion,' Calvin insisted. 'That damned quack Malleson doesn't know his knees from his elbows.'

Philip Malleson had been Calvin's greatest friend and personal physician for years. It had been Philip who'd been called to the house when Rebecca Sawyer, Tahnee's mother, had fallen from her horse. Philip who'd treated her and got the ambulance to the house so quickly. Philip who'd kept pumping air into her, when her broken back had prevented her lungs from working. But all to no avail — she had died barely two hours after being admitted. And, of course, it had been Philip who'd treated Tahnee's childhood ailments, and who now tried to treat Calvin whenever he fell ill. Not that Calvin Sawyer would ever admit to being ill, even when a thermometer insisted he had a temperature of 102, and he was sneezing and coughing loudly enough to send the family spaniels running for cover.

'Daddy!' Tahnee said warningly. 'What did Philip say exactly? And when?'

Again Calvin muttered something, his grey eyes sliding away from hers, his fingers restlessly plucking the bedsheets.

'Doctor . . . er . . . ' Tahnee struggled to recall his name, and flushed guiltily when she couldn't.

'Galsworthy,' the doctor supplied, without having taken offence. 'And don't worry, I've already put in a call asking for Dr Malleson to come in.'

'See, Daddy,' Tahnee said, looking back at her father. 'If you don't tell us what's been going on, Philip will. Come on now, 'fess up. What's he been telling you?'

Calvin grunted. 'He's a fussy old hen. Just like you. A good thing you're an only child, my girl. Two daughters would drive me insane.'

Tahnee, aware that he was stalling, slowly folded both arms across her chest, a gesture that both her father and Mike Greening recognized of old. Mike had worked for Sawyers right from college, working his way up the executive ladder to the vice-presidency he now occupied. And during that time he'd been a frequent guest at the Sawyer mansion. He had two sons and a daughter of his own, and looked on Tahnee practically as one of his own. And so both men knew that when Tahnee crossed her arms like that, wild horses wouldn't move her.

'Oh, all right,' Calvin muttered crossly. 'Phil has been muttering about ulcers for years. Telling me I have 'em, telling me to drink milk, telling me to get tests, telling me to stop eating spices, to stop drinking bourbon, you name it. Load of rubbish. I'm fit as a fiddle.'

'Ulcers. Ahh,' Dr Galsworthy said with an air of enlightenment. 'I'll just be a moment.' And so saying, he stepped out of the room and was gone.

Tahnee looked witheringly across at Mike Greening. 'Did you know about this?'

Mike, a six-foot tall man with sandy hair and freckles, held up his hands, palms outwards, in a gesture of peace. 'I know he chews antacids as if they were candy, yes, and I've been on to him for years to get it checked out. But you know your father.'

'I haven't gone anywhere, you know,'

Calvin Sawyer butted in testily. 'I can speak for myself. And there's nothing to get het up about. I'll be right as rain tomorrow, you'll see.' And then he winced as a spasm of pain lanced into his stomach, and made him sit up and forward on the bed. Alarmed, Tahnee shot off the bed and grabbed her father's hand. As she did so, Dr Galsworthy came back with two orderlies. Noticing his patient's distress, he instantly went forward and held his fingers to the pulse in the older man's wrist, ignoring Calvin, who tried to snatch his hand away.

'We're going to take you down to ultrasound and X-ray, Mr Sawyer. Also, I'm afraid, you're going to have to swallow some foul-tasting gunk. Think you can manage that?'

Calvin, who'd turned a distinct shade of grey in the last few moments, grimaced. 'Course I can, man. I'm not an infant.'

Dr Galsworthy sighed, no doubt thinking — if not actually saying — that children probably made for far better patients.

Tahnee watched nervously as they wheeled her father's bed out of the room, then walked restlessly over to the window and stared outside. It was only then that she realized something that hadn't impinged on her before.

She turned, frowning, and said wearily to Mike, 'Where's Cordelia?'

Bathsheba, Barbados

At the same moment that Tahnee Sawyer asked Mike Greening the whereabouts of her stepmother, Dylan Gale signed his name to a set of papers with a satisfied flourish.

The man who watched him pensively visibly relaxed as the last of the papers were signed, and then reached towards a silver salver resting in the centre of a small coffee table, and lifted a somewhat dusty, cut-crystal decanter. He shook the amber liquid inside and murmured, 'Sherry?'

Dylan Gale shook his head, but watched as Gordon Forboys poured himself a generous glass and took a healthy sip. Slowly, he reached into his inside jacket pocket and withdrew the thick wedge of bearer bonds that Forboys had insisted upon. Even as he handed them over, however, he felt a slight sense of unease.

This was not his usual way of doing business.

Dylan had lived on the island all his life. His grandparents had emigrated there from the UK in the 1930s, and his father,

Geoffrey, had been born there. Dylan had then attended school at the Bridgetown Academy for Boys, and had only gone abroad for a brief three years to attend university in South Virginia. He'd come straight back to Barbados, however, determined to put his degree in Economics and Business Studies to good use, and had quickly homed in on tourism as the up-and-coming market to conquer.

Although his father's company still adhered traditionally to sugar cane, molasses, cotton and bananas — the island's major exports — he'd wanted to start his own company and be his own man. And had promptly done so. It had caused a minor family quarrel for a while, but now even his father had to admit that Gale Imperial, the name of Dylan's hotel chain empire, was a roaring success.

Dylan had been clever, buying old properties with charm and grace, and keeping the number of rooms small and intimate. This way, he didn't have to deal with new builds, or compete with the big multi-conglomerates that crowded out some of the Island's beaches. He'd also catered to the very top end of the market, hiring local but gifted cooks, buying the best of ingredients, the best of linens and furnishings, and attracting the more discerning holiday-maker. With the purchase of this latest historic building, with its sumptuous views across Tent Bay, he could easily visualize how the old house would look after it had been given a make-over, and almost hear the sound of appreciative, happy guests.

Then he frowned as Gordon Forboys all but snatched the bearer bonds from him and threw back the rest of his sherry. There was something so anxious about the way the man was behaving that Dylan simply couldn't shake the feeling that there was something very wrong about this whole deal.

'Well, I must be getting on,' Forboys said, slamming his glass down. 'And I'm sure you've got things to do as well, a man of your, er . . . industry.' Gordon was a small, dapper man in his early sixties, with something of a reputation as an eccentric. He'd lived in only two rooms of the big house, employing no servants and rarely being seen during the day. Some of the neighbouring children suspected him of being a vampire, but Dylan, who'd had him checked out thoroughly before entering into negotiations for the purchase of his house, knew that the man was simply a night owl, preferring to haunt Bridgetown's private clubs and casinos, while sleeping the days away.

'Yes, of course,' Dylan agreed quietly as

Forboys leapt to his feet and stuffed the bearer bonds into the voluminous pockets of a rather ancient and battered cream jacket. 'You'll want time to move any personal items out of the house, of course,' he began, but the old man was already waving a hand.

'No, no, old boy, already got what I want. You can have anything that's left, if you want it. Ah, that reminds me, here you go.' He all but threw a big bunch of keys at Dylan, who caught them niftily, and frowned again as the old man quickly made his way to the door. He'd never known anyone be in such a hurry to leave after selling up. He listened to the patter of his small feet as they scampered across the crackling old lino that still comprised the hall flooring, and then heard the solid 'clunk' of the old oak door as it closed behind him.

Leaving Dylan alone with the 1940s serviceable furniture, fading flock wallpaper and large ceiling fan that comprised the drawing room of his latest acquisition.

Restlessly he shook his head, still feeling uneasy. Although he'd had his solicitors check out the situation thoroughly, and there were definitely no legal problems incumbent with the sale of the house, he still felt there was something definitely odd about the way Forboys had acted. Eccentricity was one thing, but even that explanation had its limits.

First, Forboys had gone to Dylan, asking if he'd be interesting in acquiring the house; for some reason, he'd refused outright to put it publicly on the market. Then he'd insisted on bearer bonds in payment, not the more usual cheque or transfer of funds. Furthermore, he'd insisted fanatically on total secrecy about the whole affair. Then there had been the matter of the asking price. True, it was fairly reasonable for both parties concerned, considering the state and upkeep of the old house. But even so, Dylan reckoned that if Forboys had haggled for longer, perhaps letting other rival hotel companies or private vendors know that the house was on the market, he could have got far more money.

It all smacked to Dylan of something underhanded. Still, whatever Forboys was up to, he, Dylan, was free and clear — he'd made sure of that. No hint of scandal — financial or otherwise — had ever touched Gale Imperial, and Dylan was going to make damned sure it stayed that way!

Shrugging off his unease, Dylan let himself out of his latest property. Outside, a beautiful Barbados breeze carried the scent of the sea and frangipani to his face, and as he gazed around the overgrown, colourful garden, he suddenly smiled. The house was his. Soon he'd send in his usual team of craftsmen — carpenters, electricians, plumbers and interior decorators — to work their magic, and then gardeners to tidy up (but not too much) the rich colourful jungle surrounding the house. Soon the property would be raking in the money for him just like all the others.

He walked towards the cliff edge and looked out across to sea, where the usual plethora of cheerful red, blue, white, yellow, pink and purple windsurfers' sails tucked and dodged across the gentle blue swell of waves, and he felt suddenly happy. Free and alive.

This afternoon he'd forget the office for once, and get into his snorkelling gear and see if he could find a deserted reef to explore. Or maybe find a beachful of beautiful, bikini-clad holiday-makers and buy one of them a coconut cocktail from a beach hut-bar. And after that . . . who knows? Life was good and full of possibilities, after all.

Florida

'I still don't see why I have to stay in tonight,' Calvin Sawyer complained, for about the fifth time in an hour. 'Even if I agree to this operation tomorrow, I can stay in my own bed tonight. I promise not to eat or drink anything.'

'No!' Tahnee said, before either Mike, Philip Malleson or Dr Galsworthy could add their own objections. 'You're staying in, and that's that! Daddy, you've got to start taking care of yourself,' Tahnee wheedled. 'You heard what the doctors said! If the ulcers perforate it could be really serious.'

Indeed, Dr Galsworthy had been very grave when, her father having been returned to his room, he'd taken her aside in the corridor for a private chat. Her father had at the very least five ulcers, two of which looked to be on the brink of bursting. Surgery was imperative, and not only that, he was to avoid all stress and have complete rest for at least six weeks. Tahnee had assured him that she'd see to it that he did, knowing that Mike and the other vice-presidents would be well able to manage Sawyer Enterprises for a few months without Calvin's guidance. And she herself planned to move back in to The Mansion until her father had recovered completely.

But this, Dr Galsworthy had told her gently, could be some time. Even after the two worst ulcers had been removed, the others would have to be closely monitored. Also, there was the gargantuan task to be undertaken of making Calvin Sawyer change his living habits. No more Cuban cigar after dinner. No more Kansas bourbon. No more Mexican spicy food. And, most contentious of all, no more sixteen-hour working days spent at the office.

Now, as Tahnee saw her father thrust forward his jaw stubbornly, she wondered, with a smile of affection and exasperation, how she was ever going to get him to agree to all of that!

'Daddy, you're going to have to get used to slowing down,' she said firmly. 'So you might as well start now. You'll stay in here until the operation, then stay in for two weeks after that. NO!' She held up a finger, rather like she'd hold up a finger to one of the spaniels that was refusing to sit. 'You will stay, and be looked after, and rest, and get well. You will not' — she held up her hand and began ticking down off her fingers — 'bully Marisa into visiting you and sneaking in paperwork. Don't think I don't know you haven't already thought about it,' she added severely, as Mike Greening and Philip Malleson struggled to keep their faces straight, and Dr Galsworthy didn't even bother. 'You will not bribe any nurses to smuggle you in bourbon. I'll pay the head nurses twice what you will to make sure they see to it,' she added severely, as her father muttered what a mistake it had been to settle a fortune on her when she'd turned twenty-one. 'You will not have a fax machine, a laptop, or any other machine in here that'll allow you to interface with your office, and when I get home I'm going to burn all your cigars, so don't even think about asking Walton to bring you some in. By the time I've finished speaking with him, he'll be on my side in all of this, you'll see.'

Walton had been the major factotum at The Mansion since before Tahnee had been born, and in spite of being several years younger than Calvin, somehow seemed to regard his employer as a naughty little boy who needed to be looked after.

Calvin muttered dire threats about sacking the butler, which everyone ignored. Then Philip said that he had to be going, and wished his old friend good night, and the hospital doctor left too. Tahnee, still sitting on her father's bed, watching him drink lemon barley water and grimacing horribly over it, said carefully, 'I see Cordelia hasn't come in yet. Didn't Marisa call her?'

Calvin shrugged, and muttered something about stringing up whoever it was who'd invented soft drinks. 'I don't think she could get hold of her,' Calvin finally added, putting the glass down and refusing to meet her eyes.

Tahnee sighed, but said nothing. She

supposed Cordelia was having a massage at her country club with her mobile turned firmly off. Or maybe getting her legs waxed, or her toenails done, or was playing tennis, or whatever it was that Cordelia did with all her spare time.

Calvin had been widowed for nearly seven years before marrying Cordelia Fox, a not entirely successful fashion model, who'd flown in from New York one winter and decided to stay. Tahnee, who'd been sixteen at the time and used to having all her father's attention to herself, had not been happy to suddenly be presented with a prospective stepmother, and had not been sufficiently mature enough to conceal it. Consequently, even after the marriage, the two women had never got on, and it had led to Tahnee going to college a year early — at the age of seventeen.

When she'd graduated with a degree in Fine Art, her father, wanting to be sure that she was safe, had bought her a penthouse in one of the most sought-after — and safe — buildings in the city and insisted that she move in.

Tahnee had chafed a bit at first, but in the end she'd been too sensible not to concede. She was only too aware of the pitfalls that could befall rich young people, and had never taken drugs, or gone out of her way to advertise who she was or take unnecessary risks with her safety. She never walked alone at night, for example, and if she wasn't driving herself, always used one of her father's fleet of cars and chauffeurs to shepherd her around. Unlike other, more notorious heiresses, Tahnee had never been a wild child, or courted fame, and her father's influence and money had succeeded in keeping her reasonably anonymous. The fact that she worked all week at her gallery, and tended to avoid the 'in' places and 'big' parties also ensured that she hardly ever ran into her stepmother socially. Which suited her just fine.

'I'll try her mobile again, shall I?' Tahnee asked now. Although she'd never interfered in her father's ten-year-old marriage, she'd sensed for some time now that all was not well with it. She was also very much surprised that Cordelia hadn't checked in with either the house or office before now, and discovered that Calvin had been taken ill. She'd always found Cordelia to be very protective of her biggest asset, and not even her worst enemy could ever accuse Cordelia of neglecting him.

'Sure, chicken,' Calvin murmured vaguely. Then he looked up as a nurse came in, and

22

grunted at the empty needle on the tray. 'Not taking more blood! I'll be anaemic before long.'

Tahnee grinned at the nurse's crisp but cheerful comeback and stepped outside into the corridor to check her mobile phone's memory before speed-dialling her stepmother's number. Cordelia was usually very careful to be seen as the perfect and caring wife, and Tahnee had no doubts that she'd be over the moment she knew Calvin was in here. She put the phone to her head, relieved to hear it was ringing.

'Hello?' she said, the moment the connection was made. 'Cordelia, it's me. Tahnee. Look, Dad's at St Mark's. It's nothing to worry about, but he needs an operation, and I think he'd like to see you. Where are you?'

'Cordelia can't come to the hospital right now,' a male voice said shortly. 'Go home, and you'll be contacted.'

And suddenly the dial tone was buzzing in her ear again. Puzzled, Tahnee snapped shut her mobile and stared at it. That was rather peremptory. Perhaps she'd been having tennis lessons and a pool boy had answered. A friend had told her recently that the Coco-de-Mer Country Club had hired a new tennis coach who was supposed to be a bit of a demon. Certainly a lot of amateur tennis players had had their level of game elevated just lately.

Oh well.

Not giving it another thought, Tahnee put the phone back in her bag, and pushed open the door to her father's hospital room. Time for round two — convincing her father to take a long vacation this summer, and to take one every year from now on.

Oxford, England

Delphine Phillips sneezed as yet more dust tickled her nose, and smiled grimly. She was wearing her oldest pair of jeans and most threadbare T-shirt, since, having put off the loft clearance for the last few months, she'd finally decided to bite the bullet and get it done.

Now she knelt on the dusty floorboards of the attic, going through the last of the trunks. So far she'd found old childhood games and toys, moth-eaten clothes, a teddy with one eye that she could only just remember cuddling as a toddler, and piles of old school exercise books that made her smile. Her mother had been a hoarder, no doubt about it! Now she smiled sadly over an old English exercise book, that had been peppered with red-inked 'A's, and put it to one side.

The Beeches, one of many old, spacious houses that lined the city's northern Woodstock Road, had been her home for all her life. Delphine could hardly remember her father, who'd died in a car accident when she'd been only six, but her mother's presence lingered now like a healing balm, bringing gentle tears of remembrance to her eyes.

Georgina Phillips had been a Classics don at St Enselm's College for most of her adult life, inheriting The Beeches from her father, and then bequeathing it to her only child in her will. She had died only six months ago, after a short illness that she had fought like a tiger, but had, ultimately, been unable to beat.

Delphine had grown up in the rarefied atmosphere that was Oxford academe, and not surprisingly had gone to college at Somerville herself. However, it had been English Literature, and not Classics, that had been her forte, allowing her to get a BA with first class honours three years ago. Now she was studying for her D.Phil, and was a Research Fellow at her mother's old college.

Today, though, on the first day of the long summer vacation that preceded Michaelmas term, her thesis was the last thing on her mind. Already she'd taken down boxes of old clothes, books, bric-a-brac and, not to put too fine a point on it, 'tat'. Tomorrow, they were all headed for the charity shops. She was hot and thirsty and her throat was parched and more than ready for a cup of tea. Thank goodness this was the last of it.

The box that had been underneath all the other boxes was obviously old, wooden, and full of papers. Stuff that would take her forever to go through. She groaned, and was on the brink of giving up on it, not having any interest in opera programmes from 1902 (but wondering whether an old historian friend of hers might have), when she spotted something right at the bottom. Perhaps it was the red ribbons holding it together, or the very official-looking, impressive, copper-plate writing that drew her attention. But when she pulled it out and held it under the bare electric light bulb, she recognized it instantly for what it was.

A last will and testament.

For someone who'd grown up with no living relations except her mother, such an intimate document, reeking of past ties and possible family connections, was too good an opportunity to ignore. Curious, she tucked it under her T-shirt, closed the box, and backed out of the attic, feeling cautiously for the top rung of the ladder as she did so. Once she'd very carefully climbed down it, she took the dusty, ivory-coloured papers to the kitchen, and made herself a drink. There, she briefly debated changing and showering before investigating her find more thoroughly, but then realized that the papers were so old and dusty that she'd only be filthy again before she'd finished reading them. So she took her steaming mug to the kitchen table, sat down and began to read avidly.

The will was dated 15 September 1932, and belonged to one Moorcroft Mowbray, who was resident at the time of the will being made, in Bathsheba, Barbados.

The exotic address made Delphine whistle silently through her lips. She'd never heard of her mother talk about having family or friends on the Caribbean island. She read on, amused by the legalese that made so little sense to her, then gave a little 'mew' of recognition as she saw a name she most definitely recognized.

Matthew Godalming.

Godalming was her mother's maiden name, and Matthew the name of her only uncle. So that would make him Delphine's great uncle, wouldn't it? She wrinkled her nose thoughtfully. Or something like that. She was not much up on genealogy. Of course, her mother's uncle had been dead for some years now. He'd died, without issue (as the lawyers would put it), some time in the 1930s.

But from what she could make of it, this Moorcroft Mowbray had left his entire estate to Great Uncle Matthew. But what was the will doing in her mother's attic? And why had she never mentioned her uncle coming into some property on Barbados? Surely she would have. Something so lucky and exotic as that would have made it into family lore. Especially family that was so sparse on the ground as the Godalmings. (Her father had been raised in an orphanage, and even less was known about his possible family ties.)

Her mother had been the only survivor of her own family tree, and Delphine herself had no brothers and sisters.

Intrigued with the thought that she might just have unearthed a forgotten family mystery, Delphine decided to show the document to Colin Farrell. It was about time she invited him out for a drink, anyway.

Colin, an old friend who'd taken up chambers in a Woodstock firm of solicitors three years ago, was always the one to keep in touch, so it would make a nice change to instigate a meeting herself. They'd dated on and off during college, but it had never stuck.

Now, she had the perfect excuse to get herself out of the house and have a night out for once. Even if it was only a drink at The White Hart, her local.

Humming to herself as she made her way upstairs towards a much deserved bubble bath, it never even occurred to Delphine that a dusty old parchment could change her life for ever.

Or put it in mortal danger.

2

Florida, USA

Tahnee watched Dorinda, her father's cook, squeeze the last of the Seville oranges, and smiled her thanks as she placed the frosted glass in front of her. She was sitting in the shaded conservatory just off the vast kitchen where she'd often eaten as a child, and pondered how weird it felt to be living back at The Mansion.

'You need more than toast and melon.' Dorinda, a Puerto Rican by birth and as round as a football, hovered over her like a mother hen. 'Let me make you some eggs, yes? I do a wonderful Benedict, you remember?' she wheedled.

'I do remember, and they were delicious, but I'm not very hungry, Dori.' She smiled at the cook fondly, remembering childhood afternoons, after school, spent in the kitchen 'helping' Dorinda to make scones, rock cakes and flapjacks. 'What time does Cordelia usually come down?'

Dorinda shrugged elaborately and turned away, back towards her domain. Her silence spoke volumes, and as she left, Tahnee wondered if her volatile stepmother had somehow managed to get on the wrong side of the normally easygoing cook. Then she realized it was none of her business. Although she sometimes still felt guilty about leaving home so early, she couldn't bring herself to regret it.

With a small sigh, she sipped the delicious orange juice and reached for the morning papers. News of her father's illness had hit the business section, and she was glad the company had no public stock to worry about. And she had confidence that her father's management team could run Sawyer's until her father had fully recovered and felt able to take over the reins again — albeit, working reduced hours.

Dismissing thoughts of her father's business, she turned instead to thoughts of her own, and checked out the arts section, reading about the latest sculpture exhibition to hit town. She'd have to go, of course. Sculpture at The Spindlewood Tree was still woefully under-represented, and she'd promised Miriam, the woman who worked full-time there, that she'd redress the balance. And there was a young artist living in Dade County that she had her eye on, and if she was exhibiting at this latest show, Tahnee

31

wanted to check her out.

Her breakfast finished, Tahnee left the table and wandered restlessly into the music room. She was not particularly musical herself, but had taken piano lessons as a child, and, suddenly swamped with feelings of nostalgia, sat down at the grand piano and picked out a half-remembered classical tune.

After leaving her father at the hospital yesterday, she'd gone to her flat and packed a large bag, returning to The Mansion at just gone eleven, much to Walton's delight. The major-domo had led her straight to her old room, which hadn't been altered since the day she'd left it, shortly after her seventeenth birthday. Luckily, Cordelia had been out, so she had yet to inform her stepmother that she'd be moving back in for the next few months or so. She couldn't see that Cordelia would be exactly happy about it, but surely two grown women could manage to coexist in a house of The Mansion's vast size without too much trouble?

She looked up as the door opened, and Walton put his head in. A tall, thin, grey-haired man, he looked like the epitome of an English butler, instead of the son of a Texas cow-hand that he actually was. 'Ah, I thought I heard you, Miss Tahnee. Debussy, isn't it?'

Tahnee grinned mischievously. 'Not that anyone would recognize it as such.' She grimaced, closing the piano lid. 'Is my stepmother up yet, Walton?' she added casually. She had to confront her some time or other.

Walton's lean face didn't move a muscle. 'I'm afraid Mrs Sawyer didn't come in last night, miss.'

Tahnee stared at him numbly. 'Not come in?' she repeated foolishly. 'Oh. Perhaps she spent the night at the hospital,' she added, but without much conviction. She'd phoned the hospital first thing this morning to check on her father's condition, and had learned that he'd spent a comfortable night. But nobody had mentioned that his wife had been in. And surely Cordelia would have called in at The Mansion, if only for a change of clothes or a toothbrush?

'Does she often stay out the night?' Tahnee asked reluctantly. It felt too uncomfortably like spying, or interfering, to ask, but she needed to know. Perhaps Cordelia wasn't even aware that her husband was ill, and if she habitually spent the nights elsewhere, she needed to know where to contact her.

'No, miss, she doesn't,' Walton said. 'Occasionally she stays with a friend, er, a female friend, that is, but she always calls to let the staff know.'

Tahnee bit her lip. 'I see. And she hasn't called?'

'No, Miss Tahnee.'

'All right. Thank you, Walton,' she said, trying to hide her consternation as the majordomo withdrew. Damn the woman! Where was she?

Feeling a vague sense of unease, she wandered out on to the patio, where a robin watched her with interest. Already the sprinklers were on throughout the vast, beautifully tended garden, and as Tahnee went back to the conservatory to fetch some crumbs for the robin, she wondered angrily when her stepmother would bother to show up.

Woodstock, England

'Coffee?' Colin asked, as Jenny, his secretary, ushered Delphine in and then glanced a query at her employer. Colin shook his head, indicating that she wouldn't be required to stay and make notes, then grinned across at Delphine as she slipped into the padded, comfortable chair opposite his desk.

'Very Dickensian, I must say,' Delphine teased, as she looked around his office. The solicitor's firm he worked for had converted what looked like an Elizabethan white-washed set of terraced cottages into low-ceilinged offices, full of original beams, fireplaces and character. The floorboards beneath her undulated as much as the old tiled roof did above, and genuine, old, if uninspiring watercolours lined the cold, bulging plastered walls. Colin's desk was of the solid oak variety, English, probably early eighteenth century. One wall was lined with bookshelves crammed with legal tomes, and a genuine antique globe sat on one side of the desk. Wide black wooden window seats overlooked the old market town of Wood-stock, and the gaggle of tourists flocking into the antique shops and quaint little 'ye olde' coffee shops.

'Don't you believe it,' Colin said, tapping the top of his very modern-looking computer. 'But a bit of dust and Chippendale does reassure our older clients.'

He looked up as the door opened and his secretary walked in with a tray. 'Thanks Jen. I'll be twenty minutes or so. Nothing urgent, is there?'

'Nothing that can't be put off.' Jenny, a cheerful divorcee of uncertain years, looked at Delphine speculatively as she put down the tray on the desk. She couldn't remember when she'd last seen a woman so beautiful, outside of glossy fashion magazines. And her boss's visitor had not been entered into the appointment book, which made Jenny wonder if she caught the whiff of romance in the air. Not that she was surprised. Her boss was relatively good-looking, young, and had a good solid job. He was also single — a rare find indeed. But even having said all that, she thought a woman like this would have been well out of his league. In spite of the casual slacks she wore with an off-the-peg blouse, she looked as if she should be dating footballers or night-club owners.

Delphine smiled a thanks as the secretary added sugar and milk to her cup and then poured. When she finally left, Jenny gave her boss a broad wink behind Delphine's back, which Colin pretended not to see.

'Well, I have to say, you certainly added a touch of spice and romance into this dusty old life of mine,' Colin said, bringing out a folder containing the will she'd given him last night at the pub. 'It isn't often I get to research missing wills, Caribbean islands, and the possible misdeeds of wealthy plantation owners.'

'Huh?' Delphine said blankly, pausing in the act of raising her coffee cup to her lips.

'I usually get to do boring divorces,

conveyancing, title of deeds transfers and whatnot,' Colin went on, a light of enthusiasm brightening his eyes. 'So perhaps it's not so surprising that I was so intrigued by this that I was up on the internet nearly all night.'

'I thought you were looking a little hollow-eyed,' Delphine chided, putting her cup back down. 'Oh Colin, I hope you didn't go out of your way just for me. I only asked you about it because I was so surprised to find it. I didn't expect you to drop everything! I was quite shocked when you phoned this morning and asked me to come in.'

'Ah, but I got hooked on it too, so it was no hardship,' Colin countered. 'Let me ask you a few things first, see if I can clear up one or two questions before we go on.' He leaned back in his chair, a slim, pleasant-faced man with dark curly hair and wide, blue eyes. 'Your Great Uncle Matthew. He died, when exactly, do you know?'

'Not exactly, no,' Delphine said, and felt stupid. 'I really should have looked all this up when I found the will, but you took me off-guard, acting so quickly. I know he died sometime in 1933. I think it might have been January, though. I remember Mum telling me about seeing a photograph of him in the family album, and her mother, my grandmother, that is, telling her that he hadn't lived long enough to see much of the New Year. Why, is it important?'

'Well, not really, but it all fits. I don't suppose you know how the will came to be in your attic, do you?'

'I've been thinking about that,' Delphine said, catching some of the excitement in Colin's voice, and leaning forward a little across the desk, her eyes shining. 'I'm pretty sure he came to see his sister, my grandmother, just before he died. Mum told me once that my grandmother was so glad he'd died 'with family'. And, as you know, the Godalmings are a little short on the ground. So perhaps he died at The Beeches. Mind you, I can't say so for certain.'

'Hmm. It's a bit of puzzle,' Colin mused. 'I can't understand why he had a copy of the will at all. I've been mulling it over, and I think, on balance, that for some reason it must have been Moorcroft himself who posted it over to him for safe-keeping — I'm sure his own solicitors wouldn't have let it out of their office. Then, when he fell ill and went to stay with his sister, he could easily have taken it with him. Perhaps asked her to put it somewhere safe, and then, with the shock of his death and what-have-you, it could have been put away and forgotten about.'

Delphine frowned. 'But why would he leave

anything to Uncle Matthew at all? As far as I know, Matthew Godalming never left the shores of England in his life.'

'Oh, because he was Moorcroft's silent partner, I imagine.'

Delphine smiled. 'Colin, start at the beginning, will you? You're not making much sense.'

'Oh, sorry, right. I keep forgetting, you don't know the story yet. Well, neither do I, not all of it, but it's amazing what you *can* find out on the internet nowadays. Anyway, what do you know about the history of the Caribbean islands? And Barbados in particular?'

'Nothing,' Delphine said ruefully. 'Ask me about Marlowe or Hazlitt, or even Langland, and I'm your girl. Geography? Forget about it.'

'Right, Bookworm, I remember,' he teased, remembering her nickname from college. 'OK, this is what I've found out so far. Back in the 1800s, one Zacharia Mowbray, a chandler's apprentice from Bristol, decided to make his way to Barbados in order to 'make his fortune', as they used to say. He stowed away on a ship called the *Alice May* and worked off his passage to the island. Poor devil, I bet they treated him like a slave. Captains weren't keen on stowaways in those days. Lucky they didn't keep hold of him and work him to death. Or maybe they tried to and he jumped ship at Bridgetown.'

'You old romantic, you,' Delphine teased, taking a sip of coffee, but feeling as thrilled as Colin about the antics of the long-dead Bristol lad.

'Anyway, there were certainly no flies on Zacharia, because the next trace I found of him had him marrying the daughter of one of the plantation owners — a sure way to start a dynasty, if you ask me.' Colin grinned. 'And sure enough, things went well for him. His father-in-law left him the plantation when he died, and his wife produced four healthy sons and two daughters. It seems he moved out of the family home when he was in his fifties, but only because he'd had a larger house built, with a spectacular view, a little further away from the sugar fields. Mowbray House, it was called, for reasons that should be obvious.'

'Mowbray?' Delphine whispered. 'As in our Moorcroft Mowbray?'

'Right, a direct descendant. However, by the time Moorcroft made this' — Colin tapped the will thoughtfully — 'the estate had all but been eaten away, and only the house itself remained, and the land it was built on. That, incidentally, is how Moorcroft and your great uncle met. Moorcroft came to England in the twenties, to try and raise some capital to keep the plantation afloat. He didn't seem to like the banks much because he preferred to bring in private investors — which is where your great uncle came into it. Somehow they must have met and become great friends, because your uncle bought into the plantation in a big way. With this money, Moorcroft was able to keep going, and your uncle got a modest but steady return on his investment for some years, until the plantation was sold just before Moorcroft's death. I imagine he must have known he was dying, because he repaid your great uncle's investment in full about three months before he died. But that doesn't explain why Moorcroft decided to leave what remained of his estate to his friend, instead of to his family.' Colin paused for a much-needed breath, and grinned at her. 'And this is where things become really interesting. I've checked with the land registry, amongst other things, and it seems that a Mr Christopher Allinson 'inherited' Mowbray House on Moorcroft's death. According to the records, however, the will Allinson produced had been made by Moorcroft in June of 1930. A full two years *before* this one. Which means, as this will was made later and revokes all previous wills, that

Christopher Allinson should never have inherited. I've checked this out, of course,' he added, tapping the dusty papers she'd given him yesterday, 'and am quite satisfied that it's not a forgery, and that the witnesses who testified to seeing it signed are almost certainly legitimate. Which means that, legally, Mowbray House and grounds should have gone to your great uncle. Unless, of course, there was a will made even later than this one,' he added, with a typical solicitor's caution. 'But that seems very unlikely. And since you're the only living descendant of Matthew Godalming . . . ' He spread his hands and shrugged, leaving it to her to fill in the rest.

Delphine, who'd been listening enraptured, slowly leaned back in her chair. 'But who is, or should I say, was, Christopher Allinson?'

Colin nodded. 'Was is right. He died in 1951, according to the death registry. As far as I can make out, he was Moorcroft's nephew; he had no children of his own. The house was then sold on the open market, being bought by a retired British colonel and his lady. I've traced its history right through to 1988, when it was bought by a Mr Gordon Forboys, a resident of the island. But, like I said, if I'm right and this will is valid, it was never Colin Allinson's to sell in the first

42

place. Of course, after all this time . . . ' Colin waved a hand vaguely in the air. 'I'm not sure how matters would actually stand. And I'm definitely not an expert on law as it's practised in Barbados. But it's all very interesting, no?'

Delphine grinned widely. 'Very interesting, yes.'

Bridgetown, Barbados

As he sensed a presence beside him, Dylan leaned back a little in his chair, expecting the waiter to place his order of fresh sea bass and caesar salad in front of him. Instead, a man slipped into the chair opposite him, took a long, slow drink from his ice-filled glass and stared at Dylan through slightly narrowed eyes.

Dylan ate regularly at The Blue Dolphin restaurant, since it was only a two-minute walk from his office, and boasted the best food anywhere in the capital. He had a corner table permanently booked, and it was usually very discerning about its clientele. Which was why Dylan looked at his unexpected table guest with barely disguised surprise.

'Bolton,' Dylan said curtly. 'I didn't know we had an appointment.' He said it dryly, because, as they both knew, no such thing would ever have been likely.

Marcus Bolton was the nearest thing Barbados had to an old-fashioned gangster. Officially a dealer in real estate, and owner of a third-rate tourist company, Marcus Bolton in reality operated crooked gambling ships, a string of call-girls, and almost certainly a thriving illegal drugs empire. So far, the hard-working Barbados constabulary hadn't been able to pin a thing on him — but it certainly wasn't for want of trying. Growing up on the island, Dylan had always made sure that none of Bolton's tentacles had been able to land on Gale Imperial. (He also had a reputation as a corporate raider that stank to high heaven.)

'I heard you just bought that old pile of brick and sawdust, Mowbray House,' Marcus Bolton said flatly, totally ignoring the jibe.

A thick-set man of five feet nine or so, Bolton habitually wore a white suit and colourful Hawaiian-style shirt. His face was a permanent reddish-brown, and only the pale blue of his eyes provided a lighter tone. His hair was almost the same colour as his skin, and a rather tentative moustache lay across his top lip like an anaemic caterpillar.

'You heard right,' Dylan said calmly, all his old uneasiness about that deal coming back to the fore as he silently cursed Forboys, wondering what kind of arrangement he'd had going with the island's premier barracuda. And how the hell it was going to affect him, Dylan, now.

'That was a bit naughty,' Marcus Bolton said, lifting one finger off the side of his glass of gin and tonic and waving it in a back and forth gesture. A thick gold signet ring winked obscenely in the light. 'I had an arrangement with Mr Forboys to buy that particular property myself.'

Dylan smiled grimly. 'Something he neglected to mention to me.'

'No doubt, no doubt,' Marcus said, smiling widely, and revealing perfectly white, capped teeth. 'Bit of a sly old dog, old Gordon. Full of surprises, it seems. Still, no harm done. I'll take it for granted that you had no idea a private arrangement had already been worked out between us. You can simply put a stop to the sale and that'll be that. I'll have my lawyers call your lawyers.'

And so saying, he put one hand on top of the table prior to levering himself up, but Dylan shook his head slowly.

'I'm afraid not. The deal's done and dusted. Papers were signed yesterday, and money's already been exchanged.'

'Cancel the cheque,' Marcus Bolton

snapped flatly, lowering his bulk back into the chair. The arrogance with which he said it, and the certainty he so obviously felt that Dylan would instantly comply, caught the younger man on the raw.

Slowly, and suddenly enjoying himself, Dylan smiled. 'No cheque,' he said.

Marcus's pale, reptilian-like eyes narrowed. 'Surely not cash? Now, what would a nice, respectable businessman like yourself be doing mixed up in a deal that required something as squalid as actual, tangible money?'

Dylan smiled grimly to himself as he felt the direct hit. Good question! The trouble was, he was in it now, and there was no damned way he was going to let this weasel muscle in. Besides, what could the island crook want with a dilapidated house? It couldn't be that important to him, surely?

'Oh, I had my solicitors check it all out thoroughly. There was nothing wrong with the deal,' Dylan said, meeting the other man's gaze steadily. And not backing off an inch.

He felt, rather than saw, the complacency suddenly drain out of Marcus. No doubt Bolton was used to his reputation ensuring that everyone quailed before him, and bowed their necks to do his bidding like alarmed sheep. Well, it was high time he realized that not everybody was willing to do so, Dylan thought grimly.

'I'm willing to be generous,' Bolton said abruptly, finishing his drink and doing the one-finger-waving trick to catch the attention of a waiter and get a refill. 'I'll match Forboy's asking price and throw in an extra grand, for your trouble. Can't say fairer than that, can I?'

For a second, Dylan was tempted. After all, nobody but an idiot went out of his way to make an enemy of a man like Marcus. And he'd made his point — shown the man he wasn't without a backbone. And a thousand dollars for one day's work wasn't to be sniffed at. On the other hand, the house was perfect for Gale Imperial. With views like it commanded, he could ask for, and get, top tourist dollars. Besides, what kind of man let someone else scare him out of doing good business? His lips twisted dryly as the answer came back to him — loud and uncompromising.

'Sorry,' Dylan said softly. 'Not interested.'

'Funny. I wouldn't have thought your daddy would raise an idiot,' Marcus Bolton said softly, with all the sibilance of a snake.

Dylan smiled slowly back. 'He didn't.'

And, for the first time in many years, Marcus Bolton felt pinpricks of real fear lance his skin.

Florida, USA

Tahnee left the gallery early and went straight back to The Mansion. She'd dropped in to see her father at the hospital, just to make sure that he'd taken all the tests the doctors wanted prior to his operation in two days' time, and that he wasn't being too much of a tyrant to the nursing staff. Now, as she walked through the cool marble lobby that was a feature of her father's house, she noticed that the afternoon mail had been left in its usual place on a tall, gilded side table.

A thick, brown, padded envelope caught her eye, and she was surprised to see her own name on it. Who knew she'd moved back home? She'd only been here a day!

Intrigued, she picked it up and took it upstairs with her, dropping it on to her dressing table as she walked past it through her bedroom and into the bathroom. There, she stripped and took a long, relaxing hot shower. She'd just received a shipment from Japan at the gallery, from an artist who painted on the finest of silk, and after an hour of unpacking and displaying, her muscles felt cramped and stiff.

She'd just finished drying her hair when she remembered the package. When she opened it, she was surprised to find a video cassette inside. She peered into the envelope but there was no accompanying note or slip of paper. The black plastic cassette had no writing on it either. Frowning in puzzlement, she walked over to the bedroom's media centre and slipped it into the VCR. Using the remote, she turned on the television, accessed the right channel, and hit the play button.

For a few seconds, there was only the usual white-speckled black static. Then, abruptly, a picture came on. A picture of her stepmother.

Tahnee stared at it for a moment, uncertain of what she was seeing.

Cordelia was sitting on a wooden chair, in front of what looked like a plain white wall. She seemed to be staring anxiously at the camera. Her auburn hair (which her publicist had insisted on calling her 'trademark Titian' hair) stood out starkly as the only colour on the screen, since Cordelia was wearing a white pants suit, and a white-gold chain around her neck. As the camera zoomed in on her, her wide green eyes sparkled, as if full of tears. Her complexion was unusually pale. Usually Cordelia was adept with blusher and foundation and it took a shocked moment for Tahnee to realize that her stepmother wasn't wearing any make-up at all. It was so astonishing to think of the carefully beautiful Cordelia without her usual 'face' that Tahnee felt eerily wrong-footed.

As if in a premonition of things to come, she felt herself sit down abruptly on the edge of her bed, her heart racing. Then, on the screen, the picture began to wobble, and her stepmother's image disappeared as the camcorder that was taking the pictures was rotated around, and suddenly a face, covered with a black balaclava, filled the screen.

'We have her.' The voice didn't come from the masked man, since his lips, barely visible in the crude hole cut out for his mouth, didn't move. It also had an electronic edge to it, and Tahnee realized that it had been altered in some way. 'We want fifty million dollars in uncut diamonds. Get it fast. You have less than two days. Then take the first commercial flight to Barbados you can find. You'll be watched. Any police, and Mrs Cordelia Sawyer gets returned to her family in pieces.'

Abruptly, the screen went black.

Numbly, Tahnee stared at the blank screen, then scrambled for the remote, and rewound it. She watched the video again, and then a third time, and then a fourth time, trying to look for clues to Cordelia's whereabouts, the identity of her captors, or anything else that could help. But there were no reflections in polished surfaces, no sound of church bells, or any of the other things she'd seen in the movies to give her any clue.

She had no idea where her stepmother was, or who'd taken her.

Slowly, Tahnee leaned forward on the bed and covered her face with her hands.

This was every wealthy person's worst nightmare.

Oxford, England

Delphine couldn't believe she was packing. But here she was, in her bedroom, throwing practically every article of summer clothing that she had into a suitcase.

Not that that amounted to a whole lot.

Her mother had always been trying to coax her into buying clothes, telling her that she looked stunning in anything, but Delphine had never been much of a clothes-horse. Perhaps growing up without any sisters, or maybe her determination to win a place at Oxford without her mother's influence, had channelled all her energies into the intellectual, rather than more down-to-earth and pleasurable pursuits. She certainly never felt as self-confident as her beautiful mother, and preferred to keep her life on an even keel.

But her mother would certainly have had

no complaints about what she was doing now. If Georgina could see her doing something so spontaneous, so romantic and foolish, she'd have cheered out loud.

Delphine herself still wasn't sure how it had all come about. She'd left Colin's office with the will and all his notes, intrigued and entranced by the tale and the mystery that lay behind her attic find. But when, and how, had that sense of wonder changed into something more solid? What exactly had made her turn on her own computer and surf the net for last-minute package holiday deals to Barbados? Certainly, when a cut-price deal for the following day had popped up on her screen, it had felt as if fate was giving her a helping nudge in that direction. And when a quick glance at her bank balance had revealed that she could just about afford it, it had seemed too much to dismiss as coincidence.

And before she'd had a chance to draw breath, it seemed, she'd booked the flight and hotel and transferred the funds.

Too late to back out now!

Perhaps there was something deeper at work, though, Delphine thought, as she put the final finishing touches to her packing.

It had been a long and dismal six months

since her mother's illness and death, and her half-finished thesis on the metaphysical poet, John Donne, had been weighing on her heavily recently. Perhaps her subconscious had simply interceded, knowing that she needed a break, and seized on the mystery of the will as a good excuse to get her out of her house of mourning and away to an island in the sun.

Whatever the reason, Delphine found herself humming as she went into the bathroom to pack a toiletries bag. The last time she'd been on holiday had been three years ago, and that had been to Cornwall. Where it had mostly rained!

As she met her reflection in the bathroom mirror, she saw a thin, pale face looking back at her. Signs of strain seemed to stare back at her like an accusation.

Well, this holiday was definitely going to be different, she promised herself — she had a mystery to solve, and pina coladas to drink. She had beaches to bathe on and coconuts to drink from. Yes, it was high time she treated herself. And she was sure her mother would have agreed.

A nice, relaxing time in Barbados was just what she needed.

Florida, USA

'Are you sure you want to do this, Tahnee? I don't like it. Let me at least find you a security guard to accompany you. We contract out to this very good firm — '

'No,' Tahnee said quickly. Then softened her voice and her face as Vince Cardwell, her financial advisor for the last six years, shook his head reprovingly. 'I know what I'm doing, Vince,' she added firmly.

When her father had settled a hundred million dollars on her when she'd reached her twenty-first birthday, he'd also recommended Vince, from the firm of Cardwell & Fortnum, to look after it for her, something that she'd never regretted. His investments were always careful and lucrative, and when faced with the problem of raising $50 million in uncut diamonds, he'd been the first one she'd called. She herself would have had no idea how to go about it, but after less than twelve hours, Vince, who had contacts in the diamond world, had come up with the package that now sat on the table in front of them.

'Of course, due to the speed of the transaction, I had to pay top dollar. Those little pebbles have made a hole in your investments to the tune of nearly $52 million.

But you did say it was urgent.' His voice rose on both a question and a growing sense of anxiety. Something was obviously very wrong with his youngest and prettiest client, and he wished she'd tell him exactly what it was. He didn't like this desperate urgency he could feel vibrating from her like visible waves. She'd always been surprisingly sparing with herself when it came to spending money, opting to live on her earnings from the gallery she ran, and only rarely indulging herself. This sudden demand for so much, so soon, was totally out of character.

'Yes, yes, I understand, Vince, and I'm sure you did your best,' Tahnee said now, reaching across to roll the yellowish, slightly milky stones around on their bed of black velvet. They did indeed look like pebbles and totally unlike the real, sparkling, carefully cut baubles that she was used to seeing women wear. Why, if she hadn't known what they were, she'd never have said they were diamonds at all.

And, of course, that was exactly why the kidnappers had wanted them. It was really very clever. Currency could always be monitored and checked, especially in this computer-dominated day and age. And gold would have to be melted down, requiring specialist equipment — something else the

FBI could check on. But uncut diamonds would be unrecognizable — and thus untraceable — once in the hands of a skilled cutter. Not that Tahnee had any intention of calling in the police.

With her father about to go under the surgeon's knife, and with his doctor's warning ringing in her ears that he must be spared any stress absolutely, Tahnee wasn't going to do anything to jeopardize Cordelia's life.

'Well, I have to go,' Tahnee said, carefully gathering the four ends of the velvet together and tying it off with a piece of string. She hefted the little package in her hands — so small, and worth so much. Yes, Cordelia's kidnappers were being very clever. And getting her to fly to Barbados — a place she didn't know, and well out of the range of Sawyer influence — that was very clever too.

And maybe dangerous.

But she couldn't think about that. Surely, as long as she followed instructions and gave them what they wanted, they'd release Cordelia. And they had no reason to harm her, did they? After all, she was the goose that was bringing them the golden egg.

No, she could deal with this. She had to. Her father must be kept in blissful ignorance of all this until it was all over, and Cordelia was safely home.

'Remember, Vince, you mustn't say a word about this to anyone.'

'My dear girl, I'm hardly likely to, am I? While you're walking around with those . . . ' He blanched as he watched her put the package casually into her handbag, thinking how vulnerable she was. 'Please, my dear, reconsider having a guard. I could make just one phone call — '

'No, Vince, thank you. I know what I'm doing.' She reached out and grasped his hands in her own. 'Please, just do as I say.'

Vince Cardwell nodded, but didn't look happy. As she walked out of his office, he collapsed back into the chair behind his desk and prayed that she knew what she was doing.

If he knew that she planned to smuggle the diamonds out of the country, without informing the customs and excise, or even insuring them, he would probably have had a heart attack.

3

Barbados

Tahnee put her small bag down beside the reception desk and glanced around. The St Michael Imperial Hotel wasn't big, and it wasn't famous, which was why she'd chosen it, but from the moment she'd stepped into the cool, white foyer, she felt oddly welcome. Large potted ferns stood amid overstuffed, comfortable-looking armchairs. An old man, happily puffing away on a pipe, read the local paper in one corner, and smiled a thanks as a pretty waitress put a cup of coffee in front of him. Tahnee could smell faint traces of the man's fragrant tobacco and was reminded of a now-dead grandfather, who had smoked something similar.

'Hello? Welcome to St Michael's. Just arrived on the island?' The receptionist, a young man with a beaming smile, looked at her one small bag and tried not to show his surprise.

'Yes.' Tahnee answered his question, then wondered if she should have done. The less people who knew her movements and her business the better. Then she realized he was just doing his job, making prospective clients feel welcome, and cursed herself for her rampant paranoia. If she was like this after only half an hour on the island, she'd be a nervous wreck before tomorrow. She had to get a grip! 'Miss Sawyer,' she forced herself to say calmly, then watched him tap the computer keyboard in search of her reservation.

She'd contemplated using an alias of course, as she sometimes did when she travelled, since the name of Sawyer wasn't exactly unknown, but had been afraid that that might antagonize Cordelia's kidnappers — perhaps make them think she was trying to put one over on them by trying to be hard to find.

'Ah yes, Miss Sawyer. You have the Indigo Suite.' The famous name apparently meant nothing to the hotel employee, however, for he simply reached across to a small, old-fashioned wooden key rack, and withdrew a small gold key attached to a long, indigo-coloured piece of painted wood. Then he came around from behind the desk. 'I'll take your bag, shall I?' he murmured, reaching down for her canvas holdall.

Tahnee had to physically stop herself from snatching it back. She could feel her neck and shoulders aching from tension, and bit her lip in exasperation. She was going to have to get tougher than this. And not drawing attention either to herself, or her meagre luggage, was probably a good start!

'Thank you,' she said brightly, and followed the young man towards an old-fashioned, iron-grille elevator. The small car arrived promptly and quietly, and decamped them, two floors up, a moment or so later. The hotel had obviously been converted from a rich man's townhouse, and stood only three floors high. In the corridor, Tahnee noted the original, slightly faded Aubusson carpet, and the old cornices where once gaslights had been ensconced. Now, beautifully shaped, clouded glass-electric lights were installed, which still managed to retain some of the elegance of a bygone age.

Original watercolours by native islanders lined the walls, and when the bellboy stopped outside a door in the far corner suite, she was not surprised to see a charming, brass plaque attached, with copperplate lettering on it, informing one and all that this was indeed the Indigo Suite. The hotel was charming. If the circumstances had been different, she'd have been congratulating herself on her good luck.

Tahnee tipped the bellboy just enough to impress but not overwhelm, and kept the smile firmly on her face until he shut the door after him. Then she let her shoulders relax and took a long, deep breath.

Her room was painted a soft aquamarine, with indigo curtains, cushions, bedspread and carpet. A large abstract in marine colours adorned one wall, and a set of French windows opened on to a balcony. Tahnee stepped out into the bright Caribbean sunshine and gave a soft murmur of delight as her nose was instantly assailed by the wild jasmine that climbed up the side of the hotel and coiled around the black wrought-iron railings that lined the balcony. Her view looked out over downtown Bridgetown, the island's capital. It looked busy, bright, full of colour and people and chatter, but she turned away almost at once. She wasn't here to see the sights, after all.

She unpacked her bag in a matter of minutes. She'd deliberately travelled light, knowing she could always buy more clothes once she was here. Now she opened a large, native fruitwood dresser to put away her few colourful skirts and slacks, and one-colour tops. They looked lost inside the drawers, which had fragrant little packets of pot-pourri in the bottom. Another nice touch. Whoever owned or ran the hotel certainly didn't miss a trick, she thought vaguely.

When her few possessions were stowed away, she turned to her toiletries bag and carefully withdrew a large pot of expensive face cream. It was a big, round, plain white jar, bearing only the maker's famous logo, and she carried it carefully to the bathroom and forced herself to put it in the mirrored cabinet, along with her toothpaste and toothbrush, deodorant and make-up bag. Then she shut the mirrored door on it and made herself walk away. It would have been ridiculous to ask to use the hotel safe, and then to deposit a pot of face cream in it! It would only have served to draw attention to it — and that was the very last thing she wanted.

Her unpacking done, Tahnee paced restlessly about her room. The telephone remained silent, and within a few minutes she was feeling as caged as a tiger at a zoo. She put a call through to the States and checked on her father, who was only six hours away from his operation now.

He'd been surprised and, she guessed, rather hurt when she'd told him she had to fly to Barbados. He'd fully expected her to be there for him, and she had felt like the worst kind of traitor when she'd had to tell his doctors she was going to be absent for a few days. But Calvin Sawyer understood business and its demands better than anyone, and when she'd made up a hot new artist that she wanted to sponsor and snaffle before the competition even knew what had hit them, he'd beamed his approval and all but commanded her to go. The Spindlewood Tree, contrary to many people's expectations, had shown a profit after only its first year in operation. It was no rich girl's hobby, as many people had thought, and Tahnee ran it along strict economical guidelines, much to her father's proud approval. Luckily, she had a good friend and workmate in Miriam, and had no qualms about leaving her in charge of it for a few days.

Over the phone, her father sounded cheerful and complacent, as always. Not even major surgery could faze him. To her immense relief, he didn't ask after Cordelia. Before she'd left, she'd told him that Cordelia had flown off on an African safari with one of her female friends who had begged her to go along for moral support after a fictional bitter divorce and emotional crisis had arisen. Rather surprisingly, he hadn't questioned it. Perhaps the thought of surgery was more on his mind than he'd tried to pretend.

She supposed, in future, she'd have to make up dodgy satellite communications or 'walkabout' to explain why Cordelia didn't phone. She only hoped the kidnappers would get in touch soon, so she could make the exchange, and get Cordelia back, before her father twigged that something was seriously amiss.

Unable to bear the confines of her room after wishing her father good luck, Tahnee grabbed her bag and went downstairs, eschewing the elevator for the wide, curved, stairs. She planned to take a quick walking tour of Bridgetown, to try and get her bearings and begin to understand her new surroundings, but to her surprise, the bellboy-cum-receptionist hailed her the moment he spotted her walking across the foyer.

'Oh, Miss Sawyer. Message for you.' He turned to the wooden mail slots and withdrew a long, slim, white envelope. Tahnee took it, trying to keep her breathing even. She'd told nobody stateside where she was staying — not even her father's secretary. It had to be from the kidnappers.

Which meant someone was indeed watching her. She felt the hairs on the back of her neck rise as she took the envelope to one of the armchairs, trying not to look around to see if someone was staring at her. It was obvious that whoever had delivered the message would be long gone.

Should she ask the bellboy who'd left it? To

describe the man or woman for her? But no — what was the point? It would only make him curious, and what would she do, even if he described someone? Search the island for a face that matched the description? It was absurd. Besides, it might antagonize them even more if they found out what she'd done. She must just play by their rules and keep calm.

She sank down into one of the big, wonderfully comfortable armchairs, and with hands that shook just a little, opened the envelope. Inside, on a plain white sheet of paper, were several lines of writing. Someone had obviously printed them off on a computer.

Quickly, Tahnee read it.

GO TO THE MARINA AND HIRE A BOAT FOR THE WEEK. DO NOT HIRE A SMALL OUTBOARD BOAT, NOR A LARGE YACHT. YOU WILL BE CONTACTED LATER AND TOLD WHERE TO GO AND WHEN. EXPECT TO TRAVEL. YOU WILL BE WATCHED. ANY SIGN OF THE POLICE AND YOU KNOW WHAT WILL HAPPEN. DESTROY THIS NOTE.

Tahnee licked her lips, unsurprised to find them as dry as dust. Then she rose shakily and went outside, walking blindly down the sidewalk until she came to a rubbish bin. There she tore the note into tiny pieces and dropped them inside.

Then, her mind made up as to what she must do next, she found a small magazine stand and bought a map of the island and the major towns. She noted the direction of the marina, and then, with a sigh of relief, found that Slipway Street was on the way.

Before she'd left the States, she'd called in a favour of a very particular kind, not sure that she'd ever need to use it, but wanting to have the option just in case.

Now, feeling totally alone and vulnerable, she was glad that she had.

The kidnappers might have her over a barrel, but she was not Calvin Sawyer's daughter for nothing. If they thought she couldn't take care of herself — as well as the business at hand — then that was their hard lookout.

★　★　★

Delphine Phillips was surprised not to be staying in Bridgetown, but the Pirates Inn in Hastings, on the southwest coast, was everything that she could have hoped for. Just 200 metres from the beach, her room was spacious enough, and had a small terrace overlooking a palm-fringed pool. The package holiday company she'd booked with hadn't let her down.

She spent the morning unpacking, then slowly reading through the printed material left on her bedside cabinet. Barbados, she soon learned, was the most easterly of the Caribbean islands, with an average temperature of a balmy 26.5 degrees centigrade. Its population consisted of 80 per cent of African descent, with only 4 per cent European, although the official language was English. The local currency was the Barbados dollar, of which Delphine had only a small supply. At some point, she'd have to find a bank and cash some travellers cheques.

She'd done a bit of research on her destination in the few hours she'd had left before having to catch her flight, and knew that Barbados had been colonized by the British in 1627, and had attained self-government in 1961. A friend, who'd been to the island several years before, had warned her to avoid at all costs the rush-hour congestion, and not to miss the impressive statue of Nelson in Trafalgar Square, which pre-dated the one in London by about twenty years!

But she'd have plenty of time for sight-seeing and shopping and beach-hopping later. Since the island was only fourteen miles by twelve miles, she wasn't far from anywhere, really, and where she wanted to go first was Bathsheba on the northeast coast.

She took a quick shower then donned a long, floating wrap-around skirt (a present from her mother) and a loose, scoop-necked lace top (another present from her mother) and grabbed her bag. Her mother had always teased her that she had all the shopping instincts of an amoeba, since she tended to gravitate towards the durable and the shapeless. Now, in the sunny atmosphere of a tropical island, she was suddenly glad to have something of her mother's legacy to wear!

She walked out past the pool, unaware of the many male eyes that watched her as she walked by, and, deciding to test out the public transport, stopped at the first bus stop she found.

She was looking forward to seeing Mowbray House at last. For the last few days it had existed only as a figment of her imagination, a sort of cross between *Gone with the Wind's* Tara and a lonely, mysterious beach house from a surfer's movie. Which was a very hard act for a real-life house to follow, she warned herself, and was determined not to be disappointed by the real thing.

Eventually a bus came and the cheerful driver told her that for Bathsheba, she wanted the next bus to come along — or maybe the one that came along after that. Probably in five minutes' time. Or maybe an hour. Smiling ruefully, Delphine thanked him. She was on island time now, it seemed.

★　★　★

'This one is small enough to fit in a purse, but still packs a lot of power.' The old lady speaking reached across a dented wooden cabinet top and pulled out a small, pearl-handled gun.

Tahnee looked at the little .22 and shook her head. 'I was thinking more in the lines of a .38.'

The old woman, who sold fruit at the front of her store, and illicit arms out of the back of her shed, shot Tahnee a look that bordered on respect. Her frizzy white hair contrasted sharply with the wrinkled ebony of her skin, but her eyes were ageless. 'You know your weapons, pretty lady.'

Tahnee smiled. 'I'm American. My daddy taught me to shoot before I could walk.' Which was something of an exaggeration, but not much. Back home Tahnee kept a .38 in the top drawer of her bedside cabinet. She was comfortable with it, and wanted something similar now.

The old woman shuffled away and came back with a cardboard box that had once stored pineapples. Now it housed just the gun she wanted — compact, black, clean, its actions were precise and well maintained. A revolver, not an automatic like she was used to, but good enough. Squinting through the empty tubes, checking for non-existent dirt or dust that could interfere with its aim or performance, Tahnee nodded with satisfaction.

'I need ammunition too.'

The old woman laughed easily. 'Course you do, child, course you do,' she said, patting Tahnee's arm and reaching into a cardboard box that had once housed bananas. 'Hollow point or regular?'

* * *

Delphine stared up at the house and felt her heart lift. In spite of her warnings not to feel let down if the house didn't live up to her expectations, it was almost exactly as she had imagined it! Big, but not huge, its once immaculate white facing was dirty and chipped in places, but that was merely cosmetic. It had a wide sweep of wooden steps leading up to a colonnaded front porch, the steps sagging a little in the middle, but

70

that too could be easily fixed. The window frames were flaking and rotten, but what did that matter when the proportions of the house were so exquisite? And the view!

Delphine turned and looked behind her. She didn't know the name of the bay it overlooked, but it hardly mattered. Sea breezes stirred the lush green vegetation in the riotous garden, and she could only imagine what the view was like from the top-floor windows. It faintly resembled the look of a plantation house, even though there was no plantation near it. Obviously, Zacharia Mowbray hadn't wanted to forget what had made his fortune — namely sugar. And had had a house built to reflect that.

Now, looking up at the blank, empty windows, Delphine could hear the house calling to her. Wild, flowering vines clung to all sides of the house, demanding to be tamed and trellised. It needed carpenters and probably rewiring, but the house was alive, breathing, welcoming. It seemed to her as if it was lonely — needing voices and laughter — children. Yes, a family. This house needed a family, a big family with lots of dogs and cats and maybe a cook to fill the kitchen with delicious, baking aromas.

She knocked on the front door but there was no answer. And in her heart, she felt just a tiny bit relieved about that. She could hardly expect Mr Forboys to welcome her with open arms, could she? After all, once she explained her reason for being here, the poor man would probably expect her to take him to court. Not that she'd do that.

Ever since learning about the house, she'd wondered what on earth she should do about it, her thoughts turning first this way, then that. But even if, technically and legally, it turned out that it really did belong to her, she simply couldn't see herself turning anyone out of their home — a home they had a moral right to expect to be safe. She knew only too well how she'd feel if somebody turned up at The Beeches and tried to evict her!

No, she would simply have to play it by ear. Perhaps Mr Forboys would be only too glad to move out — it was a huge place for just one person, and he certainly seemed to be having trouble maintaining the old place. Until they spoke and until she had a better idea of what was what, she had no real idea what she was going to say to him. If he turned out to be an old man, or in dire financial need, she might simply say nothing at all, and go home and forget about it.

To find that he was not in gave her more time to think about it.

She stepped off the porch and walked

around the front to peer into the first window she could find, surprised to see dust-sheets covering the furniture within. Slowly she circumnavigated the house, finding similar signs of vacancy wherever she went.

Empty! It was empty! Frowning, Delphine wondered why nobody was living here. Surely Mr Forboys wasn't intending to let the house simply stand derelict? It only needed some loving care. Or did he intend to sell the land to developers and let them knock the old building down and put up a luxury, soulless villa?

Feeling absurdly angry, Delphine turned away from the house and looked around. There were no near neighbours, but down a grassy track she could just see the roof of a neighbouring house through the trees. Setting off briskly, Delphine made her way towards it.

★   ★   ★

Tahnee stood on the boardwalk, watching the yachts bobbing at anchor. She'd entered the marina at what she silently thought of as 'the millionaires' corner'.

Her father owned a yacht very similar to the ones that bobbed at anchor here, so she was used to this world, where captains and stewards were hired on a more or less permanent basis so that yachts could be 'loaned' out to friends of friends, who paid well for the privilege of using them to cruise to this 'in' spot or that for a month or so. Cannes during the film festival. Cowes during the races. The Mediterranean and Monaco for a spot of gambling.

Now, without regret, she turned away from them. The note had been very specific. She wasn't to hire anything big and gaudy that might attract attention. Nor was she to hire a row-boat.

Carefully, she walked down the quayside; dressed in a short white skirt that came to mid-thigh, white strappy sandals and a bottle-green halter top that left her shoulders bare, she attracted a fair bit of masculine attention, all of which she ignored.

Passing all manner of boats, she scrutinized them all. Some had a high boat-house which she recognized as belonging to big-game fishing boats, most of which were hired out only for the day. A little further down were the bigger, more residential-style kind, for holiday-makers to hire out and live on board for a few weeks — a sort of floating mobile home. She eyed one or two of these, but didn't like the looks of them.

She'd almost reached the last of the boats,

when she saw a 'For Hire' sign on the quay, opposite what looked to her to be a modest but friendly-looking sixty-footer. It was painted white, like most of the others, but with a neat blue, black and orange sequence of stripes that lined the white hull and formed a large fake 'mouth' on the bow. Inside the mouth was the name of the boat — *Belly of the Whale* — and underneath its point of origin — somewhere Tahnee had never heard of.

It was the name that caught her attention more than anything else. Most of the boats bore either women's names, or cutsey punning titles.

Belly of the Whale sounded refreshingly different. She stopped and eyed it. Well, it wasn't big and fancy, and it wasn't a row-boat either. And it was for hire with a captain. Just what the kidnappers had ordered.

'Hello on board,' she called, and a moment later saw the hatch flip open. Then a mop of brown hair, turning almost deep blond in the sun, appeared. A pair of naked, bronzed shoulders followed next, and a young man, maybe in his late twenties/early thirties, stepped on to the deck. He was barefoot, and wore only a pair of ragged jeans, cut off at the mid-thigh to turn them into a pair of raggedy shorts. Every inch of him was lightly muscled and deeply tanned, and seemed to be covered in a film of sweat.

Tahnee, with something of an effort, raised her eyes above the level of his well-formed, hairless chest and met a pair of smiling hazel eyes.

She swallowed hard, and croaked, 'This boat for hire?'

'Sure is. You interested?'

'Yes.'

Although his accent held definite Yankee undertones, she guessed he'd been on the island a long time, for he spoke with a kind of lazy drawl that sounded slightly Calypso. 'You want to go out now?' he asked, looking out over the horizon with a seaman's assessing gaze. 'Sun's a bit high, but there's some good views to be had if you're into photography? Or is diving your thing?' He glanced beyond her, but could see none of the usual scuba paraphernalia of the dedicated diver.

'I'm interested in hiring you for the week. Is that a problem?' Tahnee clarified, realizing he was mistaking her for a bored day-tripper.

'Oh, right,' he said with a sharpening of interest and coming forward he crouched down, the better to see her, through the deck railings. 'You'd better come aboard then, make sure you like the look of her. The

Whale's comfortable, but she's definitely got her own style.'

Tahnee walked to the rear, where a simple plank of wood made do as a gangplank. This she traversed without any difficulty, but when she got to the top he was waiting for her with his hand held out, and she took it automatically.

Her fingers tingled as they clasped his, and a tiny electrical current seemed to shoot up her arm and lodge in her breast, making her nipples tingle, and she felt her breath catch in her throat. Then he gave a small tug and boosted her on board, and she was instantly aware of the power that lay latent in his arm muscles. This was evidently a man who'd earned his muscle power with years of hard manual labour — and not a few hours spent in a top-notch gym full of the latest equipment.

'I'm Jonah Rodgers. I'm captain of the *Whale*.'

Tahnee laughed abruptly. 'So that's why you called her *Belly of the Whale*. An appropriate name for a man called Jonah.'

Jonah Rodgers grinned, revealing white teeth and attractive crow's-feet at the corners of his eyes. He had a roguish, boyish quality that instantly attracted her. 'Well, that, and the fact that she's got a whale of a mortgage on her,' he admitted ruefully. But something, perhaps a glint in his eye, told her that that would not be the case for ever. This was a man who always got what he wanted.

Tahnee nodded, understanding him at once. 'But she'll be all yours one day,' she said softly, and saw him cast her a quick, surprised glance. Obviously, he wasn't expecting such perspicacity from a mere tourist. Then he smiled again, once more the charming would-be host.

'Want to look inside?' He opened the hatch, and added, 'You'd better go down backwards,' but then she was already turning and backing in, and he abruptly bit off the other words of advice that had sprung automatically to his lips. He was glad he had when she neatly ducked her head and went down the steep set of four wooden steps without a qualm.

'You've been on boats before,' he commented, joining her down below and glancing around quickly for anything that looked out of place or untidy. He needn't have worried. He always kept her shipshape.

The main room held a long padded seat that stretched under two portholes, a fixed table, and bookshelves with a glass front to keep the books from falling out during a heavy swell. He always kept the brasswork polished until it gleamed like gold, and the wooden floor was well rubbed with linseed oil; everywhere looked clean, welcoming and comfortable. 'There's a small galley with a fully stocked fridge/freezer below and one sleeper cabin forward,' he added, moving towards the bow, but his beautiful blonde visitor quickly held out a hand. 'It's fine. I'll take her. How much?'

She walked to the table and reached into her bag for her cheque book. Jonah came up to stand beside her, his eyes widening as he noticed the name of the bank. It only gave out private cheque books to very few, and very wealthy, clients.

Jonah, without a qualm, doubled the amount he would normally have charged, and wasn't surprised when his latest client wrote it off without a blink of those fabulously long, dark lashes. When she turned and handed him the cheque, however, he had to force his gaze away from the wide violet eyes looking so steadily back at him, and accepted the cheque with barely a glance. 'You do understand this isn't self-hire, and that I come with the package?' he said firmly.

'Of course,' Tahnee said calmly. 'I've been on a few cruises, but I wouldn't know the first thing about navigation or what-have-you. But for that amount I expect you to be on call twenty-four hours, seven days of this week.' She had no idea when the kidnappers would call her, or where she'd be required to go. She might have to leave at the drop of a hat, and she didn't want a snippy or disgruntled captain to complicate matters.

Jonah flushed a little as he realized that she knew he had overcharged her, and nodded solemnly. 'Three o'clock in the morning, you want to see the moon over Consett Bay — just give the order, ma'am.'

Tahnee's lips twitched. Cheeky beggar, wasn't he? But oh so attractive. And he probably knew it. She dared say that many a woman had hired the *Whale* to sample the delights and charms of its skipper, as much as its top cruising speed or fully stocked fridge/freezer.

Then she gave herself a mental head-slap. What did it matter? She was here to get her stepmother back. Not to flirt with a randy, sexy sea-dog! Abruptly, she turned away from him. 'You'll be moored here for a while?' she asked sharply.

Jonah frowned, sensing the sudden chill, and said quietly, 'Yes, ma'am. This is the *Whale*'s permanent mooring in Bridgetown.'

'Call me Tahnee,' Tahnee said abruptly. 'I'll let you know when I need you. You have a contact number?' she demanded, all business.

Wordlessly Jonah handed her a card from a small stack on top of a bookshelf. Tahnee nodded, slipped it into her bag, and headed back up the steps. Jonah couldn't help but stare at her bottom in its pert white skirt as he followed her up. Once on the deck, Tahnee walked back to the gang plank and stepped on to the quay.

Jonah watched her go and let out a long, slow breath. Those big violet eyes — and that far-out hairstyle. Then he shook his head — she probably had a sugar daddy as rich as Croesus. When she came back he'd probably be in tow, fat as a melon and wearing enough gold jewellery to sink a battleship. During his six years on the waterfront here, Jonah had seen it all.

Still, he couldn't help but watch her, willing her to turn her head and look back at him. Everyone knew what that meant. She was interested.

But the beautiful blonde woman didn't look back, and with a sigh of regret, Jonah Rodgers went back below.

★ ★ ★

Delphine stepped into the bar, blinking a little at the transition from bright Barbados sunshine to shadowy interior.

The man who lived next door to Mowbray House had told her that Gordon Forboys had just sold Mowbray House to the Gale Imperial chain. The news had made Delphine's heart sink. That wonderful family home, sold to an anonymous hotel chain! It didn't bear thinking about. Luckily, the doctor knew that the owner of the chain was an island resident called Dylan Gale.

Delphine had thanked him and returned to town, where she'd promptly looked up Gale Imperial in the phone book. She'd been surprised at how easily she'd got to talk to the great man's secretary, and even more surprised when the great man himself had deigned to speak to her. Yet more proof that things were done differently here. Had she been back in Oxford, she'd probably have had to make an appointment in writing before she could even speak to him!

But a deep, masculine voice had assured her that she was indeed talking to Dylan Gale. She hadn't wanted to say much over the phone, merely that she had some information about Mowbray House, and that it was important that she see him. She thought she'd heard him sigh heavily, but supposed she must have been mistaken. When he'd rather wearily told her that she could meet him at his favourite bar after work that day, and gave her directions, she'd jumped at the opportunity. What she had to tell him was somewhat delicate, and would probably go down better over a few stiff drinks!

Now she peered around the small, friendly-looking bar, surprised to see that it looked like a no-frills local, and not the trendy wine bar that she'd half-expected. Over the bar were hung old sporting pictures of cricket heroes, and no noisy games machines spoiled the ambience. A large ceiling fan rotated to no real effect, and venetian blinds, half-closed to keep out the sun, added to the gloom. As Delphine walked to the bar and ordered a fruit juice, she glanced around curiously. A fifty-something man, wearing a Panama hat, sat in one corner, drinking what looked suspiciously like a Pimms. Two fat women, dressed in colourful sarongs, sat at another table gossiping, and further down the bar, a lone drinker sat reading a paper.

The barman pushed her drink to her — bearing the ubiquitous paper umbrella — and quoted a price. Delphine reached into her bag and drew out her purse, and as she paid, she said tentatively, 'I don't suppose you know a Mr Dylan Gale, do you?'

Somewhat to her surprise, the barman grinned widely and pointed down the bar. As he did so, the solitary drinker glanced up, then slowly slipped off his stool. As Delphine approached him, her eyes widened slightly. The man seemed to keep on elongating as he rose, until he stood to at least six feet three. In the dim, shadowy interior, his head reached the level of a high window, revealing a halo of silver-gold hair. He was wearing a pair of pale blue slacks and a plain white shirt, rolled up at the sleeves and open at the neck. When she was just a few feet away, she stopped nervously.

Pale green eyes swept her from head to foot, and she felt her heartbeat falter.

Her mother and friends had always insisted that she was beautiful, as had Colin and a fair few other men as well. But she had never been able to see it herself — and yet something in the way this man looked at her made her wonder, for the first time in her life.

Dylan Gale watched the woman approach, and felt as if someone had just hit him in the stomach. When the anonymous female voice over the telephone had told him that she knew something about Mowbray House, he suspected it couldn't be good. She had to be either someone who knew what trouble Gordon Forboys had managed to get himself into or, worse, an intermediary for that slug, Marcus Bolton. So he'd directed her here, not wanting to taint the offices of Gale Imperial with her presence.

Now he found himself looking at the most beautiful woman he'd ever seen.

She didn't look tiny, as most women did from his vast height, so she must be at least five feet ten. She had a perfect, hour-glass figure, with long, shapely legs that were hinted at beneath a long, floating skirt of pale lilac. She was obviously new to the island, for her long bare arms were pale as milk, and underneath the white lace of her top, her shoulders seemed equally untanned. In stark contrast to the creaminess of her skin, masses of long, curly black hair tumbled down her back to her waist, while a perfectly oval face held deep, dark brown pansy eyes of liquid velvet. A long straight nose, and a perfectly shaped mouth completed the vision.

He drew in a long, helpless breath, and hoped like hell that he wasn't in as much trouble as he thought he was. Trouble that had nothing to do with Mowbray House, or Bolton.

'Mr Gale?' Delphine asked tentatively. He didn't look like anybody's idea of a hotel magnate. Perhaps the barman had got it wrong?

Her accent was as British in person as it sounded on the phone and Dylan felt his face tighten. 'I'm Dylan Gale,' he agreed flatly. 'Please, have a seat.' He moved back and pulled a tall bar stool next to his own.

Delphine smiled nervously, and climbed, somewhat awkwardly, on to it. She rested her bag and drink on the bar, and took a long breath.

Now that she was here, face to face with him, she wasn't sure where to start. She'd thought that having to deal with a businessman would be better than having to deal with a private owner, but now she wasn't so sure. There was something unyielding about this man that both thrilled and scared her.

She watched him as he re-took his seat, noting the smooth, square chin, the flat angled planes of his cheeks, the high cheekbones and thick blond eyebrows over extraordinary jade-green eyes. She simply hadn't expected him to look like this.

She could hear her heart racing, and told herself not to be silly. She was twenty-six, not sixteen! She was a mature woman, well on her way to getting a doctorate from Oxford, not some giddy schoolgirl experiencing her first crush. She had to get a grip.

But as he turned and reached for his glass, lifted it and took a healthy swallow, and as she watched his Adam's apple bob up and down in his tanned, smooth throat, Delphine realized that, for perhaps the first time in her life, she was hopelessly, sexually attracted to a man.

She'd known it happen to her friends, of course. And her own mother had often told her that when she'd met Delphine's father, it was as if the earth had moved. And, of course, as a literary graduate, she'd read all the great love stories. Cathy and Heathcliff. Romeo and Juliet. Tristram and Isolde. She knew how grand passions, love and romance worked in books all right.

But she'd never expected it to happen to *her*. Not out of the blue, not like this. Not when she was distracted by so much else. And, because she'd never really thought it would happen to her, she had no idea what to do!

Oxford was calm, studious, careful, thoughtful, and it had turned her into all of those things too. This wild heat in her blood was as alien to her as another planet.

'So, Miss Phillips, is it? What can I do for you?' Dylan asked politely. 'And what do you know about Mowbray House?'

Delphine blinked, caught totally off-guard by the cool, businesslike voice, and said the first thing that came into her head.

'Well, I think it belongs to me,' she said.

4

'I beg your pardon?'

Whatever it was that Dylan had expected her to say, it hadn't been that. He stared at her in frank amazement, and saw a tide of colour flush up from her lovely neck to stain her smooth creamy cheeks. Telling lies obviously didn't come easy to her. At least she had a little shame — that was something.

'I'm sorry,' Delphine blurted. 'But it's true. I think Mowbray House rightfully belongs to me.'

She hadn't meant to just blurt it out like that. On the way over, she'd been rehearsing this meeting over and over in her head, and in her imagination she'd always led up to it gradually, explaining the circumstances carefully and giving the man plenty of time to see beforehand just what was coming, and thus to lessen the shock. Then she planned to tell him that she hoped they could reach some sort of amicable, mutually beneficial agreement. What she wanted to avoid, most of all, was coming across like a litigious gold-digger out to snatch his property.

Obviously she was failing miserably, for his

jaw tightened and his emerald eyes began to harden until they resembled the gem stones they reminded her of. 'Like hell you are, lady,' Dylan denied flatly. 'I paid good money for that house not two days ago. The deal went through with solicitors on both sides, and is airtight. I don't know what con game you're trying to pull, but you can go back to Bolton and tell him he's out of his mind.'

Delphine blinked, totally wrong-footed. 'Who?' Who was this Bolton man?

Dylan's lips twisted wryly. Oh, so innocent. Those big brown velvet eyes, so like a puppy dog's that had been caught chewing the master's slipper. And those slender, dark brows, caught up in such a puzzled little frown of bewilderment. She should be on the stage. Or maybe she was. He wouldn't put it past Bolton to hire someone from the acting arena to try and pull something like this off. Just how stupid did he think he was? Whatever game the crook was playing, he was in no mood to play along.

'Marcus Bolton, the man who wants Mowbray House so badly,' Dylan clarified dryly and with exaggerated patience. 'You know, the man who's paying you for this con trick.'

Delphine swallowed hard. Was it possible that Dylan Gale, the hotel magnate, was as mad as a hatter? Except for the fact that she could feel the anger coming off him in waves, she might have thought so. But the way he was looking at her — as if she was something he'd scraped off his shoe — left her feeling as if there was more to all of this than met the eye.

'Look, Mr Gale . . . ' She took a deep breath, trying to keep some sort of a grip on reality, and not let the situation slide totally away from her. 'I don't know any Mr Bolton, or what's going on here. I have no idea what you're talking about, and can only assure you I'm not trying to cheat you — only inform you of the facts as they stand. I only just arrived from England, literally a few hours ago, and I swear I've never met anyone called Bolton. Perhaps I'd just better explain what's happened?' Surely, once he'd heard her story, he would realize that she wasn't part of anything shady.

She couldn't even begin to guess who this Marcus Bolton was, and what his interest in the house could be — or, far more importantly, why this gorgeous, angry man thought she was mixed up with him. But the sooner she put him right, the better.

Dylan grinned, but it was the smile of a predator rather than the smile of an amused human being. 'Go on then,' he said, slowly crossing his arms over his wide chest, pulling the material taut across his biceps to reveal lines of sculpted muscle. 'I can't wait to hear this.'

With some effort, Delphine dragged her eyes away from her appreciation of his torso, and met his eyes with a wince of dismay. Whilst she'd never thought she was the sort who turned men's heads, she wasn't used to being looked at with such outright disgust either. And as she felt herself shrivel a little inside, it sparked her first whiff of anger. Just who did he think he was to treat her like this? She'd come here in good faith, and with nothing like malice aforethought, and she simply did not deserve to be treated like dirt.

Perhaps rather belatedly, her chin came up and her dark eyes narrowed slightly.

Dylan felt the breath catch in the back of his throat and something tingled and tightened in his loins. She reminded him of a sleek, dark cat, slowly awakening to anger and the anticipation of sharp claws roused something very male, deep within his psyche. It was heady, wonderful stuff, and made him feel powerfully alive. And that alone set the alarm bells ringing. Slowly he uncrossed his arms, reached for his drink and took a long, slow nonchalant swallow.

'Please, go ahead,' he said mockingly.

'Really. I'm all ears.'

So, slowly, step by step, Delphine told him her story. To begin with, as she described her house, her mother's recent demise, and her discovery in the attic, he'd looked attentive and amused. Then, when she described the contents of the will, the names involved, and how she took it to Colin to have a legal opinion, he'd started to look downright sceptical. And when she told him about what they'd learned of the history of the house and Moorcroft Mowbray in particular, he began to shake his head. Finally, with her voice at last petering out, he gave her a slow handclap.

Delphine felt the humiliated heat sweep across her face once more, and cast a quick glance around the bar. But nobody seated at the tables seemed to be paying them any attention. Only the bartender, standing nearby and catching her eye, suddenly started and moved ostentatiously away, wiping a beer glass with a towel. Obviously, he'd been eavesdropping. It only made her feel ten times worse to think that her humiliation had been a source of his private entertainment.

Fiercely, she turned on Dylan Gale — sitting there, like some sneering Adonis. And to think that she'd been so attracted to him she'd almost swooned at his feet like some Victorian heroine! Well that would teach her to let her imagination — not to mention her libido — run riot!

'Every word is true,' she said grimly.

'Oh, I daresay much of it is,' Dylan agreed. 'I can't see Bolton failing to do his homework. I'm perfectly willing to believe that someone called Moorcroft Mowbray owned the house in the past. But as for the rest of it!' Dylan shook his head sadly. 'Just how gullible do you think I am?'

'Since I don't know you from Adam, Mr Gale,' Delphine began icily, 'and have no wish to, I'm sure I can't say.'

'Then let me enlighten you, Miss Phillips,' Dylan said tightly. 'I'm the sort of man who holds on to what's his. I'm the sort of man who doesn't knuckle under to crooked bullies of the likes of Marcus Bolton. I'm the sort of man who'll see you in court if you try to persist with this con game. In short, I'm the sort of man you don't want to mess around with.' And having said that, he tossed a bill across to the bartender, who'd wandered back up the bar to be within earshot again, nodded at her curtly and walked away.

Outside, Dylan took a long, deep breath. Damn! He'd just known Bolton wouldn't let it lie. But to come up with some cock-and-bull scam like this had been unexpected. To be frank, he'd been expecting something far more crude — something that included violence and threats. This little piece of theatre was almost tame by comparison, but the fact that he'd found himself so damnably attracted to Bolton's appointed femme fatale was so pitiful it was almost funny.

Well, at least he hadn't let it affect his judgement.

But as he walked towards his Jaguar XJS, he couldn't shake the image of two large, pansy-brown eyes that looked at him with such melting interest and then smouldering anger. Hell, that woman was dynamite on legs. But with any luck, she'd go back to Bolton with her tail between her legs, and he'd never see her again. Bolton would be bound to try something else once he'd realized he'd failed, and would almost certainly put her on the next plane out of here — if only to make sure she kept her mouth shut.

As he slipped behind the steering wheel and turned on the powerful engine, Dylan Gale tried to make himself believe that he was glad about that.

Meanwhile, Delphine still sat at the bar, shaking with anger, humiliation, and something far more painful. Eventually, realizing that she couldn't stay there all day, she slowly slid off the stool and walked, on weak-kneed legs, to the door. Outside, she stood blinking in the bright late-afternoon sunlight.

One thing was for sure. She was not about to let Dylan Gale get away with treating her like this. When she'd come here she'd been determined to be reasonable and fair. Now it was all-out war! She was going to take possession of Mowbray House come hell or high water.

So, she'd better get cracking. First she'd need to do more research, and to learn all she could about both the house and how Christopher Allinson had come to inherit it in the first place. Eventually, she'd need a good lawyer. But that could wait. She only hoped the libraries stayed open late.

Shoulders back, she set out to find the location of the public records offices. And tried to tell herself that she was only doing what was right. All those years ago, Moorcroft Mowbray had wanted her great uncle to inherit the house — and the wishes of a dead man had to account for something, didn't they? It meant nothing that she was a woman scorned; some poor deluded female who'd found herself knocked out by love at first sight, only to be cruelly rejected. That had nothing to do with it! It had merely been a momentary madness, of which she was now thoroughly cured. Next time she saw Dylan

Gale, he'd do nothing for her. Her pulse wouldn't rocket, and her heart wouldn't dance, and, most important of all, her body wouldn't melt like an ice lolly in the sun.

It damned well wouldn't!

* * *

Back in the bar, Ollie Mombar, the bartender, walked to the phone sitting at the end of the bar, and rang a familiar number.

Like many people on the island, Ollie wore many hats — and as well as being a bartender, he made a nice little profit from selling gossip to the police. It was surprising how much Ollie overheard while pouring drinks and lending a sympathetic ear. Enough to keep him in fine rum and CDs, anyway.

The phone was instantly answered by a familiar voice. Ollie had gone to school with the man on the other end of the line, and the fact that he'd once busted Ollie for possession of marijuana wasn't something that he'd ever held against him. Especially since he paid so well.

'Hey, mon, it's me, Ollie.' He wedged the phone under his ear, and reached for another glass.

'Ollie.' His friend sounded weary.

'I just heard somethin' you might find

96

interestin',' Ollie said, breathing on the glass he was polishing, and rubbing vigorously.

'Look, Ollie, I've had a long day, yeah, and it ain't over yet. So I'm not in the mood for any idle chit-chat. You got something or not?'

Ollie's round, dark face beamed. 'Oh, I got something, mon. You gonna like it. It concerns your favourite res-ee-dent.' He strung out the final word teasingly, and wasn't surprised when his policeman friend's voice suddenly sharpened.

'Bolton? You've heard something he's pulling?'

Ollie sighed. What was it with the Barbados constabulary and Marcus Bolton? Every man jack of them had the hots to put Bolton behind bars. He supposed the fact that the island's biggest crime lord was still free and leading la vida loca must really burn them. Whatever it was, he wasn't complaining. He made a nice living out of it.

'I could do with a hundred. You know, my surfboard needs waxing and that lady of mine — '

'For a hundred it better be good.' The voice cut him off warningly, and Ollie grinned.

'Listen up. I just heard this very interesting conversation. You ever heard of Dylan Gale?'

'The hotel owner? He's clean as a whistle,' the voice said dismissively. 'Don't try and sell me a pup, Ollie, or I'll have your big fat ass in jail so fast your head'll spin.'

'No, no, mon, just listen. It's like this, see . . . '

* * *

Unaware that he was being discussed with such interest by a policeman and his nark, Marcus Bolton slowly leaned back on a floating air-mattress and looked up at a glass sky.

He had a villa not far from Crabhill, which naturally came with a swimming pool, and one which he tried to use every day. Now he put a lazy hand in the water and scooped it to one side, slowly propelling himself gently towards the edge of the pool where two men waited, watching him with calm, flat faces. One was white, one black, one was a native of the islands, one was an Aussie import. One dressed in shorts and multi-coloured shirts, the other in khaki slacks and jacket that never seemed to crease. For all their differences, however, they had two things in common — both worked for Bolton, and both were good with their fists.

Marcus expertly rolled off the airbed and planted his feet firmly on the blue, black and aquamarine tiles that lined the bottom of the swimming pool. With just a little effort, he hauled his solid bulk out of the water, and walked towards a sun lounger. There he reached for a blue and white terry-cloth bathing robe and slipped it on, covering up his black shorts and podgy body.

Both men were careful not to watch him.

'I've got a job for you,' Bolton said curtly, reaching down towards a glass table and pouring himself a gin and tonic. He reached for the ice bucket and added plenty of cubes. 'There's a man called Gale. Dylan Gale. Heard of him?'

The black man nodded, the Australian just looked blank. 'Hotel guy. Legit,' the black man acknowledged.

'Right,' Bolton agreed tersely. 'He bought something that I want, and is oddly reluctant to sell it on to me. I don't like that.'

The Australian slowly smiled. He was a big man, standing at just over six feet, with short brown hair and a face that looked like it had been in the boxing ring more than was good for it.

'I want you to find him, give him a little lesson in manners, and tell him that if he doesn't sell me Mowbray House, the next time the lesson will be fatal. Got that?'

'Sure boss,' the black man said.

Marcus Bolton's lips twisted wryly. 'Repeat

it back to me. I want the message given verbatim.'

'Huh? Oh sure, boss.' The black man paraphrased the message, and Bolton sighed wearily. 'Go on. And don't be seen.'

Wordlessly, the two men left.

Marcus waited until they'd gone, then walked through the pool area into a cool, airy hall, and on through into one of the guest bedrooms.

There a beautiful woman, lying on the bed in a diminutive white bikini, glanced up from the magazine she was reading and smiled widely. 'Hope you didn't mind me coming over, baby. I get so bored in that little cabin. It's so remote and there's nothing to do.' She pouted and slid off the bed.

Marcus smiled and slipped off the bathrobe.

⋆   ⋆   ⋆

Tahnee felt her heart lurch as the telephone rang, and she ran towards it, pausing a moment to catch her breath before lifting the receiver.

'Hello?'

'Miss Sawyer. How are you enjoying Barbados?'

The voice was mocking, accentless and

slightly oily. It instantly made her feel dirty. Taking another calming breath, Tahnee replied grimly, 'I'm sure you haven't called me to find out how I'm doing. What do you want?'

'So unfriendly! But you're right. I want you to get in your boat and take in the sights at Cuckold Point. There's a rocky little inlet there and you'll see a bright red marker on the beach. You're to take the diamonds there.'

'What do I — hello? Hello?' But the caller had already hung up. Tahnee bit her lip and slowly lowered her own receiver. Then she walked to the bathroom, retrieved the pot of face cream and its precious cargo and slipped it into the voluminous beach bag she'd bought at the hotel store. Then she dialled Jonah Rodgers' number.

'Hello, Jonah Rodgers.'

'Mr Rodgers, it's me. I want to take the boat out right away. Is she ready?'

'Of course.'

Tahnee said curtly, 'I'll be there in ten minutes.'

On his boat, Jonah heard the dial tone in his ear and flipped his mobile shut. 'Yes ma'am,' he said dryly, and saluted his phone. Then he sighed, and went down to the engine room.

★ ★ ★

Marcus Bolton had his lady friend driven back to her 'cabin' and stretched luxuriously. Then he dressed in a pair of Giorgio Armani slacks and a raw silk shirt that did nothing for either his colouring or squat figure, and walked out on to the terrace.

There, sunbirds sipped from a nectar feeder that his gardeners kept topped up, while other native birds sang from well-pruned trees. Out to sea, a plethora of pleasure boats bobbed and danced, as well as a big ocean liner, bound for the docks, with its cargo of tourists, all eager to spend their holiday dollars. The scene looked like something from a dream. Not bad for a slum kid from Hell's Kitchen, Bolton thought with a self-satisfied smile.

He pulled up a chair and sat down, sunning himself like a lizard. He could still smell the stink and squalor that had been his childhood. It had been a long, hard road from that to this. And he'd earned every inch of it. Spilling blood — both his own and others', grafting, spending two stretches inside and then nearly dying from a knife wound inflicted by some drug-crazed pimp in Harlem who hadn't known who he was messing with.

A few years ago, he'd semi-retired here, keeping his hand in just to make sure that he had a ready supply of spending cash. And indulging in the odd offbeat deal now and then, like this gig he had going with his lady-friend. Now there was some wild chick. Still, he'd be dollars in before it was all finished.

Marcus liked it here. He liked being a big fish in a small pond. He liked the fact that the police were driven to a frenzy of frustration at having nothing on him. What he didn't like was being thwarted. Being defied. Even as a child, he'd had to get his own way.

OK, Mowbray House was no big deal. As far as his little empire went, it was barely a pimple. He wanted it simply because it had a secret staircase built into the cliff that led from the cellars to the cove beneath. An eighteenth-century feat of engineering by the original builder, it had probably been commissioned by the owner so that he could smuggle in dusty maidens to his private bedchamber, keeping his white, conservative and very rich wife in blissful ignorance. The fact that, centuries later, it would make an ideal arrangement for drug smugglers would never have occurred to him.

His drug runners could have moved their goods from sea to land in total privacy, without having to worry about the customs and excise men who kept such a wary eye on them. And the fact that that pain-in-the-ass, island-royalty WASP Dylan Gale had got in first, and then refused to play ball, stuck in his craw.

It simply couldn't be tolerated.

The trouble was, Bolton had always been careful not to step on the toes of the legitimate businessmen on the island. They had friends in high places who could, potentially, make trouble for him. He had no such scruples about dealing with the low-lives, the grafters and grifters and bent cops who inhabited the underbelly of the towns and capital. But Gale was a different proposition all together. His father was a well-respected businessman and came from old money and old family — or what passed for it on Barbados. Moving against him could well have repercussions. He would have to be careful.

He also didn't like the hard, cold look in the man's eye during their last meeting. Marcus hadn't met many men in his life who had been able to look at him like that. And those who had had always been trouble. The kind who wouldn't knuckle under. The kind who thought they were better than him. He only hoped an old-fashioned beating would shake the upper-class little preppy boy out of his complacency. Once he'd had a few ribs cracked, and that pretty-boy face of his rearranged, he'd probably cave like a deflated balloon.

Marcus grinned and leaned back in the sun lounger, the bright sunlight reduced to a red-orange haze behind his closed lids.

*　*　*

Jonah waited at the gangplank as she walked along the quay. He heard a long, slow wolf-whistle emanate from the boat berthed next to his, and smiled. A party of teenage lads from Harvard had hired his friend's boat and were due to sail to St Vincent on the next tide. He couldn't fault their taste.

Now, she was wearing a dark blue dress that left her arms and shoulders bare, and floated down to rest just above her knees. It was obviously that season's design, and probably cost more than he made in a month of charters. Dark blue sandals with high heels complemented the outfit, but would have to go. He couldn't have her walking around on the *Whale*'s decks in those. The sun turned her short cap of silver hair into a halo of light that almost hurt the eyes. She was carrying a large wicker beach bag slung carefully over one shoulder, and it looked heavy. What was it about women, that they felt it necessary to carry so much stuff about with them?

'Good afternoon,' Jonah greeted her politely as she walked up the wooden plank towards him. 'I'm sorry, but I'll have to ask you to take off the shoes. I've got some deck shoes here that should fit you. You're a size four, yes?'

Tahnee nodded, and wordlessly bent down to pull off first one shoe then the other. As she did so, she leaned forward slightly, and Jonah found himself looking down her creamy cleavage. He swallowed hard and jerked his eyes back up to her face, where he found her watching him with a knowing, vaguely amused look. He could have kicked himself for being so obvious and quickly glanced over her shoulder, looking for her companion but seeing no one.

'Are you alone?' he asked, puzzled.

'Yes, it's just me,' Tahnee said crisply. 'I want to head over to Cuckold Point. You know it?'

'Sure. It's on the north end of the island. Anywhere specific you want to see?'

'No,' Tahnee said, then confusingly added, 'I mean yes, but I'm not sure where it is yet.'

Seeing him raise an eyebrow in query, she smiled briefly. 'What I mean is, I'll know it when I see it.'

'OK,' he said, obviously puzzled. 'I'll just

cast off and we'll get going.' They still had nearly five hours before the sun set, which came late this time of the year.

She nodded, slipping her feet into the canvas deck shoes he'd provided, and watched him leap lithely on to the quay to unwind the mooring ropes aft and forward. By the time he'd got back on board, she'd found a padded seat under a shady awning, and was gazing curiously around the marina.

Jonah glanced at her. No doubt about it, she was something of an enigma. Why no man? And why wasn't she interested in the more usual tourist destinations? Most women he knew would be headed off to the Animal Flower Cave, Farley Hill or Cherry Tree Hill. Maybe even Morgan Lewis Mills, or the east coast, St John's Church or Sam Lord's Castle. Maybe stopping off for drinks at the Atlantis Hotel in Bathsheba. He couldn't see why she wanted to take the boat up to Cuckold Point. Unless she was a scenery freak. There were certainly some wild, out-of-the-way crags and cliffs and coves up there.

Shrugging, Jonah went down below, turned the ignition of the *Whale*'s modest but well-maintained engine, and headed slowly out of the harbour. Overhead, gulls called raucously, and he felt his heart lift, as it always did, whenever he left harbour.

Tahnee held the bag tightly on her lap, resisting the urge to check that the pot of face cream was still there. Her heart was thundering in her chest. What would she do if there was someone waiting for her on this beach with the red marker? She had the gun, but she didn't dare use it. What if they took the diamonds, and then never contacted her again? For all she knew, Cordelia could be dead already. Before she handed over the diamonds, she'd have to insist on some proof that her stepmother was all right and that she would be released. It was a gamble, but it was one she had to take.

But suppose something went wrong? Suppose she was attacked, and they stole the diamonds from her, and then demanded more? After all, she was headed for some remote spot with only a new gun for protection, and maybe Jonah Rodgers.

She studied the man in the glassed-in wheelhouse carefully. He was young and fit, probably a bit of a chancer, but she was a good judge of men, and felt comfortable in his presence. His heart was probably in the right place. But would he come to her rescue if she got into difficulties? Could she expect him to, or even ask it of him? If things turned nasty, he could be risking his life. No, she couldn't rely on him — it wouldn't be fair. Nor could she tell him that she might be expecting trouble. He might go to the police — that was what any honest citizen would do, after all, but it was the last thing she could let happen.

No, she was definitely on her own.

She didn't know that Jonah had a mirror in the wheelhouse and that for the last few minutes he'd been watching her watching him. She had no idea that her face was so expressive, or realize that she was fairly oozing tension, making the captain of the boat very uneasy indeed.

As they headed out of Bridgetown and north, towards Paradise Beach, Jonah frowned, his hands running expertly over the wheel as he mentally mapped out his course.

There was something definitely wrong with this picture. When he'd booked her in for the week, he'd expected to ferry her and some sugar daddy around the coast to various fun spots — up to St Peter's Parish, perhaps, and the nightlife spots at Speightstown and Heywoods. Maybe moor off Six Men's Bay while she and her lover held a private beach party for two. Instead, here he was taking her alone to a remote point on the north of the island, and far from acting as if she was off to have a good time, she looked far more like a girl heading off to her own execution.

He warned himself sternly to mind his own business. He was just a glorified chauffeur, after all, nothing more. If the woman had her troubles, it wasn't his job to solve them for her. But time and time again his glance moved to the mirror and he watched her.

She looked so young, so troubled and grim. It made him want to stop the boat and go to her, squat down in front of her and take her hands into his own and coax her into telling him what was wrong.

But that was probably not a good idea. Jonah had grown up poor and fast, and had quickly learned that the rich were different. And dangerous. Best just to give them a wide berth.

After an hour's steady sailing, they passed Maycock's Bay and headed up past Crabhill towards North Point. Jonah glanced at her over his shoulder and called out, 'Cuckold Point coming up on the right soon.'

'Right. Thanks,' Tahnee said, and reached into her huge beach bag. Jonah wasn't much surprised when her hand re-emerged holding a powerful pair of large binoculars.

He wouldn't have pegged her as a bird-watcher, though. And, sure enough, after watching her for ten minutes or so, realized she wasn't training the glasses on birds at all.

Nor was she whale or dolphin watching either, for her glasses regularly swept the coastal area inland, while the sun glinted off the gold and diamond wristwatch that she wore.

Suddenly, she stiffened. 'I want to go ashore. Can you get the outboard ready?'

The *Whale*, like most charter boats, went everywhere with a small tender attached. Jonah dutifully cut the engine and weighed anchor, then stepped down and went aft. There he checked the winch, and turned to help her into the small wooden boat.

'You know how to work the outboard motor?' he checked.

'Of course,' Tahnee said curtly, too wound up to be polite. 'Just lower me down. I don't know how long I'll be.'

Jonah nodded curtly and did as he was told, resisting the urge to snap off another brisk salute. He watched her carefully, but was satisfied that she knew her way around a small boat. And, sure enough, a few moments later she was headed towards an isolated beach, inaccessible by land. He thought he could see something red on the foreshore, but with the naked eye it was hard to tell. So, perhaps she was meeting a lover here after all and that was his signal to her. It must be very hush-hush if the lovebirds were going to this much trouble not to be seen together. Perhaps the man had a very suspicious wife?

Feeling oddly depressed all at once, Jonah shrugged, and stretched out on the deck. Above him a seagull called, sounding as if it was laughing mockingly at him.

Jonah cursed mildly and told it to shut up.

★ ★ ★

Tahnee ran the boat ashore and, once satisfied that it couldn't drift away, walked slowly up the beach towards a pole that had been planted in the sand. Now that she was closer, she could see that the marker was, in fact, a bright red plastic bag. The logo on it was unfamiliar to her.

Inside, was a single piece of paper. Nervously she looked around, but the beach was tiny, with no possible hiding places. Slowly she felt some of the fear ooze out of her and quickly reached into the bag and withdrew the note and read it.

GOOD. NO COPS. TOMORROW MORNING GO TO SUNBURY PLANTATION HOUSE. YOU WILL BE WATCHED. TAKE THE DIAMONDS WITH YOU.

Tahnee gave a low moan of frustration. She'd been hoping to get this over and done with here and now. Why ask her to bring the diamonds if they didn't want them to be delivered? Was it possible they were trying to figure out where she had them hidden so that they could steal them? But why bother? They only had to ask and she'd willingly hand them over.

More likely they were just playing games with her — wearing her down, trying to break her nerve and make her more compliant. Well, to hell with them!

Angrily, Tahnee stalked to the boat and pushed off.

On board the *Whale*, Jonah heard the engine and shot up, putting his hands over the ridge of his eyes to shade them. Yes, it was the boat coming back all right. She'd barely been gone five minutes!

Wordlessly, he helped her climb up the ladder on to the boat, and then winched the tender back into position.

'Where to now?' he asked, turning to look at her. She was staring out to sea vaguely, and looked at him blankly for a moment, as if she'd hardly heard him.

Then she smiled bleakly. 'Oh, back to Bridgetown, please.'

Jonah blinked, then nodded. 'Back to Bridgetown it is.'

Tahnee watched him go back to the wheelhouse and sat down wearily in her old spot under the awning. The poor man must think she was mad. Oh, how she wished it was all over. She was worried about her father too. What if something went wrong with his operation? She should be there, by his side, not here, so far from home. And so damned alone.

Jonah watched her shoulders slump forward and the despairing way in which she dropped her face into her cupped hands, and took an instinctive step towards her. Then he stopped. The woman was too beautiful, too potentially dangerous, to play around with. Already he could feel her tugging on his heartstrings, and he knew where that could lead. As his old gran back in Chicago used to say: 'Tears before bedtime.'

Turning his boat back towards her home port, Jonah Rodgers kept his eyes firmly on the sea ahead.

But every fibre of his being was concentrated on the unhappy, beautiful blonde, sitting behind him.

5

Delphine was lucky to find a library that was staying open until 7.30, and quickly made her way to the newspaper archives microfiche. There, a friendly woman wearing an enormous and colourful muumuu, proudly told her that most of the island's newspaper records were now available on computer. Delphine felt quite guilty when her face fell upon hearing that the year she was interested in was 1932.

'Ah, those are still on the old-fashioned system,' the assistant librarian admitted sadly, shaking her head. 'We have a girl come in to see to the database, but it takes so much time.'

'Oh, I'm sure microfiche will be fine,' Delphine said hastily. 'I'm an academic, so I'm used to rooting around in dusty files and things. I'm sure your system is very good.'

With the beaming smile restored, the woman showed Delphine to a machine, and helped her locate the files she wanted. Nowadays, there were only three or four major newspapers that catered to the island's needs, but in the past there were many more, smaller periodicals, and the assistant librarian was determined that the beautiful and gracious English woman would see them all! Delphine thanked her profusely and, with one eye on the clock, set to quickly.

She found Moorcroft Mowbray's obituary first, and copied down the salient details. He'd been well liked and respected, apparently, and the photograph of him accompanying the obit showed a man in his middle fifties, tanned and fit, wearing white flannels and a Panama hat. Scrolling forward in time, she found little else about the estate, however. Which only confirmed that there had been no apparent scandal or question about the inheritance of the Mowbray estate by Christopher Allinson. She was sure that scandal mongers would have loosened their tongues had there been any question about it, and one of the papers was bound to pick up on it — if only to give carefully worded hints that would keep the libel lawyers happy.

But there was nothing. Not even a sniff of a second, later will.

OK. Deciding to give her eyes a rest after forty minutes of solid scrolling, Delphine left the microfiche and sat down in front of the library's computer. There she quickly got on to the Net, typed in the words Christopher Allinson, Barbados and Mowbray Estate and sent an unfamiliar search engine on to the trail.

It came up trumps in just a few seconds.

On the screen, an old newspaper article from 1930 showed a picture of a downtown public house, with two inset pictures of Moorcroft Mowbray and another man, in his late twenties, identified as Christopher Allinson. On the night of 8 June 1930, patrons of the bar were amused to find themselves witnesses to a spectacular fist-fight between the two men, whom, the reporter believed, were uncle and nephew. Witnesses to the fight couldn't say what had started the violence exactly — but most were in agreement that Moorcroft Mowbray was angry over some kind of gambling debt that Christopher Allinson had run up, using his uncle as a guarantor of payment.

'They had a right old barney about it,' one witness, Fred Coombs, of St John's Parish said. 'Mowbray even told young Christopher that he was going to cut him out of his will. That really made the fur fly.'

When asked who threw the first punch, another witness insisted that it was the younger man, enraged by the threat of disinheritance. 'He landed one on his uncle's chin that fair knocked Mowbray

117

over,' a young man, who didn't want to be named, confided. 'Not that he was down for long. Old man Moorcroft is as tough as they come and was soon up on his feet and swinging right back. I think the young fella was surprised. Anyway, he pretty quickly got a black eye. It was a real shiner!' the anonymous witness assured me, with some admiration. 'Then the barman took exception and they took it outside.'

Delphine smiled at the slightly old-fashioned reporting style, but carried on reading avidly.

At this point, someone obviously called the police, for Constable Dean Collins and his superior, Sgt Ned Jenkins, arrived and broke up the fight. Both Mr Mowbray and Mr Allinson were bound over to keep the peace, and appeared in front of magistrates the next morning, and were each fined the sum of five dollars for disorderly conduct.
    Outside the court, Mr Allinson refused to comment, but Mr Mowbray was heard to mutter ominously that he was off to see the family solicitor.

At this point Delphine felt her hopes rise, but unfortunately, the reporter didn't mention the name of Moorcroft's legal representatives.

Instead it went on to add:

'*This reporter has since learned that Mr Allinson, a nephew-by-marriage of the plantation owner, has had a long-standing rocky relationship with his rich uncle. A close friend of Mr Allinson's, Mr Peter Purgold, told me, 'Oh, I expect Chris will make it up with the old bear. He always does'.*'

Delphine paid the few coins needed to make copies of both the obituary and the newspaper report, then, with a few minutes still left before closing time, typed in Mowbray, Court Records and Disorderly Conduct. With a bit of luck, she reasoned, the family lawyer who'd dealt with the will would also have been present to represent his client.

She was in luck. During his short hearing, Mr Moorcroft Mowbray had been represented by counsel, listed as Mr Michael Miller, of Miller, Glenross and Orlando, with offices in Broad Street. With a sigh of satisfaction, Delphine wrote down both the name and address. Although she was sure that Michael Miller himself was probably long since dead, she had hopes that the law firm, under some auspices or other, had survived. With even more luck, they might still be at the same address.

Collecting her booty, Delphine waved a thank you to the assistant librarian as she left, and, with the sun turning a golden mellow orange as she stepped out on to the pavement, headed slowly towards the town's picturesque harbour, or as it was known locally, the Careenage.

Broad Street, her map of the city informed her, was west of Trafalgar, past the House of Assembly and Parliament buildings.

*   *   *

Jonah reached for his sunglasses and slipped them on. With the sun beginning its spectacular descent, it was getting low on the horizon, and was shining right in his eyes. His brows furrowed as he steered the *Whale* towards her home port, and as the wheel slid smoothly between his hands, Tahnee watched him with gentle envy.

He was a man so at home and at ease in his own skin that she felt tears prick her eyes. If only she could say the same for herself! But such thinking was only self-pity, of course, and with a grim smile, she told herself to cut it out. It was stupid to be so bitterly disappointed that it wasn't all over by now. But just because she was feeling so miserable,

120

it didn't mean she should be jealous of Jonah Rodgers' obvious happiness.

'This boat means everything to you, doesn't it?' she heard herself ask, and when he glanced at her over his shoulder, her breath caught at his carefree smile.

'She sure does,' he admitted readily. 'I grew up on the wrong side of Chicago. It was cold and grey and vicious. Every day I'd dream of escaping, of owning a boat and sailing the seven seas.'

Tahnee nodded. Growing up rich, secure and happy, she didn't try to pretend she understood his dream. But that didn't stop her feeling glad that he'd achieved it.

'And you?' he asked, catching her unawares. She looked at him blankly, for a moment not understanding what he was asking. She was so wrapped up with her current problems it was hard to focus on anything else.

'You have a dream?' he prompted, seeing her frown of puzzlement.

'Oh, yes, I suppose so. I run my own gallery.' She'd always loved art, but knew her own modest talent with a watercolour pallet would only ever be a hobby. Running a gallery was the next best thing, and she was happy enough with her professional life as it was. But it didn't fulfil her as this boat, and this lifestyle, so obviously fulfilled this man.

She could start a gallery anywhere. Could paint anything she chose. She could uproot herself at a moment's notice without a qualm. But this man and the sea, the open skies, his boat, the seagulls and the salt in the air, all seemed to form one single creature that she couldn't imagine existing anywhere else. For a man like that, so long as he had his boat, he took his world with him.

'So what happened to sailing the seven seas?' she asked curiously and Jonah grinned.

'Oh, I did that! The moment I was sixteen I left home and school, and signed up on the first merchant vessel that would have me. It was a boat sailing to the Philippines. There I hopped an oil cruiser headed to the Gulf of Aqaba. Then I hopped a lift to the Med, and worked with this crew shipping olive oil to Jamaica. There I got a job ferrying holiday-makers around, and took the odd gig skippering boats from place to place. You know, a rich guy wants his boat to meet him in Trinidad, but it's currently moored up in St Lucia. I take it over. And then take a boat that's moored in Trinidad, but is wanted up in the British Virgin Islands. It was cool, for a while. But none of them were ever my own boat, you know?'

Tahnee watched his face, fascinated by the expressions that crossed it. His hazel eyes looked very pale in his deeply tanned face, and when he smiled, pale laughter lines appeared at the corners of his eyes and mouth. A slight dark growth on his chin showed clearly in the red of the setting sun that it was time he shaved. Abruptly, Tahnee was aware of how tall he was. His bare feet moved on the deck as it swayed, holding his body perfectly upright and it was fascinating to watch him. It reminded her of the way a kestrel would hover on the wind — wings always moving, but with a perfectly still head as it watched for prey.

Jonah Rodgers was like that. Except it was the water, and not the air, that was his element.

'I first saw the *Whale* in Cuba, of all places. A friend of mine and I were . . . well, doing a deal,' he coughed, glossing over the illegal import of Havana Cigars that had been his main source of income and the principal capital that had allowed him to put down the necessary deposit on the boat. 'She was the property of some government official who wanted to get rid of her in a hurry. Apparently Castro doesn't like his executives to be seen to be too rich.' Jonah grinned widely. 'I wasn't going to argue — it meant I got her for a song. Well, comparatively speaking,' he added, patting the well-oiled walnut wheel beneath his hands. 'I rode her over to St Vincent, not sure she wasn't going to sink on me, and spent the next three years making her sea-worthy and doing her up. I have a friend in the boatwright business who let me borrow his dry-dock. And the rest, as they say, is history.'

Tahnee nodded, and looked forward, to where the sun was just about to kiss the top of the blue-green sea. The boat seemed to meet a wave with a happy little toss of her head, and Tahnee smiled at the imagery.

'And this boat loves you for it,' she said softly. It was another whimsical thought, but it felt right. This boat wasn't made to wallow in the harbour in some Cuban official's private mooring. She was made to skim the oceans, and was happy with her new owner, who spent so much of his time, his love, and all of his money on her. Like any woman, she knew her own worth.

She hadn't realized he'd heard her until she saw him glance at her in surprise, and she flushed angrily. Good grief, he probably thought she was flirting with him!

As if she didn't have enough on her plate. Firmly, she stood up. 'I have to use the er . . . '

'Inside, first on the right,' Jonah said, watching her with wary eyes as she went inside. What had made him open up to her like that? He'd practically told her his life story. Well, most of it. He hadn't mentioned the slight brushes with the law, the fact that his father, who'd been a bit too free with his fists, had left the family destitute when he'd been only eleven. Or that his mother had died when he was only thirteen, leaving him to the mercy of the orphanage system until he'd run away. But what would a woman like that want to know any of that for anyway? Jonah shook his head at his own stupidity, and told himself to get real.

Tahnee Sawyer was beautiful, she was unexpectedly astute and maybe even kind-hearted. That remark about the boat loving him had made a tight feeling in his throat constrict so hard he'd almost choked. No other woman had seemed to understand him, or his lifestyle, so well as she had in that moment.

But it was a mirage. A fluke. He could no more hope that the beautiful blonde would even look at him twice than he could hope to one day own the *Queen Mary*. Not that any ship would have a place in his heart like the *Whale*!

He glanced around curiously as a dull thud sounded behind him, and quickly spotted the source. Tahnee Sawyer's big beach bag had fallen off the bench and landed on the deck. It had been beside her throughout the trip, but once she left it unattended, the gentle roll of the *Whale* had made it slide off. Checking there were no hazards to navigation anywhere, Jonah quickly left the wheel, and walked the few steps to the bag. He reached down and lifted the handle, and as he did so, a big and heavy pot of face cream rolled out and across towards the edge of the deck. He made a lunge for it, his fingertips just touching it and making it wobble. It was about to teeter over the edge when he made a second grab, just saving it from falling into the sea.

He opened the handle of her bag further and was just about to thrust the wayward pot inside, when he froze. For there, inside the bag and gleaming a dull but deadly grey, was a revolver.

For a second he stared at the gun, unable to believe his eyes.

But there it was; amid the make-up bag and hair brushes, the light floating scarf, the bottle of perfume and sunscreen and all the other feminine fripperies you might expect, lay the unmistakable piece of cold metal that formed what looked like a .38. A perfectly formed killing machine.

Slowly, he put the pot of face cream back,

pulled the handles together and lifted the bag back on to the bench. Then he walked back to the wheel. A moment later, a short cap of silvery hair appeared from the hatch, and Tahnee Sawyer walked back on to the deck. She glanced at her bag in passing, just to check that it was still safe, and walked calmly on to the railings.

The sun was now a half-ball of glowing red on the horizon. It bronzed the top of the sea, and turned her slight tan to a golden glow. A growing sea breeze blew her thin clothes against her, making them flap, and Jonah watched her with hot and worried eyes.

She was beautiful and in some sort of trouble. She was unhappy and was carrying a gun. And for some reason, she wanted to check out deserted, inaccessible beaches, where someone had set out a red marker for her. For a man who had a boat to pay for, and who didn't want any more trouble with the authorities, she was potentially trouble with a capital T.

Restlessly, Jonah watched her at the railing, at the way she glanced up when a noisy seagull called overhead. The swan-like lift of her neck. The wistful smile. Hell, he wanted her so badly in that moment, that he could feel himself harden. Then he turned his face resolutely away, and concentrated on bringing the *Whale* into port. After that . . . After that, he had a decision to make.

One that he just instinctively knew was going to cost him dearly, one way or another.

* * *

Delphine paused outside a small bar. According to her research, it had once housed the offices of Moorcroft Mowbray's solicitor. So much for her hope that it might still be here. With a small sigh of disappointment, she took a seat on the table outside, not wanting to walk into the bar alone. She still felt shy about certain things, and being a lone female walking into a bar was one of them.

She'd only been sitting at the table a short while when a waiter approached, and she ordered a Mount Gray rum fruit punch, and a side order of pumpkin fritters. The other tables were rapidly filling up as the dying sun blazed a final aurora of colour, and she smiled as a child laughed loudly and with obvious pleasure. The waiter, catching the tail end of the smile, felt his heart race, and when he went inside with her order, promptly told his best friend about the beautiful tourist outside. As a consequence, she had a different waiter bringing back her order, and again she smiled her thanks.

The man, a teenager working nights to subsidise his student loan, smiled promptly back. 'Madame is on holiday?' he asked amiably. More forward than his friend, and better looking, or so he always said. He was more confident than most. If he saw a beautiful woman, he talked to her — regardless of the bar owner's policy about not flirting with customers. During the holiday season he could easily get another job if he was fired.

'Sort of,' Delphine agreed. 'I was really looking for a law firm that used to have offices here. I don't suppose you'd know of it?'

The young man laughed and shook his head. But because she was so very beautiful and looked so very disappointed, he said helpfully, 'I'll ask old Henri. He's worked here so long the spiders weave webs over him. He might know.'

Delphine laughed and thanked him, wondering who old Henri might be. A minute or two later, as she sipped her drink and forked a mouthful of delicious fritter past her lips, an old man with white curly hair approached her carefully.

'Hello, missy. You the lady who wanted to know about the lawyer people?' he asked warily.

'That's right. Please, sit down, Mr — ?'

'Oh no, missy. I won't sit down. Mr Munijar, he don't like it.'

'Oh,' Delphine said helplessly. 'It was a Mr Michael Miller I wanted to learn about. He practised law here until the 1960s or so. I suppose he's passed away now?'

'Oh my, yes, missy, many, many years ago. I was only a daddy for the second time when he went. My family's lived in this parish all their lives. My father used to work for Mr Glenross's grandfather. That was Mr Miller's partner in the law firm. Never was no Orlando, don't know why that name was above the door.' Old Henri grinned, revealing a gap-toothed smile.

'I don't suppose the old firm still exists anywhere?' Delphine asked without much hope, and wasn't surprised when the old man shook his head.

'No, missy, I'm afraid not. Mr Glenross's son, Oliver, went into the building and construction trade, back in the fifties, this'd be now. Said tourism was going to be the trade of the future. Reckon he was right, cos he sure was rich when he retired. Only Mr James followed in his father's footsteps, but he retired too, must be twenty years ago now. Still lives just yonder, though. Sold the building to a place selling ice cream and soda pops and such. Now it's this bar. I likes serving rum better than ice cream cones, though,' the old man said with a laugh.

Delphine laughed too. 'I don't blame you. But this Mr James you mention — would that be James Miller, Michael's son?'

'That's right.'

'And he took over his father's business? You wouldn't happen to know his telephone number, would you?'

It was too much to hope for, as the old man shook his head thoughtfully. 'No, can't rightly say I do. But he only lives five minutes walk over that way.' And so saying, he reached out for her napkin, and taking a pen from his top pocket, proceeded to draw her a sketchy map.

Delphine thanked him profusely and gave him a big tip with which to buy himself a drink.

'Thank you, missy. Think I'll have myself a Banks beer. I do like a cold drink on a hot night.'

But Delphine barely heard him as she gathered her things together and set off into the darkening night. She was a woman with a mission — and that mission was to bring Dylan Gale to a state of grovelling apology.

* * *

Jonah Rodgers made sure that all the electrics were off, checked the bilge pump and that all of the *Whale*'s portholes were firmly secure, then hopped off the boat. He locked up carefully behind him and walked along the quay to the George and Dragon, his favourite pub. Unabashedly English, he'd been friends with the owner ever since he'd washed up on Barbados five years ago.

There he sat at the bar, nursing a cold beer and in no mood, for once, to chat. Luckily, it was a busy night, and his friend didn't seem to notice his preoccupation.

Jonah felt stiff and tired, but it had nothing to do with anything physical. Rather, the pressure that weighed on him was all mental. For, no matter how he tried to twist the facts about his latest hire, it only played out one way.

She was alone, and carried a gun. She was interested in out-of-the-way places. She could only be checking out a possible drug-smuggling route. Barbados, like the rest of the world, had its troubles, and drug-running was one of them. Jamaica was far more famous for its yardie gangsters and drugs problems, but it was rife everywhere.

What else could it be? The fact that she was obviously unhappy about it might say something in her favour, but there was no way Jonah could let it go at that.

His mother had died of a drugs overdose.

All his young life, the problems of drugs, poverty and misery had hung over him. And he hated to see signs of it here, on his island paradise. And as beautiful as she was, and as much as he wanted her, the beautiful Tahnee Sawyer was poison.

And there was only one thing to do with poison.

Sighing heavily, and feeling absurdly guilty, he walked to the telephone and called another friend. When he'd finished and hung up, he dragged himself back to the bar. It had had to be done. It was no more than she deserved.

So why did he feel as if he'd just stuck a knife into his own heart?

★   ★   ★

Delphine opened the white picket gate and walked up the dark path. The scent of night-flowering stock filled the air, and when a security light came on in the porch of the house in front of her, she saw a large, colourful moth flitter past. A bird, disturbed in its roost, chirruped softly. A big round moon was rising, casting a magical milky glow across the street.

It was a night made for lovers.

Disconcertingly, the image of Dylan Gale rose up before her, dropping a warm, white-clad arm around her shoulders. The soft sigh of his breath, as he whispered something into her ear, made a delicious shiver snake down her spine. Angrily, she took a deep breath and shook the romantic image away.

She walked up to the wooden porch and firmly rang the bell. After a moment or two, she heard a shuffling sound, and then the door was opened. The old man who stood there looked at her with some surprise. He was bald on top, but a fringe of white hair swept back over his ears and disappeared around the back of his head. A slight paunch stretched his shirt tightly over his middle, but his face was open and friendly.

'Hello? Mr Miller? This may sound odd, but I'm hoping you can help me. It concerns a case your father worked on, many years ago. Nineteen-thirty-two in fact.'

'Goodness gracious,' James Miller said, his rheumy blue eyes widening. 'I wasn't but ten years old then.'

Delphine smiled ruefully. 'I know. I'm sorry. I'm desperately hoping that, as an ex-legal man, you might have kept records?'

'Well, I don't know about that,' he said,

suddenly cautious, and eyeing her warily. Evidently, the old lawyer was still sharp as a tick, and not about to give away anything.

Delphine quickly held up a hand. 'Oh please, I don't want to do anything illegal.'

'I should hope not!' the old man said, but with a sudden twinkle in his eye. 'Well, don't stand out on the doorstep. Come on in.' Evidently, he'd summed her up and decided she was harmless.

Delphine thanked him and stepped inside, following him through a dark hall, where a grandmother clock ticked ponderously, and into a small cosy parlour. There, a beautiful little terrier dog with a silky silver head came running up, barking ferociously, but rolled on his back immediately to have his tummy rubbed. Relieved and smiling, Delphine obliged.

'Oh, don't mind Nero. He's a faker. Would you like a cup of tea? I thought I detected an English accent.'

Delphine smiled. 'A cup of tea would be lovely. I've got a little bit of a story to tell, and tea always helps, I've found.'

'Now I find that statement very intriguing,' James Miller acknowledged with a smile. 'And to an old man who doesn't get many visitors, and is plagued by insomnia, a long story sounds mighty inviting right about now. Come on through to the kitchen, you can tell me all about it. And don't mind Nero — he'll beg for a biscuit but don't you give it to him.'

And so Delphine told him about her mother dying, and sorting out the attic, and finding the will. And she did slip Nero a sneaky bite of biscuit, which his owner pretended not to see.

As she spoke, James Miller listened attentively, occasionally smiling, or shaking his head, once, when she mentioned Moorcroft Mowbray's famous fight with his nephew, gasping and then nodding. He only murmured, 'I remember that. My mother thought it was scandalous behaviour, but all us boys thought it was grand. Please, go on.'

When she came to the part about leaving England to see if she could find out more, and to talk to the current owner, a man she thought was called Forboys, she paused, her tea drunk, and waited for him to comment.

And she wasn't disappointed. 'Well, I do remember that fight old man Moorcroft had with his nephew, as I said. Well, his wife's nephew to be correct. And I do recall my father telling me about the old man storming in the day afterwards demanding to change his will.'

Delphine felt her heartbeat flutter. 'And did he?'

'My dear, I'm not sure,' James said, then

reached across to pat her hand as her face fell. 'As I said, I was only a young lad at the time. I didn't go into practice myself until I was twenty-five and passed my Bar exams. By then, the Mowbray estate had passed on to Allinson, and I think Allinson himself had died, and the house had been sold on.'

Delphine sighed but nodded. 'Would you be willing to say what you can remember? I mean, make a statement; an affidavit, do they call it? Or even testify in court if it should come to that?'

'Well, now, that rather depends,' the old man said, once more the cautious man of law. 'You see, as far as the law courts go, my testimony would be only hearsay. What you really need is to check the probate records. See when and exactly how Christopher Allinson came to inherit. You have a copy of this later will, you say?'

'Yes, I brought it with me. Would you like to look it over for me? My friend back in England doesn't know much about Barbados law, naturally. Mr Miller, I know you're retired, but would you be willing to help me? I can pay you something . . . '

'Not so fast, not so fast,' James Miller laughed. 'Of course, I'd be willing to help. Truth is, I've been bored witless ever since I gave up the practice. I'm supposed to be

137

writing my memoirs but that ain't very exciting either. Never got to defend no murderers or such. Now this little tale of yours has some very interesting points. Yes, very interesting to us lawyers. I have friends in the records offices, and both my own papers, and Father's old papers, are all stored in a shed out back. Never could bring myself to throw them away somehow. I could certainly go through them and see what I can find out. It'll be a pleasure, in fact.'

Delphine smiled tremulously at him. 'Oh, thank you! I can't tell you how much I appreciate this.'

'Mind, I'm not saying you'll end up with the house,' he warned. 'What with the probate being settled so long ago, it might come down to statutes of limitations. It'll certainly take some sorting out. You might not have a leg to stand on, young lady, you do realize that?'

Delphine quickly nodded and hastened to reassure him. 'I don't really care about that — about inheriting I mean. Well I do,' she added confusingly 'but not because I'm desperate for the money or anything. I was up at the house this morning — Mowbray House — and it's a wonderful place. I got a real sense of history about it — and that view! I'd just hate to see it turned into a soulless hotel.

I'd do anything to stop that from happening.'

'Eh?' the old man said, startled. 'I thought you said some chap named Forboys owned it?'

Delphine shook her head angrily. 'I did, but he sold it just recently to a hotel developer. Isn't that hideous? I'm determined he won't ruin it.'

'Hotel developer?' James Miller said, his smile falling away from his face. 'Do you know who?'

'Yes. His name's Dylan Gale.' As she spoke the name, she saw a look of dismay cross the old man's face, and asked tremulously, 'Do you know him?' But it was obvious that he did.

'Dylan Gale?' James Miller echoed sadly. 'Oh dear. Oh, this is awful!'

6

Tahnee left the hotel after a delicious breakfast of mango, soursop and papaya, turning down the option of grilled flying fish in favour of several more cups of coffee. She knew the caffeine probably wasn't good for her, especially under the fraught circumstances, but she needed something to give her an edge. Feeling distinctly nervous, she took a taxi to the Sunbury Plantation House, glancing casually behind her every so often.

But if she was being followed, she couldn't spot the car. At the tourist attraction, she noticed that there were champagne lunches on offer later, and wondered if she herself might have reason to celebrate by then. She hoped so. All this waiting and cat-and-mouse running around was hard. Nobody seemed to be paying attention to her, and she couldn't imagine one of the kidnappers simply sidling up to her with the latest run-around message, so she joined a guided tour. Still nobody approached her.

She stopped after an hour to have a cup of coffee, but even in the cafe, if anybody was taking any of notice of her, it was hard to see who. She felt tense and on edge, and forced herself to relax. At least her father's operation had been successful, so that was one less thing to worry about, but as the morning wore on and still no-one approached her, and no message of any kind was given to her, she felt like shrieking. It was obvious this was another wild goose-chase.

With a sigh, she paid for her coffee and left.

★ ★ ★

Just as Tahnee Sawyer walked down the graceful steps of the plantation house, Delphine stepped off the bus in Bathsheba and made her way to Mowbray House. The sun was warm against her skin as she walked among the flowering shrubs, rife with birdsong and the chirruping of some insect she could never manage to spot.

The house appeared on the near horizon, as romantic and windswept as before. That the wind was a Caribbean breeze only added to the magic, and as she pushed open the gate and walked up the weed-strewn path, a gull called lazily overhead. Then she stopped, abruptly, as the door to Mowbray House opened, and Dylan Gale stepped out. He was dressed in a pair of casual dark green slacks and white short-sleeved shirt. The sun played a silver dance with his light blond hair, and as she approached she saw his emerald-green eyes narrow warningly.

'Miss Phillips, what a surprise,' he said drolly. 'Pointless to point out that you're trespassing, I suppose?'

Delphine forced herself to smile. After last night, and what James Miller had told her, she was seeing him in a whole new light. But his sarcasm was still definitely something she could do without.

'Mr Gale, I was hoping to run into you,' Delphine replied, equally drolly. Stopping just short of the few wooden steps that led up to the house porch, she reached into her bag and drew out a dossier. She'd brought it with her, intending to drop it in at his office later. But doing it in person was better.

'I can't think why,' Dylan said sardonically. From his height advantage at the top of the steps, he watched her look up at him and flush. She was wearing a sleeveless pale coffee-coloured sundress with a square neckline and a delicate tiger's-eye pendant fell to the top of her breasts, which were only hinted at beneath the demure dress. Her mass of luxurious dark curls were piled on top of her head with a tortoise-shell comb, revealing a slender, graceful neck. Matching tiny tiger's-eye earrings dangled from each ear.

Her eyes, the exact shade of liquid brown favoured by velvet pansies, flashed in warning as she climbed the first step.

'What's this?' he asked indifferently, making no move to take the pale beige folder in her hand.

'I'd like you to read it,' she said softly, taking the next step up. 'In fact, I insist. I was left with the distinct impression that you didn't take me seriously the last time we spoke. I thought these documents might help persuade you differently,' she added challengingly.

Dylan's lips twisted grimly. If only she knew just how seriously he took her! Already he could feel the breath tighten in his chest as she came closer, and when the slight citrus scent of her perfume gently wafted past his nose as she took the final step on to the porch, he felt his loins begin to harden. To hide this tell-tale sign of his arousal, he turned and indicated an old-fashioned swinging seat set up on the porch.

'Might as well be comfortable,' he said abruptly, and took a seat on one end. With his feet planted firmly on the decking, holding it still for her, he watched her bite her lip in a classic sign of indecision and sighed elaborately.

'I won't bite,' he said roughly. He wasn't

sure whether she was pretending to be such a shrinking violet or not, but the thought that she might genuinely be afraid of him made him feel savagely angry. And not a little bit hurt. Which was utterly ridiculous.

Delphine smiled and defiantly tossed her head. 'You'd better not,' she said enigmatically, and warily sank down beside him. When he lifted his feet, the swinging bench gave a gentle sway and a delighted smile lit up her face. Oh, how she wished she'd had one of these back in Oxford when she was a child. Those long, halcyon summer vacations in the city had always been wonderful, but something like this — to a child's imagination — would have made them magical.

Dylan found himself caught by the smile, like a wild animal suddenly caught in a trap. It lit her whole face, intriguing, unexpected, and heart-breakingly lovely. It made him yearn to know what she was thinking.

Grimly he reached out and took the dossier still in her hand, and opened it up. The first pages were Xeroxes of the will she'd so miraculously 'found' in her dead mother's attic. Idly, he wondered if her mother was really dead, and she was drawing on real past experiences, or if her parents were still alive and well somewhere. Whichever it was, he'd soon find out. After leaving her in his favourite bar, he'd contacted a PI he used sometimes, and asked him to check her out. He was due to report soon. And once he had some real ammunition to deal with her, and her puppet master, Bolton, he'd feel much better.

He frowned as he read the will. It was a good mock-up, but then, he supposed, it would be. Probably the original would be good too — genuine old paper, proper legalese for that generation, the right ink and so on. Bolton could afford to buy only the best forgers.

Without a word, he tossed these to one side, and frowned down at the copies of an old newspaper story, which bore the headings of a now defunct Bahamian paper.

'What's this?' he asked rhetorically, for he was already reading it.

'I found out why Moorcroft Mowbray probably made out the later will,' Delphine explained quietly. 'Apparently, he had a rather famous falling-out with his only near relative. I think his wife must have died by then,' she added sadly. Her voice held no hint of triumph, and she was careful to keep it that way. After her surprising chat with James Miller last night, she was having to re-think many of her misconceptions about this man.

With a sense of growing unease, Dylan

read through the newspaper reports. The most ominous of which had Moorcroft Mowbray, after leaving the courthouse, heading for his solicitor's, presumably to change his will. It seemed unlikely that Bolton would go to the trouble to make mock-ups of this — after all, with a simple phone call, Dylan could find out whether this fight had actually happened. Could this wild story she was telling actually be true?

No — it was simply too much of a coincidence to swallow. Far more likely, Bolton had simply latched on to something with a kernel of truth in it, and was using it to try and sell a bigger lie. That's what a really clever crook would do, and Dylan had never had any doubts that Bolton was clever.

'Interesting, but hardly conclusive,' he said dismissively. As he spoke, he looked up and out to sea. It was a glorious view, and a glorious day. He could see the Mowbray House Hotel guests enjoying similar days as they walked through the lush, slightly tamed gardens, relaxing and unwinding from the stresses of their city lives and high-pressure jobs. He was proud of the ambience all his hotels strove to create, and genuinely felt proud when he saw tanned, fit and happy holiday-makers heading for home, after a break in one of his company's residences.

Unlike many operators, he didn't see his guests as mere commodities.

'I found out the name of Moorcroft's solicitors.' Delphine's voice interrupted his musing, and he glanced across at her, noticing the way her hands fluttered nervously in her lap, like butterflies unable to settle. They were long, slender, delicate hands, and as he watched them, he felt the sudden urge to take her fingers and kiss them, one by one.

Abruptly he looked away and forced himself to concentrate. This charming and enchanting creature was trying to take away something that belonged to him — something that he'd paid good, hard-earned money for! Something no man, business rival or anyone else, had ever succeeded in doing. He'd better start concentrating on the battle in hand, otherwise he might find himself with a knife stuck in his back!

'Oh, I'm sure you did. A proper Nancy Drew, aren't you?' he drawled mockingly.

Delphine flushed, wishing he wasn't so overtly hostile. OK, she couldn't expect him to be overjoyed, considering, but did he have to be so hurtful? 'It wasn't hard,' she said quietly, determined not to lose her temper again. 'I simply looked up the court records and found the name of his acting solicitor.

The company doesn't still exist, of course, but strangely enough, you used to do business with the son of the man who probably drew up the will.'

Dylan tensed. This was all sounding more and more involved, and he could feel the net closing around him. Had Bolton now roped in someone else to back up this outlandish claim? Some local legal eagle by the sound of it — probably someone open to a bribe. Just how many more people would he pull in on the scam, and where was it likely to end? But letting her see that it was getting to him was the last thing he was about to do, so he took a long careful breath before saying calmly, 'Oh?'

'James Miller. I was speaking to him only last night. He's retired now, of course, but told me all about how he helped you set up the foundations.'

Dylan blinked, totally wrong-footed. Whatever he'd expected her to come up with, it hadn't been this. He knew James Miller to be a good, honest, decent man. That he could be in league with Bolton was totally unthinkable.

When his company had first started making a handsome profit, Dylan had looked around for ways of making sure that not only himself and his immediate family benefited, but that the island itself also shared in his good fortune. After all, he owned his success to Barbados itself — the island, the people, the lifestyle were what attracted his paying customers in the first place. And it hadn't been hard to realize that there were obvious ways in which he could help. First he'd set up a foundation that would give grants to promising students — students who were too poor to afford a good education, and, moreover, students who wanted to remain on the island and help their own people. This first charitable trust sponsored native islanders who wanted to become doctors, teachers, engineers and the like.

Then, a few years later, it became a logical step to help support medical centres for the poor, build more primary schools in local villages, and support the burgeoning traditional arts and crafts movements that sold quality goods direct to tourists. This latter scheme helped provide many local artisans and their families with a decent living. It meant they didn't have to lose traditional skills by having to go into the cities to do menial jobs, and it also meant that many villages were visited by tourists, which had a knock-on effect of helping out the local economy. Many families grew fruit and vegetables as a sideline, which they then sold direct to people coming to the workshops.

And the man who'd helped him through all the legalities — not to mention tax laws — in all of this, had indeed been James Miller.

'His father, Michael Miller, was Moorcroft Mowbray's solicitor,' Delphine said devastatingly, not liking the way he'd gone so pale and tight-jawed. 'As a young boy, he can even remember his father saying something about Moorcroft Mowbray changing his will. So you see it all fits,' she finished quietly.

When James Miller had told her about Dylan Gale's charitable work, and all the good he did for the island and its poorer population, she'd been dismayed. The last thing she wanted to do was make things worse for anybody, especially one who obviously did so much to help so many. And when James Miller had said gently, 'Dylan's one of the good guys, Miss Phillips,' she'd felt about two inches small.

Now, anxious to try and express some of this, she impulsively reached out and touched his hand. But before she could say anything, he flinched and quickly drew it away. She winced and leapt to her feet, walking restlessly to the railing. There, unable to bear looking at him in case he should see the pain in her eyes, she leaned on the top plank of wood, and looked out to sea.

'Look, Mr Gale, I don't want to cause you

any trouble. Really I don't. But at the same time, I couldn't bear to see this wonderful house turned into some soulless money making machine. I mean, look at it.' And so saying she turned around and glanced up at the house — the exterior, once spotless white but now flaking, the big, dusty windows with their rotting window frames and the roof, missing a few tiles and slightly undulating. 'This house is over a hundred and fifty years old. It's a part of the island's history. It's crying out to be loved by somebody. Somebody who wants to raise a family here maybe. Somebody who would appreciate all this wonderful . . .' She was about to indicate the overgrown garden, the sweeping, wonderful airy views, when suddenly he lurched to his feet.

His face was tight and furious. 'You think I need lessons in restoration from you? How long have you been on this island,' he demanded grimly, before answering his own question. 'Five minutes? I've lived here all my life — I know what this house represents and what it needs. It was the home of a plantation owner — a man who understood commerce and its benefits. Look over there.' Furious, he pointed down the road, to where, in the distance, a cluster of roofs indicated a little settlement. 'The women living there, with children to clothe and feed, can earn a decent wage for themselves by working as chambermaids and waitresses here. Their husbands can earn as much tending the gardens, growing food for the kitchens and doing general maintenance. A hotel, if it's run right, is not only a place of rest and delight for its guests, but it's also a lifesaver for its employees. I don't suppose you even gave that a thought, did you?'

Delphine hadn't. In fact, it hadn't even crossed her mind. She'd simply seen the house, and like some romantic heroine from a Daphne du Maurier novel, had felt compelled to love and protect it. Had she really believed, in some part of her, that this could be her home? Was she really so hopelessly old-fashioned? She felt a mortifying shame flood over her, and took an instinctive step backwards, giving a sudden cry of alarm and windmilling her arms as she realized she was stepping back into nothingness.

Dylan shot forward, his hands hard and comforting as they grasped the tops of her arms, preventing her from tumbling backwards down the stairs. Delphine took a staggering step forward and then froze as the backs of her knuckles grazed his chest. Suddenly she was aware of the heat of him, radiating out all around her. She could smell his aftershave, something sharp and subtle, from his morning's shave. Her breath feathered around in her throat then died as she looked up into his face.

He was staring down at her as if he'd never seen her before. His anger seemed to leech out of him, and his emerald eyes became cloudy, the shade of aqua that the sea became during a storm. He said something, something she couldn't quite catch, and then his head was dipping towards hers.

Delphine's heart leapt as his lips met hers, and her surprised brain shrieked 'He's *kissing me, he's kissing me*' before something far more primordial took over. Without her knowing how it happened, she felt herself melting into his arms. Her fingers crept up to his neck, then around to loop behind his nape, bringing his mouth closer, harder, against hers. Her breasts hardened and tingled, pressing against the firmer flesh of his own chest, making tiny radiations of desire star out to nerve endings she didn't even know she had. Her legs became heavy and languorous, making her lean ever harder against him for support.

And he was holding her harder, kissing her harder, as if a corresponding male impulse answered her unspoken challenge.

Delphine had never been kissed like this

before in her life. She could feel the old order of her life slipping away. The years of careful academic research. The sensible habits of a lifetime. Her old Oxford existence. It was as if they'd never been — as if she'd been born in that instant. The house seemed to watch them, benign and indulgent. The hot Barbados sun beat down on them, as if encouraging their own internal heat. Everything felt so supremely, superbly, *right*.

With a huge effort, Dylan forced his head up and he thrust her away. A high flush of desire sat treacherously on his sharp cheekbones, and he dragged in great lungfuls of air like a man who'd just finished a marathon.

Hell, she was potent. And dangerous. Positively lethal. He stared at her, at those great pansy eyes, looking so confused and dazed and vulnerable.

If only!

Dylan shook his head, wondering how he could be so disastrously stupid. It wasn't him she wanted. At best, she wanted the house — *his* house, dammit, if this will-story was really true. At worst, she wanted Bolton's pay cheque for pulling off a scam. And making love to him was just her way of getting it.

Without a word, he turned and jogged down the steps and walked to his car. He had to get away from her fast. Before she realized just how well she had him hooked.

Delphine watched him go and shivered, hugging herself as she felt suddenly cold. He despised her, he couldn't have made that more clear. Well, of course he did! First she showed him the weapons she'd been ranging against him, then she threw herself at him like some sex-starved vamp. No wonder he thought she was up to no good.

Oh, what was wrong with her? She behaved like a raving lunatic whenever he was around! Grimly, she gathered up the beige folder that he'd left behind and walked disconsolately back to the bus stop.

She had an awful lot to think about.

★ ★ ★

Dylan parked the car behind his office, and automatically locked it. Gale Imperial shared an old, one-time governmental building with a big real-estate corporation and a private bank, and seeing as it faced on to a busy main road, finding a daytime parking spot was always next to impossible, so he'd taken to parking in the back alleyways, and now barely gave it a thought.

His mind was still centred firmly on Delphine Phillips and all the problems she brought with her. He'd had his share of relationships, of course he had, one of them even becoming serious enough to involve the purchasing of an engagement ring. But none of them had ever worked out. His erstwhile fiancée had moved stateside, wanting a bigger arena for her corporate ambitions, and until he'd met the rapacious English woman, no woman had ever knocked him for six before. He'd always been the one in the driving seat, the one firmly in control, and that's how he'd liked it. The prospects of marriage and a family had always been so far in the future as to be almost invisible. And if he ever did stop to think about it, he supposed that he'd eventually find some local girl, one with an easy-going nature and sense of humour, someone practical and sunny, who'd make a home for himself and their children without any fuss. Someone easy to live with.

To find himself so unexpectedly bewildered wasn't something he knew how to deal with. Delphine left him hot and cold and bothered in a matter of seconds. Hell, he'd almost ravished her right there on the spot!

Because he was still thinking about that, and not paying attention to his surroundings, the first indication he had of trouble was when a hand shot out of nowhere and hit him hard in the back and side, low down, and right above his kidneys. He gave an instinctive yell, and went down on one knee, unable to prevent himself as the paralyzing pain sapped all the strength straight from his knees.

Abruptly, his brain went into high gear. He was in a series of narrow alleyways, with high walls that led to the rear entrances of a row of businesses, but he might have been on the far side of the moon for all that. Blank windows might give way to offices, but unless one of the workers inside happened to glance out and see what was happening, he was on his own. The busy main street only a few hundred yards away was full of cars and pedestrians, but he wasn't sure if anybody would hear him if he cried out. If he even had the breath left to cry out with! Besides, he didn't have time for that. Already his attacker was stepping forward, one foot rising in order to kick him in the stomach.

That mustn't be allowed to happen. A well-placed kick could rupture his spleen, break his ribs, cause internal bleeding and all other sorts of damage.

Quick as a flash, Dylan sat back on his heels and grabbed the booted foot as it swung towards him. He grunted and heaved up, yelping as fresh pain radiated out from his injured back, but hearing, with a savage grin of satisfaction, his attacker giving out an ever more agonized yell when he fell back heavily on to the edge of the kerbstone.

But then someone was grabbing him from behind and pulling his head back, an arm around his throat viciously and competently cutting off his air.

There were two of them!

Dylan tried to grab a lungful of air, but couldn't, and felt his head tighten. Dark spots of colour flashed across his vision and a hot, tight feeling constricted his chest. *Don't panic!* The voice of his one-time judo instructor sounded so loud in his head that the man, now dead, might as well have been stood right beside him, issuing instructions. Because Dylan now knew exactly what he had to do next.

Instead of straining backwards, giving his second attacker even more leverage to use against him, Dylan slumped forward, grasping the tops of the man's arms and forcing him to do the same. Then, on knees that screamed their protest, he lifted himself off the ground, bent sharply forward and brought the man behind him up and over, and rolling off in front of him. His purchase on Dylan's throat was lost when he found himself suddenly airborne, and now Dylan was able to stagger to his feet and drag in some much-needed air.

But he was given no time to recover. The

first man was getting up, rubbing his back where the edge of the kerb had bruised him, and ripe Australian-accented curses filled the air.

Dylan glanced around quickly, but there was no-one in sight. He realized at once that if both attackers were allowed to get on their feet together he'd be in dead trouble, so before that could happen, he went on the offensive. It wasn't something the Australian thug had been prepared for, and his eyes widened in almost comical disbelief as Dylan grinned savagely at him and let out a blood-curdling yell. It was a judo trick, of course, the yell designed to momentarily paralyze an opponent. It obviously worked, for Dylan got in a fast kick to the big man's shins, making him crash on to his knees in front of him. He aimed a kick under the big man's chin, and heard a tooth crack as his jaws connected, but then he screamed himself as a white light flashed in his head and his back exploded in pain. His second attacker had come up behind him and once again hit him over the kidneys in the exact same spot.

Knowing he couldn't afford to go down again, animal instinct telling him that once he was down they'd never let him get up again, Dylan put his hands in front of him and half-crawled forward, putting some space between them, then turned, crouched, to face the man rushing towards him. He was big and black, and dressed in something colourful, and that was all he had time to register, before he was upon him.

He felt his opponent jab some left hooks into his ribs, and forced himself not to bend double. Instead he timed it perfectly, then dipped his head forward in a vicious and well-placed head-butt, his stronger forehead smashing just above his opponent's weaker temple area.

The other thug, about to deliver a roundhouse punch, gave a sudden grunt of surprise as he suddenly saw stars, and then felt his cheek connect with the concrete. Groggily, he shook his head and tried to get up, but couldn't. All strength seemed to have left him.

Dylan took an agonized step back as the big Australian walked past his fallen comrade, a look of sheer murder on his face. Bruised, finding it hard to breathe from a cracked rib, almost bent double in pain, Dylan watched him warily. Feint left or right? He was sure the man was right-handed, so . . .

'Hey! What's going on here?' The voice was so welcome, so outraged and normal, that Dylan wasn't sure that it was real. Only when the Australian stopped dead and then backed up, did he realize it was all over. The bleeding man bodily lifted his comrade from the pavement to half-drag, half-carry him away, mentally cursing that fool Bolton for not warning him the mark had martial arts training.

Wearily, Dylan began to turn around, trying to take shallow breaths. A red mist swam in front of him, as he slowly went over on one side on to the cool concrete pavement. He saw someone running towards him — not a policeman although he was in uniform. A traffic warden, perhaps? Come to the alley-ways to see if he could find a vehicle illegally parked — like Dylan's own XJS!

Dylan couldn't help but give a small laugh. Somewhere he heard someone telling him that it was going to be all right, that he was calling an ambulance. Then he closed his eyes and went to sleep.

* * *

Marcus Bolton stood just inside the door, wondering what had brought such a beautiful woman to such a nondescript bar. He watched her for a few minutes as she sat on a tall bar stool and ordered a second glass of mixed fruit juice, then made his move.

Delphine took a long cold sip and sighed

heavily. She wasn't sure what had brought her back to this bar — except for the fact that it was the first place she'd ever set eyes on Dylan Gale. Now how pathetic was that?

The same barman who'd pointed him out to her now watched her with a curious look, and who could blame him. The lunchtime crowd had been and gone, and apart from a few tourists, dazed from the sun and tired from a morning's sightseeing and shopping, she was the only one in the bar. In the back of her mind lurked the possibility that she'd only come here because this was his local bar, and there was a chance that he might pop in here during his lunch break. That she was so desperate to see him again even after their debacle that morning was a mortifying thought and one she didn't let herself dwell on.

The fact was, she was feeling at a loss as to what to do next. She'd come to Barbados for a holiday, and to perhaps find out the answers to an intriguing little mystery. She hadn't expected to wander into a battlefield, or fall prey to some kind of exotic virus! For how else could she explain her behaviour towards a perfect stranger?

Now she glanced up as a heavy-set man took the stool beside her, and smiled casually her way. He had dark hair and eyes, and was probably somewhere in his fifties, with an unmistakable aura of power about him. Most women, she thought, would find him attractive, but she barely glanced at him.

So she was astonished when he held out his hand towards her and said amiably, 'Miss Phillips, isn't it? Delphine Phillips?'

Delphine stared at him blankly. 'Er . . . yes. How did you . . . I mean, have we met?'

The man smiled, waving a vague hand at the bartender who'd wandered closer. 'Scotch on the rocks,' he said, then turned back to her. 'No, we haven't met. But I think we have a mutual interest in common.'

Delphine gazed at him helplessly. 'We have?'

'Mowbray House. I was interested in buying it. I heard from the realtor that you were interested in it too,' he lied glibly.

Delphine frowned. 'I don't know the realtor,' she said suspiciously, and Marcus Bolton grinned.

'Ah, but you don't know Barbados yet, Miss Phillips, and how she works. Nobody's business is their own here. It's a tiny island, and people like me, with a vested interest in knowing what's going on, learn all sorts of things, very fast indeed.' He smiled. 'Please, let me introduce myself. I'm Marcus Bolton.'

Delphine, in the act of automatically

putting out her hand to take his, froze. Marcus Bolton. That name was familiar somehow. Then, in a flash, she realized why. It was the name of the man Dylan had accused her of being in cahoots with.

Realizing she was being rude, she quickly shook his hand but looked at him warily. 'As I said, Mr Bolton, I don't know you.'

'No, but we have a mutual acquaintance in Dylan Gale, I think.'

Delphine sucked in her breath. 'I'm not sure I can discuss Mr Gale, Mr Bolton,' she said, sounding unbearably prim and proper even to her own ears. She wasn't that much surprised when Marcus Bolton grinned widely.

'You British! Still, I thought I'd introduce myself. I've lived on the island some years now, and thought I'd better give you a little heads up.'

Delphine blinked. 'What?'

Again, Marcus Bolton grinned. When he'd heard from his snitches that some English broad had been giving Gale trouble about Mowbray House he hadn't been that impressed but had decided to check it out nevertheless, just in case it had any possibilities. Now, having seen her for himself, Marcus was even more interested. He liked dealing with women. Especially with

164

ones like this one — so innocent, they shouldn't be let out without their mothers. 'Look, Miss Phillips, I'm not sure what your interest in Mowbray House is, but please, let me just give you a little bit of advice. Dylan Gale is a major player on Barbados — he has friends in high places, a lot of money to back him up, and what he wants, he gets. If you're going to take him on, you need someone in your corner. A backer, say. I just wanna help.'

Delphine sighed softly. 'Mr Bolton, I don't think that's a good idea,' she said, wondering if she was making a big mistake. But she didn't think so. Whoever this man was, he was no friend of Dylan, and whatever their problems were, the last thing she wanted to do was get in the middle of it. She was already in enough hot water as it was.

To her surprise, Marcus Bolton merely shrugged. He hadn't struck her as the type to give in so easily. But he said cheerfully enough, 'OK, fine. But if you ever change your mind — and I've got a feeling you might — call me.' He handed her a card, drained his drink, and sauntered away.

In the back of his big black limousine, he lit up a cigarette and smoked thoughtfully.

He'd have to look into this more carefully.

* * *

In the bar, the barman sauntered into the back to make a telephone call. With a bit of luck, his policeman friend would give him a big enough reward to enable him to buy tickets to next Saturday's cricket match.

★ ★ ★

Delphine left the bar soon afterwards, pushing all thoughts of Marcus Bolton firmly away. Perhaps she should just forget all about Mowbray House and about Dylan Gale and get on with her life. Perhaps the best thing to do was simply have her holiday and then go home where it was safe. Where she knew who she was, and what her life was all about.

It would certainly be the safest thing to do.

With a small sigh, she walked down towards the harbour and tried to do some window shopping.

And convince herself that being safe was all that she really wanted from life.

7

Jonah walked briskly along the darkening street towards Tahnee Sawyer's hotel, even though his feet felt as heavy as lead. Beside him, and easily keeping pace, was a tall, dark-skinned, dark-haired and dark-eyed man, whose head was constantly on the move. He noticed a car that almost ran a red light. He noticed a woman, dressed in a very tight and very short skirt, turn a corner and quickly disappear when she saw him. He noticed an alley cat about to leap on to the rim of a public rubbish bin in search of food scraps.

Sergeant Flloyd Turnbull, one-time LAPD cop, had spent many, many years noticing such things. Since moving to Barbados and joining the police force here, he had less things to notice, it was true. And the slower, more laid-back pace suited him, on the whole. But tonight, because of what his friend Jonah Rodgers had told him, he felt the old familiar prickle under his skin. The slight dampness of his palms that told him that something big might be in the offing. It reminded him of the old days patrolling areas that were prone to rioting, the stakeouts that might turn unexpectedly violent at a moment's notice, or the domestic call-outs that always had the potential to turn nasty.

'That's her hotel just up ahead,' Jonah said reluctantly, nodding at a small but beautiful converted townhouse over-looking a leafy square.

Flloyd looked at it and felt his pulse rate pick up a beat. 'That's one of Dylan Gale's hotels,' he said sharply, and some of the surprise must have sounded in his voice because Jonah glanced at him curiously.

'So?' he asked, a shade testily. He knew he sounded surly, but the simple truth was that he was feeling angry at his friend for making him come here. It was an anger that was generated by the fact that he felt so damned guilty. He felt like the worst kind of heel, sticking the law on to Tahnee Sawyer. And yet what else could he do? If she was up to something illegal, and somebody else got hurt or even died because of it, how would he feel then?

'Oh, nothing,' Flloyd said, with an elaborate shake of his shoulders. 'Just one of life's funny little coincidences, that's all.' And added 'maybe,' very softly, under his breath. But he was not about to tell Jonah that one of his snitches at a certain bar downtown had recently passed on some interesting gossip about trouble brewing between Dylan Gale, and that worm-about-town, Marcus Bolton. That was strictly police business.

When Jonah had told him about the curious behaviour of his latest client, Flloyd had agreed that it was curious but not in itself necessarily incriminating. But it was certainly worth checking out, which was why he'd insisted on Jonah taking him to the client's hotel, and pointing her out in person. He doubted that his immediate superior officer would consider it worthwhile — or worth the overtime money — to sanction a watch being put on her, so Flloyd was going to have to do this in his own time. Which meant he wanted to be sure he was tailing the right girl! Now, finding the mysterious Tahnee Sawyer holed up in a Gale Imperial hotel touched his funny bone. Could it all be connected, somehow?

'Let's go inside and have a drink at the bar,' Flloyd said, smiling across at his old friend, who scowled and then shrugged. Flloyd was not insensitive, and he was very much aware that Jonah Rodgers would rather be anywhere else right now. From one or two things he'd picked up from reading between the lines, he was sure that his friend was more than just a little attracted to the mysterious Tahnee Sawyer.

The two ex-pat Americans had met at a regatta a few years ago, and had immediately hit it off. If Flloyd had picked up on some of his new friend's less than razor-straight past, he'd made no mention of it, and Jonah, for his part, didn't hold Flloyd's profession against him. In spite of the vagaries of their natures and lifestyle choices, the friendship worked. Flloyd was reluctant to put it in jeopardy now, but he sensed Jonah's growing unhappiness. He could only hope that there was some innocent explanation for the girl's weird behaviour.

'This girl, she's really pretty, huh?' he asked nonchalantly, ignoring the sharp look Jonah shot at him.

Jonah didn't reply as they pushed through the doors of the hotel and entered a small lobby, before veering off to the right, where they could see the entrance to a small, intimate bar. 'I'll have a Falernum,' Jonah told the barman heavily, and sensed his friend's surprise at the order. Falernum was a liqueur concocted of rum, sugar, lime juice and almond essence. Made right, it could be fairly potent, and wasn't something he'd normally drink. Tonight, though, he wanted the bite of it sitting in his stomach when he pointed out Tahnee Sawyer. When it came he grimly tossed it off, not commenting on the fact that Flloyd had ordered a Mauby, which was another native but non-alcoholic drink, made by boiling bitter bark and spices, which was strained and then sweetened.

'I hear Carambola used to make a killer Falernum,' Flloyd said casually, mentioning a famous and romantic restaurant where he often took his first-time dates.

Jonah, thinking how well Tahnee Sawyer's chic sophistication would complement the ambience of the restaurant, wished suddenly that he was there with her right now, sharing a meal of oysters and christophines and eddoes with her, perhaps served with a side order of buljol. Introducing her to the local culinary delights that the island had to offer would have been something special.

Instead, here he was, about to finger her to the cops.

Ordering another potent drink, he let it sit on the bar in front of him, then stiffened as, out of his peripheral vision, he caught a movement of silver. They were sitting at the far end of the bar, in the gloomiest corner, and he knew she hadn't seen him as she hesitated in the doorway.

'That her?' the ever-observant Flloyd asked quietly, then slowly whistled under his breath when Jonah nodded. The woman who walked towards a table in the centre of the room

171

wasn't tall, but she seemed to fill the space around her. Part of it was the geometric, silver haircut, of course, some of it the thousand-dollar electric blue cocktail dress, but most of it, Flloyd had to admit, was sheer sexiness.

'No wonder she's got you tied up in knots, my friend,' Flloyd said softly. Jonah watched her sit and order a drink, and hunched down further over his own glass as she slowly let her eyes sweep the room. Sitting right next to, and partly concealed by, Flloyd, he hoped she wouldn't spot him.

She didn't. When he looked back again, the waiter was delivering her drink — something tall and cold, with fruit in it — and she was glancing out of the window at the darkening sunset.

'So, you let me know when she next calls you to take the boat out, yes?' Flloyd said calmly. 'I've got a friend with a small speedboat who owes me a favour or two. We'll follow you out and see if anybody else is watching. Or does anything interesting.'

Jonah nodded silently, and was relieved when his friend tossed back the last of his drink and slid to his feet. 'Well, I've got to get going. Hey, Jonah,' he added softly, and waited until the other man had glanced up at him before saying softly, 'you did the right thing, yeah? You know that, right?'

'Yeah, I know that,' Jonah agreed heavily, and watched Flloyd saunter casually past Tahnee's table on the way out. The blonde girl glanced at him briefly in passing, and smiled slightly. Jonah felt his gut twist as his sense of guilt deepened. For the next ten minutes or so he was forced to sit in the gloom, waiting for her to leave. When she finally got up, picking up her clutch bag and walking towards the door, he let a few minutes pass, then got up himself. At the doorway, though, he suddenly moved back, for he spotted her standing at the reception desk.

Damn! He'd assumed she'd gone straight up to her room.

That had, in fact, been Tahnee's intention, but as she crossed the foyer the receptionist had called her over and handed her a message that had just been delivered.

Now she stood at the counter and read it for a third time.

GO NOW TO BARCLAYS PARK, TO THE PUBLIC GARDENS. YOU WILL FIND THE SIDE GATE ON THE EAST SIDE OPEN. FOLLOW THE RIGHT-HAND PATH AND WAIT ON THE FIRST BENCH YOU FIND. YOU

WILL BE CONTACTED. BRING THE DIAMONDS.

Tahnee licked her lips nervously, and glanced over her shoulder towards the door, realizing it was already fully dark outside. She didn't notice a man duck back inside the bar room, and wouldn't dare have challenged him if she had. She had to assume she was being watched and followed all the time now. And to confront someone might spell disaster for her stepmother.

She glanced once more at the note, in an agony of indecision. She didn't like the sound of this. Before her little tasks had all been performed in broad daylight, with either Jonah there, or plenty of other people around, which made her feel if not safe then at least less alone.

But to meet a kidnapper in a dark and deserted park?

For a moment she leaned against the reception desk, a momentary wave of weakness sweeping over her. She didn't think she could do this! Surely, if she called home her father would know someone . . . but Tahnee's thoughts stopped right there. No, she couldn't call her father — his doctors had made it plain that he was to have no stress. And she couldn't really call anyone she trusted from back home — even if she made them promise to keep her request for help a secret, word might still get back to her father. But there had to be private security companies located here on the island, surely? The rich and famous came to Barbados all the time, and probably needed bodyguards. But what if the kidnappers spotted him following her around? They might decide to call the whole thing off, and what happened to Cordelia then?

'Are you all right, Miss Sawyer?' the receptionist asked, snapping her out of it. She forced herself to smile brightly, and straighten up from the desk. Her shoulders came back and her head came up.

'Yes, yes, thank you.' She reached for her bag and headed towards the lift.

She needed to retrieve the pot of face cream.

And her gun.

★   ★   ★

Delphine Phillips pushed open the door in a side ward and glanced inside. It was a private room, with only one bed, and one figure, sleeping on it.

She'd been in her room, with the local radio station playing in the background for company, when the news programme had come on. She'd been about to order room service, feeling too dispirited to dress up and go out, when the newscaster's voice suddenly made itself heard. Before, it had only been a drone in the background, an anonymous source of human contact. Then the pleasant, female voice had mentioned Dylan Gale's name, and suddenly it sounded loud in her ears.

She'd gone across to it at once, staring at the innocuous radio in disbelief as the programme continued, informing her that local resident and businessman, the hotelier, Dylan Gale, had been attacked and injured during an apparent mugging earlier that day.

She'd immediately felt a cold hand clutch her insides and twist them, and she'd sat down abruptly on the bed. Dylan, hurt? Before she could process that thought properly, the bulletin was speeding along.

He was said to be recuperating at the JDC Hospital in Bridgetown, and that his family had been informed.

His family. Suddenly, it occurred to Delphine that he might have a wife. Children even. It was not something she'd thought of before, and she felt herself catch a huge breath of air.

She buried her face in her hands and tried

to get a grip. Someone had hurt him — she had to go and see if he was all right. She'd never be able to close her eyes, let alone sleep, until she had. And if, when she got there, he wasn't alone — well, that was all right too. So long as she could just look through the door and see for herself he was going to be OK, that was all she could reasonably ask for.

So she'd hailed a taxi, inquired about him at the desk, reassured the porter on duty there that she wasn't press, and now here she was.

The room was painted a pale lemon-cream colour and a large bunch of exuberant, native flowers displayed their colours from on top of his bedside cabinet. Lying in the bed, Dylan Gale had a white gauze pad on his forehead and left cheek, and under a pale blue pyjama top, she could see that his ribs had been tightly bound. A drip was attached to one arm, but he seemed to be sleeping peacefully.

The nurse at the reception desk had told her that his parents had already been and gone that evening, and that visiting hours ended at 9.30.

She was about to pull her head back and close the door when he suddenly opened his eyes.

'Who's that?' he asked sharply, and

Delphine quickly pushed the door open again. 'It's only me. I wanted to see how you were.'

Dylan Gale smiled wryly. 'Well, as you can see, I'm all right. No thanks to Bolton's bully-boys.'

Delphine came in slowly and pushed the door shut behind her. Warily she walked forward, hooking a chair from where it had been placed with its back to the wall, and moving forward with it. When she was a few feet from his bed, she set it down and sat in it.

Dylan watched her and couldn't help but grin. She wasn't going to get too close, was she? But then again, who could blame her for wanting to keep her distance? If she was hooked up with Bolton, she might reasonably suppose that he might feel justified in lashing out and dishing out some of their own medicine.

But she was, of course, perfectly safe. Dylan had never hit a woman in his life, and didn't intend to start now.

'I still won't bite,' he drawled mockingly, as Delphine watched him with big, solemn, brown eyes.

'The radio said you were mugged,' she began carefully. 'But I take it you don't think there was anything random about what happened to you?'

Dylan watched her closely. He'd had a visit from his PI that afternoon, who'd reported in on his findings about her. Contrary to what he'd expected, Delphine Phillips had checked out. She was exactly who she said she was. Her mother *had* died six months ago, she *did* live in Oxford, and she was currently working on her D.Phil thesis. So she was as intelligent as she was beautiful. No mere actress, hired to play a role then. It was beginning to look more and more as if at least part of her story was true.

But that still didn't mean she wasn't working for Bolton. Until he was able to check out her research for himself, and more importantly, have a word with James Miller, he'd be a fool to trust her.

'How are you feeling?' she asked carefully. 'Have your ribs been broken?'

'Only cracked,' Dylan corrected grimly. But it still hurt like crazy every time he forgot himself and breathed in too hard. 'A few scrapes and bruises, nothing to worry about. I'm being discharged tomorrow, all being well. The two thugs Bolton hired to do this got a little more than they bargained for,' he added with a wolfish grin.

Delphine shuddered. If he'd really been attacked on purpose, how could he laugh about it? What if, next time, they really hurt him?

'I wish you'd take this seriously,' she heard herself say angrily, then could have kicked herself as he turned his head sharply on the pillow and speared her with a steely-eyed look.

'Oh, I take it seriously, all right,' he said softly. 'You can assure Marcus Bolton of that.'

'I've barely spoken to the man!' Delphine said hotly, then flushed as his eyes narrowed.

'Oh? So you *have* spoken to him, then? Some refreshing honesty for a change. Last time we met, you said you'd never even heard of him.'

'He introduced himself to me in a bar,' she said, a shade defiantly. 'I had no idea who he was until he said his name. A rather squat, sturdy-built man, in his early fifties, very tanned, with thinning dark reddish hair?'

'That's our Marcus,' Dylan agreed grimly. 'What did he want?' He wasn't sure yet that he was buying into any of this, but at least he wasn't bored any more. He'd been going crazy lying in bed all day, doing nothing. Now, his blood was singing and he felt gloriously alive again. Sparring with the beautiful English girl sure beat staring at the ceiling.

'He warned me about you, actually,'

Delphine said quietly, and saw him give a genuine start of surprise.

'*He* warned you against *me*?' he repeated incredulously. 'Of all the damned cheek!' He had to laugh, then winced as his ribs objected in no uncertain terms. Seeing the spasm of pain that crossed his face, Delphine half-rose, then sat back down again as he shot her a quick, fulminating look. Obviously, he was not a man who liked to be fussed over. Which was just fine with her! She had no desire to play Florence Nightingale.

But the harsh overhead lighting showed up a golden sheen on his chin where he needed a shave, and she had to fight back the urge to push back a lock of damp hair that kept falling over one eye.

'He said you played hard and rough, and that I might need someone on my side before this situation about Mowbray House was all finished with,' Delphine continued. 'It was a bit creepy, actually. He seemed to know all about me.'

Dylan's cat-green eyes narrowed. Interesting. Was this some game of double bluff? Or was it possible she really was the innocent in this, and that Marcus was playing her? He didn't like that last thought at all. Bolton played dirty.

'Be careful of Bolton, Delphine,' Dylan

181

said harshly. 'I mean it — even if you are working hand in glove with him, you can't trust him. He's vicious, and has no moral compass at all. He'll turn on you without a moment's thought, when it suits him.'

'Once and for all, I hardly know the man,' Delphine said hotly. 'Believe it or not, I'm not used to being called a liar!'

Dylan grinned at the sudden fire in her face. It seemed to light her up, to smoulder from within. Already he could feel its heat, burning him.

'OK, OK, peace,' he said, holding out a hand. He shifted a little in the bed, trying to sit up a little, but the soreness in his ribs made him give a small gasp.

'You should keep still,' Delphine said with a small sigh of exasperation, getting off the chair and going over to him. 'What's wrong? What are you trying to do?'

'Sit up,' Dylan said shortly. He didn't like having to lie down, while she was free to move about as she liked. It made him feel vulnerable.

'Isn't there some sort of lever under the bed that does that?' she asked, bending down, then spotting a short-handled crank. Cautiously she turned it, then looked up and nodded as the back of the bed began to bend. 'Yes, this'll do it. Tell me when it's upright enough for you.'

Dylan looked down at her bent dark head as she turned the handle. She was so close he could smell the sweet fragrance of freesias from her shampoo. For a giddying moment he had to fight the urge to bend forward and plant a kiss on top of all that glorious dark hair. When she glanced up at him in question, he blinked hard. 'A few more degrees, please,' he said through slightly gritted teeth, then added, 'That's it, thanks.'

Delphine smiled and stood upright. For a brief instant, the intimacy of the moment paralyzed her. Here he was, lying helpless in bed, wounded and hurt, and she had only to reach out and . . . Watching, she saw slim pale fingers push the fair hair off his brow. Dylan went as still as a hunting heron, but his green eyes widened and began to glow like back-lit emeralds.

Slowly, his larger, tanned hand reached up and grasped her wrist; his grip was strong and firm, but somehow wonderfully gentle and tender. Holding her eyes with his own, he turned her hand over and drew her naked, vulnerable palm up to his mouth. When he planted a small kiss there, she felt her breath catch in her throat, and her knees turned to water. Helplessly, she felt herself lean against the side of his bed for support.

By applying a downward pressure on her

wrist, he forced her to bend forward, closer, and closer.

'Are you married?' she blurted out.

Dylan, after a startled second, slowly smiled. 'No.'

His hand moved from her wrist to the back of her neck, his fingers curling around the nape and gently stroking the pulse point at the side of her neck. It was fluttering wildly, like a trapped butterfly. He didn't care how good an actress she might be, he didn't believe she could fake a reaction like that, and a primordial, masculine sense of triumph flooded over him.

Yes! She wanted him.

Urgently he reached up and kissed her — long and hard. Delphine gave a barely muffled yelp, then moaned softly, their lips foraging, tongues duelling, as he pulled her closer and closer. She put a hand out and pressed it against his pillow, trying to stop herself from putting pressure on his tender ribs. Ignoring her thoughtfulness, Dylan dragged her closer still, barely registering the pain it caused him.

He was lost in the scent of her, the taste of her, the thrill of her.

A loud, amused cough rudely shattered the moment. Delphine, her face flaming, shot up and away, turning bewildered eyes to the doorway, where an amused woman in a nurse's navy blue uniform watched them.

'Sorry — I wouldn't have walked in if I'd known,' she apologized cheerfully, giving Delphine a broad wink. 'Time for meds, Mr Gale.'

Dylan scowled and was about to say something very uncomplimentary about meds, then bit it off as Delphine muttered something incomprehensible and made a dash for the door. He watched her go, fighting the urge to call her back.

Damn the woman! Just wait until he was feeling fighting fit again. She wouldn't get away from him so easily the next time.

* * *

Tahnee wasn't sure which direction was east, and consequently had to tour the perimeter of the public garden, pushing at each gate until she found the right one.

Jonah, walking about twenty yards behind her, wondered what the hell she was doing.

When he'd seen the look on her face as she turned away from the reception desk, he'd wanted to walk straight across the room and take her in his arms and shake her, and demand to know just what the hell was going on. She looked both afraid and yet grimly determined at the same time. Instead, instinct told him to collect his motorbike and wait outside, on the dark street, and keep watch on the entrance, and sure enough, a few minutes later, she came out and hired a taxi.

Jonah had never felt the need to own a car before — after all, what did it matter to him? He didn't have a wife or steady girlfriend, and he lived on board the *Whale*. So long as he had a means of getting from A to B whenever he needed to, the small Japanese bike was perfectly adequate. But now, as he followed the taxi across the island towards Morgan Lewis Beach, he wished his vehicle wasn't quite so conspicuous. He had to keep well back in order for the distinctive sound of a motorbike engine not to reach her, and once or twice thought he'd lost her.

When he'd seen the taxi's brake lights up ahead, and realized it was dropping her off in a deserted part of Barclays Park, he turned off the engine right away, and slipped off his helmet. Locking the bike to a nearby set of railings, he sprinted down the road, glad he was wearing deck shoes that made no echoing sound on the tarmac.

He was just in time to see her walk around the perimeter of the public gardens and disappear round the corner.

He watched her try the first gate in the

railings she came to, but it was locked. He could have told her that — most parks on the island were locked when it became dark. Undeterred, she walked on and turned the corner on to the south side of the park. Again, keeping to the shadowed areas unlit by the street lamps, Jonah followed her. When she tried, unsuccessfully, to go through the next gate, Jonah began to get a very bad feeling.

Why was she so determined to get into a locked public garden? There was nothing in there. During the daylight it was packed with native islanders and tourists, but at night it was locked, so there were no drug users or traffickers, no lonely, desperate men trying to meet like-minded men in the public toilets. Unless she wanted to steal some of the plants, he could think of no good reason why she should go inside. Or why anybody would want her to go inside either.

Except as a meeting place that was guaranteed to be private. Was that it? Was she meeting somebody here in order to discuss whatever it was that was going on? But why go about it in such a weird way?

Puzzled, he looked around, but the night was deserted. He could hear the occasional hum of traffic, sometimes a human voice far away, laughing, probably somebody leaving a bar a little the worse for drink. Then he ran forward as he realized he'd lost sight of her, and found her again, as he'd suspected, on the far side of the park; the east side. This time, when she pushed against the gate, it opened.

Luckily there was a bright moon, and her silvery-blue cocktail dress showed up well. One moment he could see it, the next he couldn't. Which had to mean she'd gone inside.

Grimly he followed. Somehow, what happened to her had become his business. Quite how Tahnee Sawyer had become his concern, he wasn't sure. He only knew that she was. And if she was in trouble, he was going to help her — and damn the consequences.

Inside, the pale gravel paths and flowering bushes gleamed ghostly in the moonlight. He looked left, but could see no movement, then right. And there she was. Walking down the path. She walked slowly, her head constantly turning, almost as if she expected someone to leap out at her. Her hand rested on her bag, which was slung over one shoulder. Even in the dark, and from this distance, he could sense her tension.

His own throat dry, Jonah followed her deeper into the dark park.

Tahnee saw the bench a moment later and stopped to stare at it. In the daylight it was probably a delightful spot to sit on, the back facing the street, the front view stretching off across the park. It had bushes behind it and a large herbaceous border on the left. In sunlight they were probably full of bees and butterflies and singing birds. Here, in the dark, they only spread deep, dark shadows. Shadows where anybody could be lurking.

Reluctantly she approached the bench and sat down, furthest from the bushes. Her legs were shaking so much she was glad to sit, but now the worst part had come.

Waiting to see what would happen next.

Jonah, having seen her stop, had stepped instinctively off the path and into a flowering, fragrant shrub. He peered around it cautiously, and saw her sit down.

What was she doing?

He waited.

On the bench, Tahnee waited.

About ten minutes later, she jumped as an owl called and swooped low across the grass in front of her. In his hiding place, Jonah watched and waited some more.

Somewhere in the night, a Bridgetown church chimed ten.

189

Tahnee fingered the gun in her bag. She was sitting with the bag on her lap, her fingers curled comfortingly around the handle. Luckily, her finger wasn't on the trigger, for she might have pulled it in the next moment, as, right beneath the bench, a mobile phone suddenly rang. It sounded strident, almost angry, in the soft velvet darkness of a Barbados night.

She nearly leapt off the bench in fright, and from his position a few hundred yards away, Jonah clearly heard its ringtone. He'd assumed it was her own until he saw her shoot off the bench, back away, and stare at it.

Tahnee, her heart thundering, slowly walked back to the bench, bent down and reached underneath. She gave a brief thought to spiders or poisonous nocturnal creepy crawlies, but her fingers encountered only grass and good, fertile earth, before it hit the smooth metal of a manmade object. Taking deep, slightly panicky breaths, she picked it up, stood up, and turned it on, then held it to her ear.

'*Good*,' a voice whispered, making a shiver run down her spine. '*You know how to follow instructions. For that, you get a little reward.*'

There followed a muffled sound, then a short pause, then a voice, scared and female

190

and instantly recognizable, filled her ear.

'Tahnee! Tahnee, is that you? Oh, please, Tahnee, please do what they say. They scare me. Tahnee, they hurt . . . '

There was a muffled squawk, then sudden silence. Tahnee felt the nape of her neck go cold. 'Cordelia,' she said sharply. 'Cordelia!'

'*That's all you get for now. Sleep well.*'

There was a click in her ear, then an eerie silence.

In the darkness, Tahnee stared helplessly at the phone in her hand, her brain working overtime.

She'd spoken to Cordelia, so she was alive. That was good. Very good. They were pleased with her for following instructions. Another good thing in her favour. And now she had a mobile phone. Could she trace it back to the owner? No, surely, they wouldn't be so stupid as to use a traceable phone. It had probably been bought from a pay-as-you-go shop, with cash. Besides, if she tried to trace the phone, and she was being watched and they learned what she was doing, they'd probably be angry.

OK, so nix on tracing the phone. What next? Was she supposed to leave the phone here or take it with her? They hadn't given her any specific instructions about that. But suppose they wanted to contact her again

— it made sense to keep the phone, right? Numbly she slipped the phone back into her bag, and then looked back at the bench.

They hadn't told her she could go either, but surely she wasn't expected to wait here any longer, was she?

For a moment she hesitated, plagued by indecision, then told herself to get a grip. They'd accomplished what they wanted. It was time to go back to the hotel.

She turned and began to walk quickly back along the path. So quickly that Jonah, still concealed in his hiding place, had no chance to slip out and get away before she passed him.

He'd watched her answer the phone, but apart from saying 'Cordelia' twice, she hadn't said a word. What was that all about?

Now she was drawing level with his hiding place, and he held his breath, keeping himself perfectly still; then, to his abject relief, she was going past.

He let out a long, slow breath of relief, then waited a few minutes before stepping out on to the path. When he turned, about to head for the gate where he'd come in, she was waiting for him.

Stood in the middle of the path, the moonlight silvering her head like the halo of some pagan high priestess, she was stood with her shapely legs slightly apart, arms fully extended.

And in her hand was a gun. A gun that was pointed, unwaveringly, at him.

Tahnee saw his face and a split second later, recognized it.

And something inside her curled up and died.

8

Tahnee felt the gun waver slightly in her hand as she recognized him, then she took a firm breath, raising the gun a fraction and closing her fingers more tightly around it. Of all the people in all the world she thought might have come walking down that dark path behind her, Jonah Rodgers was not one of them. And she felt a sharp, heart-rending sense of betrayal that took her totally by surprise. After all, she barely knew the man!

Jonah, his heart thundering in his chest, slowly raised his hands, feeling both foolish and fascinated. She looked like some avenging moon goddess, and in spite of the dangers of the situation, felt something hard and warm stir in his loins.

'I'm harmless.' He tried to smile brightly, and waggled his naked fingers. 'See?'

'What are you doing here?' Tahnee asked rhetorically, her voice emerging like a scratched record. She cleared her throat, and tried to put some threat and more energy into it. 'Did you see what you wanted?' she demanded scornfully.

Jonah frowned, aware of a growing sense of

bewilderment. Why was she sounding so mad and so hurt? She was the one up to no good. She was the one holding the gun on *him*! 'I'm not sure what I saw, exactly,' he said at last. 'Tahnee, what are you doing here in this place in the middle of the night? Don't you realize it could be dangerous — the island has its fair share of muggers and crime you know. And how did you get in, anyway? These public places are usually locked at night.'

Tahnee blinked, surprised by the puzzlement in his voice. How did she get in? Surely he knew if he was one of the kidnappers. But what else could he be? Why else would he be following her? She shifted her feet a little restlessly, feeling as if the situation was fast slipping away from her. And now that she came to think of it, why *would* the kidnappers have her followed anyway? They'd know at once whether or not she'd followed instructions, because if she hadn't, she wouldn't have been there to answer the phone. Why risk exposure by putting a tail on her? If she had called in the cops or the FBI, they'd only have been in danger of being picked up.

And yet, when she'd walked past the bushes and sensed a presence there, her heart rate had gone into overdrive. Unless it was some tramp bedding down for the night, who else would have a reason to be in the park except for one of them? And when she'd waited on that dark path, gun ready, heart sounding like a gong in her ears, and had first seen Jonah, she'd felt poleaxed. Her first thought had been to wonder how they'd known she'd pick his boat. Her second was to wonder how could she ever have been so foolish as to trust him. To start liking him, even.

Out on his boat, she'd felt an almost glorious sense of freedom and relief in his presence. Probably because he'd seemed so uncomplicated and happy in his own skin, so much at ease with life, which was in such a contrast to herself and her situation.

She'd felt utterly betrayed to know that, all along, he'd been working for the enemy. But now she wasn't so sure that things were as they seemed.

'The gates were left open for me, I presume,' she said cautiously, feeling her way around this new situation.

Jonah frowned, sensing her distrust and wishing it was different. 'Why would a park employee unlock a gate for you?' he asked curiously.

Tahnee took a long, slow breath. 'Why don't you just tell me what's going on, Jonah?' she said softly.

Slowly, Jonah lowered his arms, letting

them fall to his side. As he did so, he was relieved to note that she lowered the gun until it was pointing at the ground. Finally, he shrugged. 'I don't know what's going on,' he admitted simply.

Tahnee sighed. If he was one of them, why didn't he just demand the gun from her and berate her for disobeying instructions, or threaten repercussions? 'Why don't you start by telling me what you're doing here?' she said flatly.

Jonah nodded cautiously. 'All right. I was in your hotel tonight, having a drink, and I saw you at the reception desk. You looked really bad; almost like you were ill. Afterwards, when I saw you walk outside, I was concerned. So I followed you.' It sounded, even to his own ears, so lame. But he could hardly tell her he'd been fingering her to the cops, could he?

'I see,' Tahnee said wryly, her lips twisting in disbelief. 'A proper good Samaritan, in fact?'

Jonah sighed heavily, realizing it was time for some twisting of the truth. 'It wasn't only that,' he admitted reluctantly. 'But you've got to admit, you've been acting kind of squirrelly ever since you hired me. Going out to deserted beaches. Acting like a cat on a hot tin roof. Frankly, I was worried you might be up to something that could come back on me.'

Tahnee cocked her head to one side and thought about that. Now she was more curious than afraid.

'What do you mean?'

Jonah shrugged helplessly. 'Look, I haven't paid off my mortgage on the *Whale* yet. I need to keep my nose clean and my business dealings dead straight. Not being a native of the island, I could be deported for any irregularity. And as for getting mixed up in anything faintly illegal — forget about it! I just didn't like the way things were looking, so I thought I'd follow you and check things out. And here we are' — he allowed his voice to harden a little — 'in a dark and deserted park. With you holding a gun on me.'

Tahnee stared at him from her big, violet-coloured eyes. Put like that, it certainly sounded reasonable enough. Was it possible he was telling the truth? Or was he only trying to save his own skin? After all, he could hardly admit he was one of the kidnappers, could he? After this was all over, and she had Cordelia back and they had the money, he'd want to be sure that she couldn't point her finger at him.

On the other hand, she wanted to believe him. As ridiculous as that was, she wanted to be able to trust him. She was feeling alone and scared, and there'd been something solid and trustworthy and basic about him that had attracted her right from the first. It made her want to walk into his arms and be soothed and petted, like a stray cat who'd found a warm home. She could even imagine his fingers on her, his hands on her back, stroking, his voice in her ear, murmuring how he'd take care of her, protect her, and love her.

Which was madness. Pure and simple. Either he was a kidnapper, in which case her own life might now be in danger, or he was telling the truth, really did have suspicions that something was up, and was putting his nose in where it definitely wasn't wanted. Which, in a way, was even more dangerous — for both of them! What if the kidnappers realized what he was doing and decided to do something about it?

Either way, she had to end this now. It was best they just parted, and had nothing more to do with each other.

But even as she thought it, she realized she couldn't do it that way. If she told him he was fired, and sought out a new boat and skipper, what would happen? If he wasn't a kidnapper, they'd soon realize what she'd done and wonder why. Perhaps sense a trap. Maybe wonder if her new boat and skipper were undercover FBI. In which case, the consequences for Cordelia didn't bear thinking about! And if he was one of them, telling him she was going to someone else might precipitate a catastrophe as well. What if they decided things had got too hot and scrapped the kidnap attempt altogether. Cordelia might get killed. *She* might get killed.

No, there was no way out.

Whether he was a good guy, or a bad guy, Tahnee was stuck with him.

Wearily, she opened her bag and put the gun away. 'Look, what do you say that we just forget about this, huh?' she begged helplessly. 'I just wanted to get some air and stretch my legs. You startled me, skulking about in the bushes, and I decided to protect myself. No harm, no foul. All right?'

Jonah, glad though he was to see the gun disappear from sight, felt oddly deflated. The explanation she'd just given him was no explanation at all. Did she really expect him to go along with it? And yet what else could he do? Flloyd had made it clear that he wanted him to keep on reporting in. Not that he cared about that any more. As far as he was concerned, he'd done his civic duty. Let the cops on this island do their own dirty work.

But if he told her to go find another boat, he'd never see her again. And she was in trouble, big trouble, that much was obvious. And she needed him. Big-city girl, touting a gun, and acting as if she could handle the whole world — ha! She wasn't fooling him. Inside she was a tired, scared, little girl and Jonah was beginning to feel mad. Mad at whoever was doing this to her.

So he smiled and shrugged, and once again spread his hands in a 'peace' gesture. 'Sure, Tahnee,' he said softly. 'Whatever you say.'

And so, neither trusting the other, they turned and walked away into the soft Barbados moonlight. Jonah wanted to reach out and take her hand, but didn't. Tahnee walked beside him, wishing with all her heart that he would take her hand, and telling herself that she was glad when he didn't. And somewhere, overhead, an owl hooted in avian derision.

*   *   *

Delphine awoke just after seven to the sound of an unknown bird singing outside her window. The scent of frangipani wafted in on the breeze, and she slowly stretched, before taking a shower and sitting at the dressing table to brush her long, dark hair. She'd just finished, and was about to tie it back with a tortoiseshell comb, when a hard knock came at her door.

Surprised, since she always went down to breakfast, and hadn't yet requested room service for anything, she walked to the door and opened it, and felt her spirits sink the moment Marcus Bolton smiled back at her.

'Sorry to wake you at such an unearthly hour,' he said smoothly, 'but I'm afraid we have a problem. May I come in?'

Delphine instinctively took a step forward, not wanting this man in her room. Catching a fleeting look of chagrin on his face, she forced a smile. 'Sorry, I was just going down to breakfast. Why don't you join me?' Not that she wanted his company, but better that than be alone with him.

Marcus inclined his head sardonically and followed her through to the inn's near-deserted dining room. She helped herself from the buffet to some mammyapples, a basket-ball sized, thick-skinned fruit with giant seeds, and added some papaya and mango. Her guest, she noted, opted simply for coffee. Once seated beside a raffia partition that was host to a climbing morning glory plant, she sipped her own coffee and eyed him warily.

Marcus reached into his inside jacket

pocket, and withdrew a long, legal-looking document. 'I had to work fast to get this. Did you know that Dylan Gale is sending in the heavy squad? In fact, they're due to start work' — he turned his wrist to check his watch, — 'promptly at nine o'clock this morning.'

'No,' Delphine blurted, confused, then frowned. 'What's the heavy squad?'

'Manual labourers. Probably to clear the Mowbray House gardens, and start digging an Olympic-size swimming pool.'

Delphine felt herself shudder. A swimming pool? In her mind's eye she saw once again the charming, overgrown tangle that surrounded the house. Saw it all cleaned up with an antiseptic pool, complete with black, white and blue tiling all around it. Saw the native flowers gone, replaced by well-maintained, easy-access concrete paths.

'He can't do that!' she wailed softly. It would spoil the whole look of the house!

'He will, unless we stop him,' Marcus shot back. 'That's why I got this,' he added, handing the piece of paper over. In fact, it was a series of papers, almost impossible for her to read, the legalese was so impenetrable.

Seeing her difficulty, Marcus smiled smugly. 'Basically, it's a temporary restraining order, banning Gale Imperial from doing any maintenance and/or cosmetic work on Mowbray House until the issue of ownership can be decided. I had this lawyer I know make it up, using your name — since you're the one with the claim to it,' Marcus added quickly, as she opened her mouth to object. 'It obviously wouldn't carry any weight if the courts saw that I was the one trying to stop it. After all, I've got no legal rights in this matter. But I explained your situation to this lawyer I know, and he was able to get a judge to grant a temporary stay of execution for the house. But you have to appear in court this morning to confirm it. You'd better take all the relevant documentation with you. Without it, the judge might decide you don't have a strong enough claim and then' — Marcus shrugged his wide shoulders helplessly — 'Mowbray House gets a makeover, whether we like it or not.'

Delphine bit her lip, and pushed her breakfast plate away untouched. Suddenly, her appetite had fled.

On the one hand, since speaking to Dylan in hospital, she wanted nothing to do with Marcus Bolton. A small voice at the back of her mind was insisting that she had to find a way to make Dylan trust her. And consorting with his enemy was hardly the way to do it.

On the other hand, didn't she owe something to Mowbray House? To her dead great uncle, and the man who'd left the place to him? Didn't she owe it to them to keep the house safe?

And, another little voice piped up mischievously from the depths of her heart, at least, while she was making a nuisance of herself, she'd have another excuse to see Dylan again. And this way, he wouldn't be able to forget about her in a hurry. After all, a man like that wouldn't think twice about a nobody like her — unless she gave him a reason to. But such a thought was despicable. And childish. It was . . .

'Look, I don't want to rush you,' Marcus snapped heavily, 'but if we're going to move on this thing, we gotta go now.'

Sighing wearily, Delphine nodded.

* * *

Dylan was in Fairfield, in the parish of Saint Lucy, when he got a phone call from the foreman of the landscaping company he used. Mike Tyler, a dour Scot in another life, now married to a native woman and happy to exchange a North Sea oil rig for a spade and a bag of fertilizer, sounded unusually curt.

'Dylan, we seem to have a problem. I'm out at the new site in Bathsheba. We can't get in.'

Dylan, who was looking into the idea of converting an old sugar mill into holiday flats, frowned and nodded to the real-estate agent with him that he needed to take the call. Tactfully, the young man walked away a few yards, and Dylan began to walk slowly back to his car. 'What do you mean, you can't get in?' he repeated flatly. When he thought back to Mowbray House, he could remember only a ramshackle and largely falling-down wooden fence ringing the perimeter.

'What's the problem? I can't remember any padlocks anywhere. If you have to, pull up some fencing — it's going to be replaced by a native-stone wall anyway. You have the specs, right?'

'No, mon, ye dinnae understand.' Mike's voice became even more Scottish. 'It's not that we cannae physically get in. We've been issued with a writ to stop all work. Not that we'd really got started anyway. Look, Dylan, I think ye'd best get over here, mon. Sort this out. I'll tell the lads to stand by, but if there's no work here, I'll have to get started on that job down at Crane Bay. I cannae afford to have me workers standing idle, ye understand?'

'No, I understand that. I'll be there in twenty minutes,' Dylan agreed tersely and hung up. Then he called across to the estate agent that they'd have to reschedule the appointment and drove off the lot with an angry spin of his wheels that shot gravel across the deserted mill's forecourt.

* * *

Delphine slowly walked to the easternmost part of the garden, where the sound of the sea was so loud she could almost believe it was just a step away from her feet. Here the garden was salt-sprayed, the flowers mostly succulents and hunkered down to withstand the wind. There was something almost pagan about the wildness, and behind her, when she turned, the house seemed to be a part of that wildness too. And yet, at the same time, a sanctuary. It just broke her heart to think of it rendered into a soulless compartment of rooms for strangers that came and went, and left nothing of themselves behind. A house like this one deserved to be loved and cherished. Not simply made use of.

She could hear the murmur of the men who were still parked out front. They'd broken out their thermos flasks and were drinking tea, some looking amused, others angry or worried, by the turn of events. She'd felt undeniably guilty when she'd walked up the path half an hour ago, and asked to speak to the foreman. She hadn't expected a tall, blond, Scot to greet her, and when she'd handed him the injunction, and explained that he wasn't legally entitled to do any work there, she hadn't been able to meet his eyes.

Her appearance in court that morning had been very brief; the judge, a middle-aged black woman, seeming to be very busy. So Delphine had simply confirmed the salient points in Marcus Bolton's document, and handed over copies of the will and notes on her research so far. She now had another court date in two days' time.

Marcus had introduced her to his lawyer, Frederick Cramer, a tall, thin, white-haired man in an expensive suit, who'd hardly spoken two words. According to Marcus, Frederick did a lot of pro-bono work, and was something of a specialist campaigner in this area, being determined to keep Bahamian history, architecture, culture and lifestyle from being eroded.

Once outside the court, Marcus had wanted to come with her to the house to see that the injunction was enforced, but Delphine had insisted she go alone. She tried to tell herself it was only because she wanted to avoid a scene, but deep inside, she knew that what really mattered to her was that Dylan Gale didn't see her and Marcus together.

She'd have preferred to go her own way, and do her own battling, but as Marcus had pointed out, by the time she'd gone through the courts and repeated the process he'd already gone through, Mowbray House might already be transformed beyond recognition. But although she might be forced to accept Bolton's help this time, she was determined to have nothing else to do with him. And she had to make Dylan understand this.

Now she heard the low, throbbing hum of a powerful sports car engine split the morning quiet, and she took a deep breath. Walking to a gnarled tree-stump, she sat down on legs that suddenly felt watery, and tensely waited.

A few minutes later, she saw him, walking through the garden, thrusting aside flowering branches and vines laden with colourful butterflies and bees, and step out into the open area. He spotted her at once, of course, and walked straight over, his body moving in a tight, careful way that told her he still felt the pain of his injuries. His lips twisted into a wry smile as he approached.

'When Mike said some woman had stopped him and his men from working, I knew it had to be you. Just what are you playing at?' He came to a stop in front of her, six feet of angry male. He was wearing a plain white shirt, open at the neck, and rolled up at the wrists, to reveal tanned, muscular arms. With it, he wore a pair of loose black slacks that rippled in the breeze from the sea, clinging to firm calf and thigh muscles. His green eyes blazed down at her like an angry cat, and she could almost imagine a long, sinuous tail flickering angrily at the tip.

She felt her breath catch in her throat.

'Why don't you sit down?' she asked softly, her eyes searching his face, which seemed paler than usual. There was still a plaster on his forehead, only half-hidden by the fall of his blond hair. 'You don't look well. Should you really be up and about so soon?'

Dylan grinned savagely. 'Your concern is touching. Or at least, it would be, if you weren't trying to put me out of business. Come on, then, let's have it,' he added, holding out his hand imperiously, wagging the fingers in a 'give me' gesture. Reluctantly, she put the injunction into his hand.

Wordlessly he read it, then slowly folded it into quarters and slipped it into the back pocket of his slacks. 'So, you're actually going through with it,' he said, shaking his head, his voice a mixture of disbelief and grudging respect. 'Do you really think any court on this island is going to just hand over Mowbray House to you? A property that I bought in good faith, and paid good money for? On the basis of a questionable sixty-year-old will, that's been out of probate for nearly as long?'

Delphine sighed softly. 'I don't know. But at least it'll stop you building a swimming pool here for a little while. Just look at it, Dylan — look around you. Can't you see the house doesn't want that?'

Dylan blinked. 'Swimming pool? What swimming pool?' He glanced across her shoulder, at the wide blue expanse of the Caribbean sea. 'Why the hell would I put a swimming pool in here? This place comes with access to its own private beach.'

Delphine opened her mouth, then closed it again. Marcus must have got it wrong. 'But those men out there — what are they going to do?'

'Well, nothing now, it seems,' Dylan grunted, but not without a savage smile. You had to hand it to her — when she went for the jugular, she didn't shilly-shally about. 'And that reminds me.' He pulled out his mobile, pressed a speed-dial number and said laconically, 'Mike? It's me. You'd better get the gang down to Crane Bay Beach.' He paused, listened, then smiled grimly. 'Yeah, looks like it. I'll let you know when work can start again. I'm sorry to mess you about.' Again he paused and listened, then smiled. 'Thanks, I appreciate it.' He flipped the phone shut, slipped it into his shirt pocket, and shook his head.

'Mike's a landscape gardener. He and his crew were going to clear the jungle a bit, add some more plants, put down some chipped bark paths, repair the derelict pond, add a stone wall perimeter and some climbing plants, and generally make this place beautiful again. If you look closely' — He turned and indicated the garden behind him — 'you can see how the original owners had the grounds mapped out. Follows an old Gertrude Jekyll plan, if I'm not mistaken.'

Delphine swallowed hard. 'Oh. I thought you were going to put in a big swimming pool.'

He turned on her abruptly, his face tight and angry. 'You really see me as some sort of visigoth, don't you? Some vandal with the sensitivity of a Mongol army. Have you even taken the time to visit any of my hotels? No, I can see you haven't,' he added savagely, as guilty colour flooded her face.

'I'm sorry. Really, I am. It's just this house!' Delphine said helplessly. 'Ever since I first heard about, I knew I had to see it. And now that I have, it's calling to me. I just can't let it down.'

Dylan, surprised by the sudden passion in her voice, felt his anger evaporating. 'You really do care about it, don't you?' he said, with something like wonder in his voice. He turned and stared at the house. It was old, slightly ramshackle, a bit shame-faced, as if it knew it had been neglected and wasn't looking its best. But it was a proud old girl.

He smiled wryly. 'Have you even seen inside it yet?'

Delphine felt her breath catch. She wasn't sure whether it was the sudden gentleness in his voice, or the smile that finally reached his eyes. She only knew that her mouth had gone as dry as the Sahara, and her heart had taken wing. Mutely, she shook her head.

Slowly, he held out his hand to her. 'Well, I just happen to have the key,' he said softly.

Wordlessly, Delphine reached out and put her hand into his.

★ ★ ★

Tahnee Sawyer was staring aimlessly at a selection of the frozen yoghurts to be found at Toppings, when her world suddenly came to a shocking, crashing halt.

She'd chosen the Quayside Shopping

Centre as the ideal place to pass a few hours, figuring that nobody would be contacting her so soon after last night's episode. And, in truth, she needed to get out and do something normal. So she'd decided to combine some business with a little pleasure, and had spent the morning trailing around the hand-made articles to be found in ARTWORX in Shop 5, wondering if it might be worth setting up something similar at the gallery.

Needing to drink something cold, she'd wandered into Toppings. One moment she was contemplating lemon sorbet, and the next, casually glancing up and through the window, she saw a woman stroll past who could only be her stepmother.

Cordelia!

That trademark mass of Titian hair was unmistakable. She was tall, as Cordelia was, and walked with that same catwalk grace that was so typical of her father's second wife. She thought she saw the woman begin to turn, as if sensing someone watching her, and the profile too was the same. Or seemed to be. The next moment, the woman was out of sight, and suddenly Tahnee wasn't so sure.

Without even thinking about it, Tahnee shot out of the aisle, dodging the freezer sections as she zigzagged desperately to the shop door, where she turned and looked left, in the direction Cordelia had gone. The shopping mall was packed, however, full of tall, long-limbed graceful natives, brightly clad tourists, and browsing shoppers. And the head of chestnut-coloured hair was nowhere in sight.

Stepping out into the milling throng, Tahnee dodged and swerved through the crowd, trying to recall, desperately, just what it was that she *had* seen.

The woman had been tall and lean, but her hair had been the most noticeable thing about her. And she was well dressed, smart, chic and groomed, just as Cordelia invariably was. But there had to be lots of wealthy women on the island, surely? And some of them must, by law of averages, have auburn hair. And she hadn't seen her face — not full on. Was it possible that it had been just wishful thinking? For the past few days Tahnee had been desperately worried about her stepmother. Had her tired mind simply seen a passing resemblance in the face of a stranger and played a trick on her?

Frustrated, standing on tiptoe and trying to see over the heads of her fellow shoppers, Tahnee scoured the crowds. Dammit, where had she gone? Logically, she knew, it couldn't possibly have been Cordelia she'd seen. And yet . . .

Tahnee peered into the cafe nearest her — it was small, and she could see every table. There was no-one inside who looked remotely like her. Next, she shot into a small boutique — gave it a quick, almost manic look much to the proprietor's surprise, and shot outside again. There, she almost cannoned into Flloyd Turnbull, who, taken by surprise by her sudden manoeuvre, just managed to avoid a collision.

He'd been watching her all morning, and had just been about to give it up as a lost cause. Obviously, the lady was only window shopping. Then, without warning, she'd gone all psycho on him. He'd been hanging out by the freezer section when he'd seen her race out of the shop. For a brief second he wondered if she'd been shoplifting, then realized that wasn't the case at all. No, it had seemed as if she'd suddenly seen something that had galvanized her into action. Now, she was obviously looking for someone in the crowd. But who? And what was she so het up about?

Puzzled and intrigued, he followed her for the next few minutes, but slowly, she began to wind down.

Tahnee, not sure any more of just what it

was she *had* seen, made her way to one of the outdoor cafes and sank down on a chair. She must be going mad — thinking she could see Cordelia in the crowd. She was cracking up. It was time to get a grip.

When her waiter came, she ordered a gin and tonic. From a table opposite, Fleyd noted the order and raised a quizzical brow. The little lady had definitely got into a flap about something.

He would be glad when he got the gen on her from the mainland. He'd already contacted some friends of his, sending her picture and name. If she had a rap sheet, he'd know soon enough. Then he might have a better idea of what all this was about!

★   ★   ★

Delphine stood at the top landing window, staring out towards the sea. The house smelt of old wood and dried flowers, and seemed to whisper with memories of the past. And breathe promises of the future. From the moment she stepped through the front door, it felt as if she was being welcomed home.

Behind her, she was very much aware of Dylan standing close, his body almost brushing her own. If she took just the tiniest step backwards, she knew, her back would be pressed against his chest, her derriere into his groin. Would his arms then come around her? Would he lean forward and perhaps whisper something in her ear? The thought made her swallow hard.

'The house is perfect,' she said softly, curling her fingers around the windowsill in an effort to deny her increasingly erotic thoughts.

'A bit dark,' Dylan said, teasingly.

'Atmospheric,' she corrected firmly.

'It could do with re-wiring.'

'But nothing glaring.'

'Floorboards creak.' He carried on with the game, reaching out to brush a stray strand of hair off her cheek. He wanted to lift the mass of dark hair and plant a kiss in the nape of her neck. He wanted to reach out with his hands and run them up her bare, pale arms, perhaps nibble on her ear. He took a harsh breath, and told himself not to be such a pushover. He'd had women before — lots of them. And he'd always been in the driving seat. But this woman was driving him crazy. What would it really hurt to flirt a little . . .

'It's talking to us. Making friends,' Delphine whispered throatily.

'It needs redecorating throughout. Treating for damp here and there.'

'It needs some tlc,' she agreed. But it didn't

need to be turned into a hotel. And the house seemed to agree; it felt as if invisible arms enfolded her, thanking her, and begging her to stay.

Downstairs, Dylan had shown her the kitchen, with its vast, old-fashioned range and big, scrubbed table. The living room, musty with dust motes dancing like miniature angels in the morning sun. The hall, where a clock should be ticking, but wasn't. The winding staircase, almost grand and not quite elegant. And finally, upstairs, with its mass of bedrooms and single antiquated bathroom with a slight mould growing between the aqua tiles, and an old, claw-footed bathtub with the original taps.

She'd loved it all.

'Delphine,' he said huskily. And suddenly, she felt him pressing into her, his chest warm and hard against her back, his arms coming around her to gently loop around her waist. She felt the slight stubble of his chin as his face brushed against her cheek, and his breath fanned her hair at her temples as he looked out across the tangle of gardens towards the sea.

'That's lovely,' she said softly.

'So are you,' he murmured, and felt her turn in his arms. The next moment her breasts pressed tenderly against him, and when he looked down, he saw her dark velvet eyes melt in invitation.

With a muffled moan that was half-curse, half-defeated laughter, he kissed her long and slow, and hard. And when it was over, he kissed her again.

Delphine closed her eyes, clinging to him helplessly, utterly lost. She kissed him so passionately, giving so much of herself, that he could almost forget the piece of paper she'd handed over to him that morning.

Almost, but not quite.

And he wondered — even as he kissed her and held her ever more closely — just how much she wanted this house.

And just what she'd be willing to do to get it.

9

Tahnee opened up her portable laptop and took a deep breath. What if she was making a big mistake? Then she shook her head, telling herself that she couldn't keep on doubting her instincts like this. In the past, she'd always followed her feelings, and it felt right to do the same now.

She was back in her hotel room, having taken a taxi from the shopping centre. She'd had a quick shower and had changed into a short, scarlet-coloured dress with a square neckline and bias-cut skirt. Quickly, she tapped out her own business e-mail address at the gallery and left a message for her secretary. She knew Gina, who worked three afternoons a week, always kept a watching eye on the computer, and sure enough, within a minute, she received a reply.

For just another moment longer, she hesitated, then typed out her message.

Gina, do me a big favour. Look in top drawer of my desk for 'Opening Night' File, and find photo of myself, Dad and Cordelia taken at gallery opening party. Send me large-print copy ASAP.

She tapped her silver-painted fingernails nervously on the side of the machine as she waited, then breathed a sigh of relief as the photograph appeared on screen. She saved it into a file, tapped out a thanks, and logged off.

Taking the laptop downstairs, the receptionist was happy to oblige her request for use of their office printer, and within a moment or two, she was staring at a large, A4-sized printed photograph. It had been taken at the party which had launched her new gallery, and her father's face beamed with pride as he stood beside her, one arm looped lovingly across her shoulder.

She'd called him that morning, and knew he was chafing to get home from the hospital, but she'd persuaded him to stay where he was, as per his doctors' instructions. It was strange that, yet again, he hadn't mentioned Cordelia's absence, and she was beginning to wonder if that wasn't significant. In fact, if her growing suspicions turned out to have any basis in fact at all, it might explain a lot of things.

But first things first.

Since she was still in the hotel's admin office, she begged the use of a pair of scissors from a polite, but slightly intrigued secretary, and quickly cut both herself and her father from the picture, leaving a full-length, full-face likeness of Cordelia remaining. This she carefully slipped into her purse and, thanking the secretary for all her help, left the hotel.

She had a long afternoon's work ahead of her.

As she left the hotel, she didn't notice Flloyd Turnbull strolling casually behind her.

★ ★ ★

Marcus Bolton regarded the two men he'd called into his study thoughtfully, and wondered why it was he could never remember their names. Both the big Australian and his companion still looked a little worse for wear, one sporting a black eye, the other still holding himself stiffly from the bruises that covered his body.

Marcus smiled grimly. Who'd have thought that Dylan Gale, spoil rich brat hotelier, would be made of such steel?

'It's all right,' Marcus drawled sarcastically, as he saw the Australian shoot his comrade a wary look out of the corner of his eye. 'I'm not going to ask the two of you to take on one spoilt little rich boy again.'

The shorter, dark-skinned man opened his mouth to protest, caught his boss's gimlet eye, and snapped his jaw shut again. And winced. Ever since his altercation the other day, he was sure he had a loose tooth. He only hoped it didn't fall out.

'This is something I'm sure even you two morons can't fail to cope with.' And he gave them terse, easy-to-follow instructions. When they were gone he sighed, then reached for the telephone and dialled a familiar number. When a subdued female voice came on the line, his face twisted into a vicious sneer.

'Just what the hell do you think you're playing at?' he snarled. 'Pull another stunt like that, and they'll be pulling your stupid, worthless, pretty little hide from the sea. Understand me?' He listened in silence for a while as the desperate, wheedling voice sounded in his ear, and smiled grimly. Then, cutting her off in mid-flow, he slammed down the phone.

Why was it that nobody could simply do as they were told?

★   ★   ★

Delphine took a walk along the beach near Bathsheba, smiling at the children playing in the surf, patting out buckets of sand for sandcastles and cajoling parents for money for ice creams, and wondered what it would be like to have children of her own. Would they have Dylan's fair colouring or her own?

Then she stopped stock-still in the sand, and shook her head. Where oh where did such thoughts come from? So they'd kissed. So it had been wonderful. But hadn't he then told her he had to get back to the office, and left her, without, apparently, even a moment of regret? Had he by any word, deed or signal indicated that the events of that morning by the landing window had meant anything to him other than a pleasant, adult flirtation? A fun way to while away a few minutes?

No, he had not.

And yet here she was, fantasizing about a future that almost certainly would never happen. Where was her cool, academic mind? What had happened to all her sensible, reasonable ways?

She caught a sunbathing woman looking at her curiously, and smiled an apology for blocking out her sun before quickly walking on. She was acting like an idiot!

Restlessly, she walked the length of the beach, then started to turn back, noticing a set of wooden stairs that ran up the side of the cliff. A gate at the bottom had a notice hung on it and, curious, she walked up to read it.

PRIVATE: MOWBRAY HOUSE RESI-DENTS ONLY

Of course, she thought. The house must be just above, and Dylan had said something earlier about the house having its own private access to the beach. Unsure whether such an act constituted trespassing or not, she opened the gate and began to climb the stairs. The wood was old and bleached with age, but the stairs seemed safe enough. And as she climbed, she felt her heart lifting.

Perhaps it was the playful call of the gulls, or maybe the warming glow of the seemingly never-ending sun. But somehow, she suddenly felt that everything was going to be all right.

★   ★   ★

In Mowbray House, a big Australian man poured cooking oil into a pan and turned on the heat, while his companion watched, and sighed.

'I don't get why we don't just toss some turps or gas around the place and set light to it.'

The Australian shrugged. 'Boss wants it done this way. Guess he doesn't want the cops to suspect arson.'

'But nobody lives here,' his companion pointed out reasonably. 'So who's gonna believe some tramp broke in, decided to cook himself some chips, and then left the pan on?'

The Australian, noting the heat begin to shimmer across the surface of the pan, grinned widely. 'Nobody, I reckon. Boss wants to let Gayle know he's behind it. But at the same time, make sure nothing can lead back to him.'

'Smart, I suppose,' the other man muttered, but without any respect. The fact was, he didn't like Bolton. If he could find other work, perhaps in Mystique, maybe Trinidad, he'd be off like a shot.

The Australian, noting that the pan was beginning to smoke now, said casually, 'Time to be going, I reckon.'

Outside, Delphine Phillips stepped on to the top wooden stair and glanced across the grassy cliff top towards Mowbray House.

★ ★ ★

Tahnee went back to the shopping centre and tried the cafe first. She showed Cordelia's picture to both the waitresses, but none of them remembered seeing her, or serving her that morning.

Outside, Flloyd watched her carefully,

reflecting that at least she was easy to follow and spot, what with that flame-coloured dress that showed off every sexy curve, and that weird haircut that suited her so perfectly. She was some sexy babe all right. No wonder his mate Jonah had taken such a header.

★ ★ ★

Delphine walked slowly across the grass, watching as a small, azure butterfly flitted in alarm from a wildflower in front of her, was caught by the sea breeze, and wafted closer to the house.

She suddenly stopped and frowned, when she thought she heard a door slam shut. But how could that be? There was only Mowbray House close enough to be the source of such a noise, and Dylan had locked it up that morning. Curious, she began to walk towards the house a bit faster. In her mind, she was worried about vandals, or maybe squatters.

Being at the side of the house, she didn't notice smoke slowly begin to seep through the cracked wooden window frames in the kitchen, which was at the back.

★ ★ ★

Dylan Gale threw down his pen in disgust and pushed back his chair. He'd been trying to go through the lease agreement on some land near Rockley Beach, where he planned to built some holiday chalets. But for all the progress he was making, he might just as well be beachcombing, a favourite pastime of his from childhood. Every time he tried to concentrate his mind on the business in hand, he kept seeing a pair of dark velvet eyes. Whenever he tried to concentrate on architects' plans, he felt soft, mobile lips beneath his own.

Dammit, the woman was getting under his skin. He walked restlessly to his window and looked out on downtown, baking, cheerful Bridgetown.

Perhaps she was still at Bathsheba? She'd said she was going to hit the beach, maybe do some sunbathing. He might still catch her.

If he hurried.

Feeling like a fool, but knowing he was going to do it anyway, Dylan left his office and, for the first time in his life, chased after a woman.

★ ★ ★

Flloyd Turnbull watched, puzzled, as his quarry entered the same boutique she'd

229

dashed into just a few hours earlier and moved closer to the window. Feeling slightly embarrassed to be seen peering into a women's fashion shop, he saw Tahnee Sawyer reach into her bag and pull out what looked like a piece of paper. She handed it to the shop assistant, who took it, looked at it, and shook her head.

Flloyd had done enough footwork in his time as a police officer to recognize the procedure for exactly what it was. For some reason, Tahnee was showing a photograph around the place, trying to get an ID, maybe?

Now why would she be doing that? What the hell was going on? This was not the behaviour of someone setting up a drugs run, or anything else criminal that he could think of. Was it possible that Jonah's gorgeous and mysterious lady was a PI? He couldn't think of anyone else who might be going around trying to get a line on someone.

Now wouldn't that be a kicker?

Thoroughly hooked now, he stood to one side, casually strolled towards a hawker selling straw hats, and tested one, liking the look of it. Looking in the shop window opposite, he saw Tahnee leave, hastily paid for the hat, and began to stroll after her.

* * *

Delphine walked up the porch steps and tried the door. It was locked. Still, the house had to have more than one door, and she was sure it had been a door slamming shut that she'd heard. She stepped back off the porch, and walked to one side of the veranda and peered around the side. No doors, only windows.

Re-crossing the porch, she turned and looked down the other side. Again, no doors, only windows. She was just about to pull her head back around, when, out of the corner of her eye, she thought she saw movement.

She looked again, more closely, and saw nothing. Perhaps she'd seen a shadow, or maybe a bird flitting by.

And then she saw it. A wispy, dark, ethereal movement of smoke.

Fire!

Mowbray House, her beloved Mowbray House was on fire! With a cry of alarm, she shot off the porch and sprinted around the back.

* * *

Out on the road, Dylan Gale turned off on to the now familiar private road that led to his latest acquisition. He had a pair of binoculars which he always kept in the back of the car, and which would now prove ideal.

He'd go to the head of the steps and scan the beach below. It would be the quickest way to see if she was still there. And if she wasn't, at least he'd have saved himself the humiliation of scouring the sand looking for her in person.

★   ★   ★

Tahnee, her feet sore after so much walking, stopped for a cup of coffee, and to re-think her strategy. Going from shop to shop was getting her nowhere. Nobody in the shopping centre had seen Cordelia, which probably meant that the woman she'd seen hadn't been her stepmother after all.

She stirred sweetener into her cup and took a sip. And yet, no matter how it was beginning to look, she was still sure, deep down, that it was Cordelia she'd seen that morning. Which could only mean that, far from being kept a prisoner, Cordelia was as free as a bird — for no kidnapper was going to let his victim out to do some window shopping!

Which in turn meant, of course, that the kidnapping was a hoax. And the only one who could perpetrate such a hoax was Cordelia herself. But why would her stepmother do such a thing? She'd never risk such an outlandish undertaking unless she was truly desperate. Unless she knew, or suspected, that her husband was planning to divorce her, say.

Tahnee knew that her father always employed the very best lawyers, and had insisted that she sign an air-tight pre-nup before their marriage. So there would be no gigantic pay-out should they part. A fake kidnapping might be the only way for Cordelia to get some money. And this might explain why her father seemed to have no interest in the whereabouts of his wife. Perhaps they'd already split up?

If only she could just call him up and ask! But she didn't dare. She knew her father was a fiercely proud man, and having to admit his second marriage was a mistake and a disaster would be hellish for him. And it would raise his blood pressure at the very least, and who knew what else? So soon after his operation, she simply couldn't risk asking him about it.

And what if all this was wishful thinking on her part? She'd never liked Cordelia, and nothing would suit her better than to have her out of her father's life. Could it be that she was letting herself be persuaded of the woman's guilt on nothing but a half-glimpse of a woman in a busy shopping mall, and circumstantial evidence?

OK, time to take stock, she thought. This was getting her nowhere. She had to think like her stepmother. Just suppose, for the sake of argument, that Cordelia was on the island, and free as a bird. Where would she go? What would she do?

Well, her stepmother liked the good life. She liked to spend, spend, spend and be pampered. Spend and be pampered. Of course! She shouldn't be trailing around a shopping centre. What she needed was to hit the spas and beauty treatment centres. The most expensive boutiques, the jewellery shops! That's where she should go.

With renewed vigour, she got up and walked purposefully through the door. A moment later, Flloyd Turnbull rose to follow her, then stopped, surprised, as a small Asian man, dressed in a nondescript pair of khaki shorts and loose flowered shirt, rose from a table in the corner and did the same thing.

He might, of course, have been a customer, simply leaving the shop. But Turnbull, who recognized the man, knew better. Alec Singh was well known to his colleagues in Vice, although Flloyd had never had dealings with him personally. A fact for which he was now heartily grateful, for it meant that the little crook hadn't made him as a cop.

Sure now that he was on to something very

interesting indeed, Flloyd Turnbull followed the man who was following Tahnee Sawyer. And wondered just what Marcus Bolton's interest in the American tourist could possibly be.

For the little Asian was a pimp who not only kept an eye on Bolton's stable of girls, but also did other odd jobs for his boss, when called upon.

★ ★ ★

Delphine found the back door easily, but it was locked, and she almost sobbed in frustration. From the back of the house she could clearly see dark smoke seeping from a window now, and desperately she stood back a little, trying to see if there was an open window or another way in. But there was nothing.

Without another thought, she glanced down, searching the garden for a rock. Finding one, she went to the nearest window and, taking a sharp breath, smashed the rock through it. It made her feel ridiculously criminal even as she did it, and the sound of breaking glass made her wince.

Too late, she wondered if the added oxygen now seeping into the house would only make the fire worse. Oh why, oh why, hadn't she brought her mobile phone with her? Then she wondered if 999 would even be the right number to call over here on Barbados. Even as she was thinking all this, she was smashing the glass into the house, creating a shard-free access through the window. Then levering herself carefully through the frame, she wriggled inside, and immediately began to choke.

She found herself in a room that had, at some point, been a study, for an old writing bureau stood to one side, and a stack of bookshelves, now mostly empty, lined one wall. Holding her hand over her face, she made her way to the door. Opening it, she almost gagged, for out in the hall, the smoke was worse.

Far worse.

It stung her eyes, making them run, and further impeding her vision. It caught at the back of her throat, making her gag and want to vomit. Grimly, she fought down the urge to cough, knowing that, once started, she'd never stop.

The kitchen. The smoke had to be coming from the kitchen. Groping her way along the wall, she began to make her way there. Her chest was beginning to feel tight and painful, and her head began to pound. Her instincts screamed at her that she didn't have long, that she should get out. NOW!

But she wasn't going to let Mowbray House burn!

★ ★ ★

Dylan parked the car in front of the house, reached for his binoculars, and opened the car door. He was acting like some ridiculous, lovelorn swain from a bad movie and it wasn't improving his temper. She was probably long gone, anyway.

As he trotted across the grass clifftop he glanced back at Mowbray House and froze. Black smoke was billowing out of the back of it.

Bolton! With a curse at his own stupidity, he dropped the binoculars and raced towards the house. He should have known Bolton would try something else after beating him up had failed. He should have hired security guards to keep an eye on the place. As he raced around the back, he was trying to remember if the house was still insured for fire.

And then he heard a woman scream. And all such mundane thoughts fled.

★ ★ ★

Tahnee smiled at the beautician and showed her Cordelia's picture.

'Ooh, what lovely hair,' the young girl said enviously, surreptitiously fingering her own dyed blonde locks. 'No, I'm sorry, I'd surely have remembered if madam had been a client,' she said regretfully, and handed back the photograph. Sighing, and thanking her wearily, Tahnee wandered back outside.

She'd consulted a phone book to make a list of all the places she thought her stepmother might visit, and was about to hail a taxi to try out the next one when suddenly her phone rang. It sounded wrong, somehow, and it took her a moment to realize that it wasn't her phone's usual ringtone. The noise issuing from her bag was a rather tinny version of Beethoven's Fifth. And suddenly, she understood.

It was the mobile phone from the park! She went everywhere with it now. Her heart suddenly thundering in her chest, Tahnee scrambled one hand into her bag.

From his position across the street, Flloyd Turnbull looked from Tahnee to Alec Singh, who'd followed her here. Singh was talking on his mobile, and for a moment, he wondered if it was he who was calling Tahnee Sawyer. Then he noticed that the little man was already talking, while Tahnee was still fumbling to answer her own phone.

So, Singh was watching her and reporting

in to someone else, was he? In that moment, the policeman would have given a month's salary to be close enough to overhear what he was saying.

Tahnee, oblivious to being the object of so much interest, lifted the phone to her ear and said breathlessly, 'Yes?'

'*Stop what you're doing at once,*' a metallic voice hissed into her ear. '*We've been watching you. If your activities come to the attention of the police, you know what we'll do to your stepmother, don't you?*'

Tahnee swallowed hard. 'I'm not doing anything.'

'*Don't lie to me!*' the voice hissed, with all the venom of a cobra. '*Go back to your hotel at once. We've left a little present for you.*' And then the voice chuckled, making an icy trickle slide down her back. '*But you won't like it,*' the gleeful voice warned gloatingly. And then, abruptly, Tahnee was listening to nothing more than the dial tone.

With shaking fingers, she folded the mobile away and put it back in her bag. What had she done? Oh, what had she done? So much for following her instincts! If anything happened to Cordelia because of her horrible, suspicious mind, she'd never be able to live with herself. White-faced, shaking, she hailed the first taxi that came into view and gave him

239

the address of the hotel.

She felt physically sick.

From across the street, Flloyd could see how upset she was, but stayed at his post. Once the taxi was gone, he watched Alec Singh say something more into the phone, nod, and hang up. When he moved off up the street, Flloyd followed casually behind.

*   *   *

Dylan Gale found the broken window at once, and quickly slipped inside. 'Who is it? Who's there?' he bellowed into the smoke-filled room, then, seeing that the door was open, made his way out into the hall.

In the kitchen, Delphine stared at the blazing chip pan in dismay. When she'd found the kitchen door and opened it, she'd been taken by surprise by the sudden 'whoosh' that the opening of the door had caused. And the burning flames had suddenly leapt to the height of the ceiling, making her scream in panic.

For a second or two she simply stood there, fascinated by the sight. She thought she heard a voice somewhere in the house, and wondered if whoever had set the fire was still here. But she couldn't think about that now. The house was counting on her to save it. Already the walls behind the cooker were darkening, the paint blistering with the heat. How long before the curtains caught fire too?

Quickly, coughing and choking now, she ran to the sink and turned on the water, praying that something would come out of the taps. If the water had been cut off, all would be lost. But the taps, after shuddering for a second, began to produce a sluggish flow. Looking around for a towel, she spotted an old cloth apron hanging from a closet door instead, and grabbing that, wetted it under the tap, wrung it out loosely and, smoothing the now-damp cloth out, turned back to the stove to confront the fierce heat. But even as she steeled herself to take a step towards that frightening inferno, she felt a presence beside her and cried out.

She spun around and found herself face to face with Dylan Gale. Wordlessly he took the damp cloth from her and none-too-gently pushed her back towards the door. Then he stepped forward, threw the cloth over the pan, smothering the flames, and reached down to the cooker knob to turn off the heat.

Then he stepped back, coughing and choking as the steam and smoke fought each other with a noisy hissing roar. It sounded like two animals fighting, and over by the door, Delphine shuddered. She felt weak-kneed and curiously boneless, and knew it was due to nerves and shock.

If Dylan hadn't been here, she'd have had to do this all alone. But she wasn't surprised that he'd been here for her, and it didn't even occur to her to wonder why he'd come back. Somehow, she knew, Dylan Gale would always be there for her.

She watched him take off his shirt and run it under the tap, then add it to the apron already on the pan. Then, finding an oven glove on the draining board, he put it on and carefully reached for the chip-pan handle. Picking it up, he carried it carefully to the back door and Delphine rushed to help him, turning the key in the lock and holding the door open, standing well back in order to let him and his dangerous cargo get through.

Once outside, he walked a fair way from the house, and then set the pan down on the bare earth.

Delphine staggered out after him, and stood crouched over, taking in great gulps of air. Her eyes were streaming, and when she looked up at him, his image was impossibly blurred. She wiped her eyes and straightened up as he stormed over to her, his face livid.

'Just what the hell were you thinking of?' he roared at her, making her flinch. 'Why didn't you just call the fire brigade? What madness possessed you to go in there?' he raged, pointing at the house. 'Do you love the damned place so much you're willing to burn with it?' And he reached for her shoulders and shook her. 'You could have been killed!' he snarled. 'I might have lost you! Don't you realize that?'

When he'd stepped into that hell-hole of a kitchen and seen her approaching the flames, it felt as if his whole world was in danger of crashing down around his ears. Now that she was safe, he felt like killing her!

Then her big brown eyes filled with tears, and she began to shake, and he groaned helplessly.

'Oh no, love, don't,' he murmured hoarsely, and dragging her close, enfolded her in his arms. Feverishly, he began to rain tiny kisses down on the top of her head.

★　★　★

Tahnee's legs were shaking as she approached the reception desk. She managed to smile, however, as she asked if there was a package for her. The receptionist checked the pigeon-holes and withdrew a small box, wrapped in brown paper and tied neatly with string.

Tahnee accepted it with hands that trembled noticeably, and turned away before the concerned man could ask her if everything was all right.

As she climbed the stairs, however, she had to grip the banister hard to prevent herself from falling. She dreaded opening the package, not knowing what she would find, but knowing it wasn't, *couldn't* be, anything good.

Outside, Jonah Rodgers pulled up on his bike and shut off the engine. Leaving his helmet on the pillion, he walked quickly into the hotel and headed straight for the stairs, ignoring the surprised shout of the receptionist.

He'd been checking the air filters on the *Whale* when Flloyd had called him and told him to get over to Tahnee's hotel right away. The policeman hadn't been very forthcoming, only saying that he'd been following her and it had looked as if she'd had some bad news and could probably do with some company. He'd told Jonah her room number at the hotel, and to wait for her if she wasn't already there.

Although Jonah had demanded more information, Flloyd had been unwilling, or unable, to tell him more. But the tone of his voice had been enough. Now, he mounted the stairs two at a time, heading for the top floor, his eyes counting off the room numbers as he went.

Upstairs, Tahnee opened her door with the key and walked straight to the bed, letting herself down on it before she fell. Knowing if she put it off, even for a moment, she might not have the courage to ever open the box, she ripped off the paper and slipped off the string, revealing a small cardboard box. With a bravado that was not quite real, she lifted the top off and looked stoically inside.

And found herself staring at a small gold ring. Puzzled, she took it out, then noticed a folded piece of paper underneath.

She took it out, put the ring back inside, and opened it up.

RECOGNIZE THE WEDDING RING? ANY MORE FOOLISHNESS AND THE NEXT TIME YOU GET THE FINGER THAT WORE IT.

It took a second for the words to sink in, and when it did Tahnee felt her heart leap. They were threatening to cut off Cordelia's finger!

Suddenly the world tilted and darkened at the edges.

Jonah reached the top floor at a dead run and saw a door ajar. Without pause for thought, he ran to it and pushed it open. And instantly saw her on the floor, her white-blonde hair a stark contrast against the dark carpet, her scarlet dress like a pool of silken blood splayed out around her.

'Tahnee!' He ran to her, picking her up and cradling her in his arms. For one awful, world-shattering moment, he wondered if she was dead — if some intruder had broken in and killed her. Then she moaned, and her eyelids fluttered open.

She looked at him, confused, afraid, then blinked. 'What . . . what?' she mumbled. The box! The ring!

She struggled in his arms, and he helped her up and on to the bed. 'It's all right, it's me. You're safe,' Jonah said frantically, rubbing her cold hands between his, then lifting his hand to cup her cheek against his palm. 'I won't let anything happen to you,' he promised her huskily, and knew that he meant it. No matter what trouble she was in, no matter how bad it got, he'd do anything to protect her.

Anything.

Tahnee, spotting the piece of paper and box on the bed, reached behind him and quickly grabbed them. When he turned around to see what she was doing, she thrust the box into the drawer of her bedside cabinet.

And although his heart sank at this sign of how much she still distrusted him, it made no difference. For a bare moment he'd thought she was dead, and he knew now how bereft his life would have been if that had been true. 'I'm not even going to ask,' he said softly, and saw her luminous violet eyes turn to him. 'I don't care what's in the box, and you don't have to tell me anything. Not one thing. I only care that you're all right. But you're not, are you?'

His voice was so full of concern, so tender and so very much what she needed to hear right then, that Tahnee burst into tears.

Helplessly, Jonah held her close and rocked her. Not only did he have to save her from whatever trouble she was in, he had to keep Flloyd Turnbull away from her as well.

'Why don't we just get in the *Whale* and sail away,' he said softly over the top of her head, once her sobs had died away into sighs of exhaustion. 'We could go north, up to the British Virgin Islands maybe, where nobody knows us. You could be my ship's mate, and we'd eat fish caught fresh from the ocean, always anchored a mile offshore. We could sleep out on the deck under the moonlight, and drink mango juice and champagne. Nothing and nobody would ever be able to find us, or bother us.'

With her cheek pressed to his chest, Tahnee dragged in a ragged breath. He smelt of the sea and sun, and hard-working male. 'That sounds divine,' she whispered. And because she wanted so much to do just that, pushed herself away from him. 'But I can't.'

Jonah sighed heavily, and when he went to pull her back to him, she pushed him away again. '*I can't*,' she said, even more forcefully, and getting off the bed, walked to the window, hugging her arms around herself, staring out unseeingly across the town.

Jonah watched her wordlessly for a few moments, bitterly aware that there was nothing he could do, then got up and slowly left. But as he went down the stairs, he was already making promises to himself, and to the woman he now knew that he loved.

In utter despair, Tahnee leaned forward, letting her forehead rest on the cool glass of the window. A moment later, she saw him emerge below, climb on his motorbike and roar away.

And wondered. Would she ever see him again?

10

Marcus Bolton paced his terrace, oblivious to the spectacular sunset all around him as he listened to the nervous voice of the law clerk on the other end of the telephone.

'You know, Jacob, for a man who owes thousands in gambling debts, I'm surprised at this attitude of yours, I really am,' Marcus interrupted. 'Have you heard about the man, not so long ago, who owed even less than you did, who slipped and fell one dark night, and ended up in hospital with both his kneecaps smashed? Can you imagine that?'

He walked to the railing encircling his terrace and leaned on it as the terrified bureaucrat on the other end of the phone line gabbled almost incoherently. Marcus sighed elaborately.

'But surely you know a judge who's got some little skeleton in his cupboard that he doesn't want rattled? Yes.' Marcus grinned, as the terrified squawking abated somewhat. 'I thought you might. Your sort always does.' It was a fact of life he'd learned long ago, that it always paid to have friends in high places. Or rather friends of friends in high places. It was surprising how often it was the little man, not the bigwig, who could get things done.

He listened for a few moments, then smiled again. 'Get the case moved up to the day after tomorrow, and I'll write off your slate. Clean as a whistle.' He listened for a few more moments as the little clerk told him how impossible it was, then said casually, 'You know, smashed kneecaps aren't the 'in' thing this year for some reason. I heard on the grapevine it was smashed elbows that were more popular now. Something to do with losing mobility in both arms. It concentrates the mind, or so they say.' He listened for a few more minutes, smiled, said softly, 'Yes, I thought you'd see it my way,' and hung up.

He sighed heavily as he stared out over the spectacular view. Then he glanced at his watch and realized that he was going to be late for his dinner date; but so what? She would wait. Marcus grinned wolfishly. She had no other option.

He raised his phone again, but hesitated. Although he was sure now that Delphine Phillips' law case would be heard the day after tomorrow, he was not confident that things would turn out as he hoped. Oh, he was pretty sure things would go the English woman's way all right — the little law clerk was not the only one who knew where some skeletons could be found and rattled. But would that necessarily put him any further forward? Theoretically, it should be easier to bully or threaten Delphine Phillips into selling Mowbray House to him than persuading Dylan Gale. But he'd detected a certain cooling in the English woman's attitude towards him lately, and if he was any judge of character, the dark-haired beauty was beginning to become a little too fond of Gale for his liking. He'd had them both watched, and there was something in the surveillance photos that rang alarm bells.

Who knows, the silly little bitch might even fancy herself in love with him. And as everyone knew, a woman in love was like a stick of dynamite. You never know when it was going to go off, and who it was going to blow up.

No, it was probably a good idea to have a contingency plan in operation. Just in case. Making up his mind, he quickly dialled a number in New York. One he'd dialled only once or twice in the past, but which he'd been careful to memorize, and not write down anywhere.

A female voice answered promptly and cautiously, citing neither name nor telephone number.

'Hello, it's Mr Cornelius Smith,' Marcus

said blandly. 'We've done business in the past,' he added. He'd chosen his alias to be memorable, and was not disappointed when the voice of the female broker became a trifle warmer.

'Oh yes, Mr Cornelius,' she said. 'I trust the service we provided was satisfactory?'

'It was,' Marcus said. 'Both prompt and as advertised. I'd like to place an order for the same service, please. In fact, two orders.'

'Our fees have risen by ten per cent since we last had business dealings, Mr Cornelius.'

Marcus sighed. Typical — prices always went up. Never down. Be it the price of bread, lawnmowers, or pedigree dogs. Or ordering a hit.

'That's fine,' he responded impatiently. 'Do I send photos and details to the usual PO box?'

'That will suit us admirably, Mr Cornelius.'

'I want to place the order overseas. Not a problem, I hope?' The last time he'd made a call like this, he'd been stateside and had wanted a particularly dim and recalcitrant rival rubbed out in Detroit. But he need not have worried.

'That presents no problem at all, sir. I look forward to hearing from you. You may remember we require a deposit? A show of good faith, if you will?'

Marcus grunted. He knew only too well, and wouldn't normally pay up front for anything. But in cases such as these he had no choice. 'Fine, fine. Bearer bonds all right?' He had no intention of signing a cheque or dealing in vast sums of cash, either of which could come to the attention of nosy Feds.

'Very satisfactory, Mr Cornelius. A pleasure to do business with you, as always.'

Marcus grunted and hung up. Of course, he had people on the islands who'd be more than willing to earn some extra bucks by killing Gale and the English woman for him. But it needed to be air-tight and professional. And, above all, to have no leads trailing back to him. And for that you needed out-of-town, anonymous professionals.

Business concluded for the day, he went indoors to shower and change, whistling a half-forgotten tune under his breath as he did so. He used copious amounts of mouthwash and deodorant because he fancied his chances of getting lucky tonight. His dinner companion owed him some attention, and he felt in just the mood to collect.

He drove to the far east of the island, not far off Ragged Point, and turned off on to a private road that ended in a small valley, surrounded by trees. He parked in front of the only dwelling, a simple, single-storey building that he often rented out to 'guests' from the US, who needed to lay low for some reason or other.

When he walked to the front door, he knew she must have heard him coming, and imagined her dismay. And after the stunt she'd pulled today, she had good reason to be nervous. Hadn't he expressly told her not to set her dainty little foot outside the door?

When she opened up for him, however, she was dressed to kill in a low, white sequinned dress that hugged her magnificent breasts and revealed a deep cleavage. Her glorious red hair was piled on top of her head in a careless mass of ringlets and waves. She smiled provocatively, but Marcus was aware of the flicker of fear in her eyes. And it pleased him.

'Hi, Cordelia,' Marcus Bolton said laconically.

* * *

Jonah spent a miserable afternoon on the boat, creating jobs to do but feeling the time drag. He hadn't wanted to leave Tahnee after she'd pushed him away, but he could see that she was at the end of her tether and needed some space.

As the light began to fade, however, he

wondered if he should call round at her hotel, just to see if she was all right. But he was afraid it was still too soon. He'd go round first thing tomorrow. And if she chucked him out, he'd try again tomorrow night. And then the day after. If he had to, he'd simply pester her into confiding in him.

He prepared himself a lacklustre dinner of clam chowder, which he then couldn't eat, and feeling too restless to stay in, took the bike to Paynes Bay, where he sat on the pillion, staring at a half-moon, and wondering how the hell he was going to get Flloyd Turnbull off her back.

*   *   *

Flloyd Turnbull, unaware that his friend was thinking of him in less than flattering terms, was about to leave his desk for the night, when a Fedex came in from LA. The return address was that of an old buddy, the one he'd asked to run a background check on Tahnee Sawyer.

Sitting back down eagerly at his desk, he tore it open and tipped it up. The first thing to fall out was a handwritten note from his old friend. As he read it, a puzzled frown tugged at his dark brows.

Hey, Flloyd old buddy! What you doing mixing with the great and the good, all of a sudden? Not that I blame you — she's a looker. But you know what they say about girls who have rich daddies! Watch your back, old buddy. — Fritz.

Puzzled, Flloyd began reading the report, and slowly leaned back in his chair, blowing out a long, low whistle as he did so. When he'd finished, he leaned forward and stared unseeingly at a filing cabinet placed just beside the entrance.

For the daughter of a billionaire, Tahnee Sawyer sure kept a low profile. Flloyd thought he probably knew all the really big players by sight, but as Fritz had pointed out in his report, the Sawyers didn't play the 'look-at-me, I'm-rich-so-I'm-a-celebrity' card. In fact, they flew so low under the radar, they were practically invisible.

No wonder Tahnee was able to move around unrecognized.

But that still begged the question — what was she doing in Barbados, all alone, and running around doing odd things in the middle of the night? What did she want with Jonah Rodgers? Why visit deserted beaches, or show a photograph around town? And why was Marcus Bolton so interested in all this?

Suddenly Flloyd stiffened. Was Bolton interested in lifting her? As far as he knew, the crook hadn't ever stooped to kidnapping — but the daughter of a billionaire made for a pretty tempting target. Especially one as alone and unprotected as this girl seemed to be. Come to think of it, just what the hell was she doing wandering around without protection anyway? Where was her driver, her bodyguards?

The more he thought about it, the less Flloyd liked the way this was looking.

* * *

The next morning, Dylan Gale hammered on the hotel door, and scowled down at Delphine as she opened it. She'd obviously just got out of bed, for she was wearing a pair of ridiculously large and loose lemon-coloured pyjamas, and her hair, gloriously mussed and falling almost to her waist, was hopelessly tangled. There was not a scrap of make-up on her face, and she looked adorable — sleepy-eyed, all warm and cosy from bed. It made him want to take her straight back there and . . . He cut the thought off abruptly.

'Sorry to interrupt your beauty sleep,' he drawled sardonically, 'but it's already seven-thirty in the a.m., and some of us who work for a living need to be getting on.'

Delphine blinked and stepped back. 'Come in. Do you want coffee? I could always order room service. Or some fruit? Toast,' she offered desperately, suddenly aware that he was now in her room, and she was standing there wearing nothing but silk pyjamas. She could feel her nipples tightening and wondered if they were visible beneath the material. What was it about this man that sent her hormones into overdrive?

Nervously, she brushed her long black hair off her face, unaware that lifting her arms to do so made the lemon-coloured silk cling in several interesting places. Dylan, dry-mouthed, turned abruptly away from her and paced the room.

'I didn't come for breakfast,' he rasped. 'I came to get some explanation for this!'

She gaped at him, then blinked as he thrust out an envelope at her. 'It was couriered over to me this morning. Couriered, you'll note. Not posted.'

Delphine, who had no idea why that should be so significant, took a step closer and reluctantly took the envelope from him. She could tell that he was mad, and obviously at her, but she honestly had no idea what she'd done this time. They seemed to spend all their time either arguing, at loggerheads, or dancing a waltz of misunderstanding and attraction. It was heady stuff, of course, but once, just once, it would be nice to have a peaceful, civilized conversation.

She unfolded the official-looking piece of paper and read it. Then, unable to believe what it said, read it again. 'The day after tomorrow!' she squeaked. Their case was being heard the day after tomorrow?

'But . . . but, I thought it would be weeks,' she gasped. 'Months yet, even. I was prepared to come back in the Michaelmas term vacation,' she said, glancing up at Dylan in dismay. 'This isn't nearly enough time! I don't have half the documents I need, and I haven't even heard back from James Miller yet. He was going to go through his father's old papers. Is this your idea?' she asked grimly. 'Do you think rushing me will give you the edge?'

Dylan, who'd been watching her like a hawk, and growing more and more puzzled at her bewilderment and genuine anger, laughed harshly. 'Me?' he all but yelled. 'Don't look at me — this isn't my doing. It's that shyster you hired! It's his signature on the documents — see?' And so saying he walked up beside her, scanned the court letter, and slapped a finger on the relevant signature. He was so close, Delphine could smell the tangy pine scent of his aftershave, and her knees gave a little warning wobble.

Then she forced her mind to keep on track, and read the signature to which he was pointing. And it was indeed cosigned, on her behalf, she noted angrily, by Frederick Cramer.

'But I don't understand,' she murmured helplessly. 'I didn't know he was going to do this. I didn't ask him to.'

Dylan stared at her for a few more moments, and slowly let out his breath. Delphine saw the way his shoulders slowly relaxed, and only then realized how tense he was.

'Bolton,' he said bitterly. 'He'll be behind this, no doubt. I've asked around about Cramer and he's as big a crook as Bolton.'

Delphine opened her mouth to point out that Cramer was supposed to be a campaigner on cultural issues, then closed it again. Of course Bolton was lying about that too. 'I don't get it,' she said at last. 'Why is he so determined to help me?'

Dylan glanced at her sharply, a sudden fear lancing through him. 'You're really not in this together? No, don't get mad,' he said, coming across to her and placing his hands on tops of her arms as she began to turn on him angrily. 'I'll believe you if you say that you aren't.

Only, in a way, that makes it worse, don't you see?'

Delphine, suddenly overwhelmed by his nearness, licked her dry lips nervously. 'Worse?' she echoed breathlessly. He was wearing his usual casual uniform of light-weight slacks and plain white shirt. She had only to lean a little inch or two forward and she'd be able to undo the shirt buttons with her teeth. Perhaps flick her tongue under the plain white cotton, lick his skin, taste the salt and . . . She shook her head.

'If you're not in it together,' Dylan said, 'then he wants you to get ownership of the house so that he can get his hands on it.'

'But that makes no sense!' Delphine said. 'If I don't want to see it turned into a hotel, then I really, *really*, don't want to see someone like Marcus Bolton get his hands on Mowbray House! I'd never sell it to him — never. And I'll make that damned well clear to him, the next time I see him,' she added defiantly, and Dylan felt his heart both lift, and constrict, at the same time.

Lift, because of her bravery and defiance, but constrict, because she obviously had no idea who she was dealing with. And if Bolton wouldn't hesitate to have him beaten up, or resort to arson to burn down the house, what might he do to Delphine?

'Sweetheart, listen to me,' he begged urgently, his hands digging hard into her arms. 'Bolton's dangerous. Promise me you won't ever meet with him alone? If he calls you, promise me, you'll call me right away?'

Delphine's eyes blazed. Sweetheart. He'd called her sweetheart!

'Delphine!' He gave her a little impatient shake as she continued to gaze wordlessly up at him. 'Are you listening to me?'

Delphine nodded. 'Call you. Right,' she echoed vaguely. Or did he use the word sweetheart casually? Did he call his cleaning lady sweetheart? Or the woman who sold him his morning paper?

'We've got to get to the bottom of this,' Dylan said grimly, staring down at her. 'Why does Bolton want the house so badly? He's currently living in a ritzy villa, so he sure as hell doesn't want to move into it. He's not in the property business as such. Unless he wants to use it as a cat house,' he mused, and saw her eyes widen in dismay. 'It's possible, but it's just too damn old-fashioned for him. It actually smacks of having a little class. No, I just can't see it.'

'Is the area due to be re-zoned or something?' Delphine asked vaguely. 'You know, will he be able to make it into a casino or something?'

'No,' Dylan said flatly. 'Besides, he already owns a casino boat. One of his flunkies takes it out into international waters every night, then brings it back in with the dawn tide.'

'Oh,' Delphine said blankly.

'Come on,' Dylan said, reluctantly lowering his hands. 'Let's go back out there and see if we can figure it out. There has to be some reason he wants that house so badly.'

Delphine nodded, but for once, she wasn't thinking about Mowbray House. She wanted him to stand closer. She wanted him to touch her, to kiss her again. She wanted him to be so lost in wanting and desire that he couldn't see straight!

But of course, that simply wasn't going to happen. She'd never been the kind of woman who could inspire such passion in a man. And here she was, without a scrap of make-up on, with mad hair, and wearing pyjamas, of all things. His usual kind of woman probably wore baby-dolls to bed.

Miserably, she turned and walked to the wardrobe, while, behind her, Dylan watched her with hot and hungry eyes. It was all he could do not to grab her and rip that ridiculous lemon-coloured outfit off her body, and ravish her. With a curious noise that was half-muffled groan, half-repressed laughter, he walked to the door and let himself out.

Jonah noticed that the door was open the moment he reached the top of the stairs, and his heart shot into his mouth. Quickly he walked forward and pushed it open — and saw Tahnee Sawyer's delightfully rounded derriere, waving at him from the side of the bed.

She was down on her hands and knees, and scrambling frantically to look under the bed.

'What have you lost?' he asked, and winced as he heard her head 'thunk' against the underside of the mattress. Tahnee quickly pulled her head back and looked around.

She was wearing a turquoise pair of shorts, and a skimpy, scallop-necked top that started as turquoise at her stomach and rose in various shades of blue to pale lilac before it reached the shoulder straps. The last layer of colour matched her violet eyes perfectly. Her geometric cap of silver-blonde hair shone in the morning light, but her beautiful, triangular-shaped face was pale and tight with tension.

'My pot of face cream,' Tahnee said. Her voice was so tortured and panic-stricken that for a moment he couldn't make sense of what she'd said. He expected to hear that tone from someone who was telling him that a violently catastrophic hurricane was on its way, or that someone they loved had been involved in a car crash.

'Face cream?' he echoed blankly. 'Did you say face cream?'

'Yes, I always keep it in the bathroom c-c-cabinet. But it's gone.' She looked so frantic, Jonah still wasn't sure he was hearing her right.

'Tahnee, darling, you can always buy another pot of face cream,' he pointed out gently. He walked towards her and helped her on to the bed, alarmed by how cold her hands were. Was it possible she'd suffered a mental breakdown of some sort? Why the hell had he left her? Doctors. He needed to call a doctor for her.

'The maid!' Tahnee suddenly cried out. 'She came in this morning. Could she have taken it?'

So saying, she shot off the bed and dashed out into the corridor. He saw her grab the arm of the young maid who was just pushing a cart of towels from the opposite room. He heard Tahnee's high-pitched voice, then the maid say something in response, then Tahnee came running back. She pushed past Jonah, who was still standing in the doorway, and ran to the bathroom. When Jonah followed her to the door, she was kneeling down at the small wooden cabinet under the sink, and she gave a small sob as she reached inside to bring out the big, heavy jar.

She hugged it to her chest, and slowly sank back down on to her haunches. Then, perhaps realizing how absurd it all was, she looked at Jonah and began to laugh.

But big, fat tears rolled down her cheeks as she did so.

'She thought it was too heavy for the cabinet on the wall,' Tahnee explained, laughing harder. 'So she moved it.'

Jonah nodded, humouring her. 'Huh-huh, it probably was,' he said softly, walking to crouch down in front of her. 'Why don't we put it back, and then go and lie down, hmm?' he asked, reaching for the pot.

Tahnee blinked, suddenly focusing properly, and reached up with a shaky hand to wipe her face. 'It's all right,' she said briskly. Before he could reach for the pot, she put it back in the wooden cabinet beneath the sink, and firmly closed the door. Then she scrambled to her feet. 'Don't worry, I don't need the services of a shrink just yet,' she said, in a much firmer tone of voice. She even managed a wobbly smile. 'I know how it must have looked.'

When she'd returned from breakfast that morning, and out of habit had checked the cabinet, she simply couldn't believe it had gone. She'd searched her handbag, the bedside cabinet, everywhere for it. Even under the bed, thinking it might have rolled there. That was where Jonah came in.

Now, reliving her actions through his eyes, it was no wonder he was treating her as if she needed the attentions of a straitjacket and a rubber room. 'Really, I'm all right,' she said again, and to prove it, straightened her top, ran a quick hand through her short cap of hair, and walked calmly into her bedroom. There she sat down on the chair in front of her dresser and regarded him with still-wet, violet eyes.

'I wasn't sure I'd ever see you again,' she admitted flatly.

'Oh?' he asked warily. Although she certainly seemed to have pulled herself together, he still felt as if he needed to walk on eggshells. 'And why wouldn't you? You still want use of the *Whale*, don't you?'

'Yes, please,' Tahnee said calmly. 'I just thought, well, most men I know after being, well, rejected . . . ' She took a deep breath and stared down at her hands. 'They tend to go off in a huff.'

Jonah grinned widely. His brown hair was a little stiff from the salt breeze, and one knee, showing beneath his coffee-coloured shorts, had a healing scab on it. He looked like a gorgeously sexy ragamuffin. His rope-soled sandals looked ready to fall apart, and his blue T-shirt was so old and faded it looked almost white. But it stretched tightly over his chest and upper arm muscles and made her want to trace them with her fingertip.

'Don't worry about that,' Jonah laughed. 'I'm used to being given the elbow by beautiful women. It's like water off a duck's back by now.'

Tahnee laughed wryly. Yeah, right. Sure he was!

She was about to say something when the telephone rang.

She glanced at it, and a tight, grim expression grabbed her face. The light of teasing laughter fled from her eyes, and Jonah felt the temperature in the room drop, several icy degrees. He wanted to reach out and snatch the phone away. To make whoever was on the other end of it go away. To stop hurting her. But already she was reaching for it, and Jonah knew, with a pang of real pain, that she had already forgotten him.

'Hello?' Tahnee said, as calmly as she could.

'*Take the boat to Six Men's Bay. Tell your little Cap'n Ahab to anchor the boat a hundred yards off the first marker buoy. He'll know it. Then take a little swim out to it to see what's there. You'll be watched.'*

The digitally altered voice was replaced by the dial tone, and Tahnee hung up. She wasn't aware that, apart from the greeting, she hadn't said a single word. Or how strange that must seem to the man who'd been watching her.

Taking a long, slow breath, Tahnee got up and began gathering her things together. It was a good thing she was a fair swimmer, otherwise she'd need to buy some sort of swimming aid. She went into the bathroom, and remembered to close the door behind her before retrieving the pot of face cream and pushing it into her bag. The kidnappers might want her to leave the diamonds tied up to the buoy. It made a perfect retrieval point, after all. If they had a fast boat, they could grab the gems and be out into international waters before any watching police or FBI could catch them.

When she walked back into the bedroom, Jonah was standing by the window, tense and grim-faced.

'I'd like to take the boat out,' Tahnee said, her chin coming up, defying him to question her. She didn't realize how tired she looked, or how tense. She'd lost weight since coming to the island, and looked more vulnerable

269

than Jonah had ever seen her.

Well, if she wouldn't tell him what was going on, or let him help her in any other way, he could at least do this for her. To be there for her, and make her job, whatever the hell that was, easier.

'Of course,' he said with a smile. 'Where would you like to go?'

★   ★   ★

Dylan and Delphine had searched Mowbray House from top to bottom. The attics had been largely empty, likewise the cellars.

Now, outside, on the veranda, dusty and hot, they sank down on the swinging porch chair. 'Well, if there's something here for Bolton, I can't see it,' Dylan said.

Delphine sighed, and reached out to take his hand. 'Dylan, about this court thing. Can't we come to some sort of arrangement?'

Dylan glanced at her curiously. 'Like what?'

Delphine shrugged. 'I don't know. I don't want you to lose out. I mean, I know you paid a lot of money for the house. If you promise not to turn her into a hotel, I'd be more than willing to let you keep the title to her.'

Dylan smiled wryly. 'That's very generous

of you,' he drawled wryly. 'But if I can't turn 'her' into a hotel, what good is she to me?'

Delphine shook her head helplessly. Couldn't he see that this house cried out for a family? For people in love to come here and live here and share some of their love on the house. To restore, and polish, re-furnish, and cherish it. What would he say if she told him what was in her heart? That she wanted to come and live here with him, to love him, marry him and have children with him?

He'd run a mile, poor man.

Dylan watched her walk to the railing and lean on it, looking out over the tangle of garden, her long, dark hair gleaming like ebony in the sun.

She was really in love with this house.

Damn her.

Why wasn't she in love with him?

The thought jolted him, bringing him to his feet, a feeling close to panic lancing through him. 'I've got to get in to work,' he said abruptly. 'Want a lift back to town?'

Delphine shook her head miserably, and watched him walk away from her. Again.

He seemed to be farther out of her reach than ever.

Dylan got behind the wheel of his Jag and shot off towards the open road. How

had this happened? How had he managed
to fall in love with a woman who only
wanted him for his house? If it didn't hurt
so much, it would be funny.

Absolutely bloody hilarious, in fact.

11

Jonah went up the gangplank first and leapt lightly on to the *Whale*'s deck, then turned and offered her his hand. When she landed beside him, Tahnee's knees buckled slightly, and she fell up against him. He caught her, and his lips thinned.

'You look exhausted,' he accused quietly. 'Why don't you go lie down on the bunk and catch a little sleep? It'll take a while to get around to the other side of the island anyway.'

Tahnee was feeling tired, and since she'd have to go swimming later, realized that it was probably a good idea to catch forty winks. She'd be no good to anyone if she drowned!

'I think I will,' she murmured, and disappeared below. Jonah went to the wheelhouse and turned on the radio, first to check the weather forecast, which sounded good, then to tune into the harbour master's channel to see if there were any hold-ups or problems. There were none — so it would be, literally, plain sailing.

Next he went through his routine set of checks, and after he'd started up the engine a couple of minutes later, steered the boat skilfully through the channel. He noted, but didn't particularly pay attention to, a fast little speedboat that idled out behind him. The island was full of fast boats and rich boys who liked to play with them.

Flloyd Turnbull had once done a big favour for one such man, which was why he was now hunkered down out of sight in the passenger seat of the boat. Ralph Moran, the rich boy who'd been saved a lot of embarrassment, not to mention a couple of days' community service, due to Flloyd's influence, glanced at him now with a cocky grin. 'I feel like that guy out of *Miami Vice*. You know, the good-looking one,' he said happily. 'We after drug-runners, smugglers or what?'

Flloyd grunted. 'Never you mind.'

Ralph shrugged, but grinned. 'You got a gun?'

Flloyd rolled his eyes. 'Just don't get too close. I don't want him to spot us,' the policeman warned laconically.

*   *   *

Jonah waited until he had a totally clear path, the radar telling him there was nothing for a good half-mile either side of him, before he dropped the boat down to idle, and then roped off the wheel. He went below quickly and quietly, and found Tahnee, as he'd hoped, fast asleep in his bunk.

The same bunk he'd crawled out of this morning, her silvery head on the same pillow. She looked as if she belonged there. One arm was flung up and over her head, her honey-coloured skin patterned by the reflection of light and water coming through the open porthole.

Carefully, he went to her bag and, keeping one eye on her sleeping face, rifled quickly inside. It didn't take him long to find it. Just as he thought, the pot of face cream was in the bag. He carried it outside the sleeping berth and into the main living quarters, where he sat down in a leather swivel chair, placing the pot on the smooth, oval table facing him.

Then he took the lid off and stared down into a white, fragrant cream. It made him smile slightly. So what else had he expected?

Carefully, he inserted first one finger, then two, delving around in the gunk, then caught his breath as they encountered something other than greasy, smooth paste. Carefully, and with a little sucking sound, he pulled out a tiny polythene bag. Since it was covered in gooey cream, he went to the sink and grabbed a couple of squares of kitchen roll, then returned to the table and popped his find into the middle of them. Then he wiped the excess cream off his fingers, and as much off the bag as he could.

Examining it carefully, he saw that the bag had a sort of pocket-shape that allowed itself to be turned inside out, and it took him a few moments to get it open. Then, taking a deep breath, he carefully upturned the bag and blinked as a little cascade of brown pebbles spilled out on to the table top.

For one moment, he thought he was seeing some kind of crystalline drug — so deeply enmeshed in his head was the idea that Tahnee had somehow fallen under the influence of drug-runners. Then the bright sunlight hit one of the stones, which glinted oddly. Slowly he reached out and picked it up.

He'd never seen one before, but he knew, almost at once, that he was looking at an uncut diamond. He held it to the light, peering through it, and a small rainbow flashed and was gone. Yes.

Diamonds.

He stared at the stones, trying to gauge their weight. One thing was for certain, they must be worth a fortune. A very large fortune. Carefully, he put the stones back, refolded the slippery polythene envelope with some difficulty, then gouged a space into the gloop in the pot, popped the envelope back in, and smoothed the cream back over. When he was sure everything looked the same as when he'd first opened it, he put the lid back on, and carefully pushed open the door to the sleeping cabin.

As he walked the few steps across to her bag, Tahnee stirred and turned in her sleep. He watched her, almost hoping that she'd wake up, thus forcing a confrontation, but she simply sighed a little and settled back against the bunk.

Jonah slipped the pot back into her bag, then went thoughtfully back up on deck. As he unhitched the rope from the wheel, he saw a speedboat, way back. It wasn't unusual to see one, even out here. Advanced waterskiers liked the deeper swells out at sea.

He put the engine back into gear, and headed once more into open water.

* * *

Dylan Gale looked at Gabby Motulo and smiled grimly. 'No sign of him at all then?' he asked, without surprise.

Gabby, whose real first name nobody seemed to know, was a big man, a native islander who'd once, in his youth, been a member of the police force, but had for

277

nearly twenty years or so enjoyed the reputation of being the only private eye on the island. Now that wasn't so, for he had rivals, but everyone who was anyone knew that Gabby was the man you called if you wanted things found out.

Now the PI shrugged his massive shoulders helplessly. 'Your man Forboys should be called 'The Great Magnifico'. The only man who can truly vanish without a trace.'

Dylan sighed. 'He had to get off the island somehow, Gabby,' he said chidingly.

Gabby spread his big hands, his fingers like sausages as they spread out in a telling gesture. 'He never flew, and certainly not under his own name. But I have people at Grantley Adams' — he smiled widely, naming the island's main airport — 'and I can tell you he never left under another name either. But alas, the island is full of people who own boats.'

Dylan smiled wolfishly. 'I know that. And quite a few of them will island hop, no questions asked, if the price is right.'

Gabby shrugged, a knowing one-man-of-the-world gesture to another. 'And I know most of those as well.' He laughed like a barracuda. 'But none will admit to it. I think Mr Forboys must have paid well — really, quite extraordinarily well indeed if nobody is willing to talk to Uncle Gabby.'

Dylan nodded. 'What about your contacts on the other islands? If he wanted to leave the Caribbean, he'd surely have had to use his passport somewhere?'

Gabby raised one white eyebrow. 'You know how many islands there are. Think how many bribes I'd have to flash around. You really want to spend that much money just to find out where your boy has flown?'

Dylan sighed heavily. 'No, I suppose not. No, leave it.'

Gabby sighed, not without sympathy. He'd done a few jobs for Dylan Gale over the years, and respected the man. He was both legitimate and honest — not something you could say of all of Gabby's clients. It grieved him to see the man in difficulty. 'Word is, Mr Forboys was being hassled by Marcus Bolton,' he said, but he could see that this came as no surprise.

'He's not the only one,' Dylan said. 'OK, forget Forboys. I want you to research a house for me,' he said, succeeding, for the first time in years, in surprising the PI.

'A house,' Gabby squeaked.

'Yes — one I bought off Forboys. Mowbray House, near Bathsheba. I want you to find out if there's anything special about it.'

'That's rather vague.'

279

'It's all I can tell you. Except that Bolton wants it badly. And I want to know why.'

Gabby's usually cheerful, big, round face creased into a frown. 'You getting into something bad, Dylan?' he asked quietly. 'You don't want to get mixed up with the likes of him. Your daddy won't like it. No sir.'

'I'm trying to keep *out* of anything bad, Gab,' he corrected wryly.

'Ah well. In that case — consider it done.'

As Dylan watched the big man shuffle out of his office, he leaned back in his chair and sighed.

And wondered what Delphine was doing right that moment.

★　★　★

Tahnee slipped into the water from the *Whale*'s rope ladder, and sighed in pleasure. The water was warm, even out here, and felt silky against her skin.

She was wearing a plain white bikini, and when she pushed off from the boat, she knew Jonah was watching her. He hadn't liked it when she'd told him to moor up about a hundred yards off the first marker buoy because she was going swimming. He'd tried to dissuade her, even resorting to scare tactics by mentioning sharks. But she had no other choice.

She felt safer knowing that he was watching over her and keeping a lookout for the fearsome fish, but even so, she tried not to think about it as she set off in a competent overarm crawl towards the buoy. It was red and white, and bobbed in the distance, reminding her of a giant traffic cone.

Tahnee reached it a while later, her arms and legs just beginning to feel heavy with the effort. As she grabbed the base of it, smelling rubber and plastic and salt, she saw a small white box, tied round the middle of the buoy with string. Her heart lurched as she thought that a severed finger might lie within. And it would be all her fault.

She swallowed hard and forced her hand up to reach and untie it, her fingers slippery with seawater. When she got it down, she trod water, letting the box rest on the rim of the buoy, before reluctantly opening it.

Inside was nothing more horrific than a small cassette — the old-fashioned kind of mini-cassette tape businessmen used to dictate to secretaries. She didn't have anything that would play it, but she supposed she could buy one in an office supply store somewhere. Almost giggling with nervous relief, she popped the cassette back into the box, which was waxy and waterproof, she noticed now, and swimming awkwardly with one hand curled around the box, made her way slowly back to the boat.

On the speedboat idling a fair way off, Flloyd Turnbull lowered his binoculars and frowned. Whatever she'd recovered from the buoy had been small.

'Interesting,' he said to himself, but beside him, Ralph eyed him warily. He was spread out on the seat, catching some rays, already bored with the 'stakeout'.

'Huh?'

'Nothing,' Flloyd said softly. 'But start her up. Unless I miss my guess, we're heading back to harbour.'

★ ★ ★

Jonah carefully judged the distance to the mooring dock, turned the wheel hard starboard and shut off the engine. Out on the deck, Tahnee watched, admiringly, as he brought his beloved boat home with barely a nudge of her fenders against the wall.

When she went into the wheelhouse, he was already turning off the engine. She watched him through the glass window as he leapt from the *Whale* on to the dock, his bare feet, brown as a nut, landing on the wet wooden planking as surely as a gymnast dismounting from the parallel bars. He quickly and competently looped rope, fore and aft, around the white-painted iron stanchions, and when he came back on board, Tahnee felt the breath catch in her throat.

He looked superb, in cut-off jeans that were white and ragged at the hem and clung to his hard, male, brown thighs. A loose white shirt, with frayed cuffs and collar, hung on him like an afterthought, snapping around him in the breeze, at first showing then hiding the hard upper body muscles that he'd accumulated over the years. The creases at his eyes showed in pale laughter-lines when he squinted in the bright sunlight, and his unruly hair was slightly salt-stiffened and called out to her itching fingertips to come and play.

Restlessly she went down to the main living area, looking around the small but homely space with a smile. It was tiny compared to her condo back in Florida. In fact, the *Whale* — square foot per square foot — could probably fit in her place four times over. But for all her penthouse's luxury and designer chic, Tahnee knew she'd rather be here.

And suddenly, without warning, she realized that she never wanted to go home again. Didn't want to go back to her big apartment that was always so empty. Go back to her life that seemed to be going nowhere on well-oiled, easy paths. Oh, she wanted to see her father, of course. And the gallery. But she could open a gallery here, and her father could visit here too.

Then she shook her head, wondering why she was thinking such thoughts. She didn't belong on Barbados — she'd only set foot on her soil a week ago. Then she felt the boat move, and behind her heard the steady rhythmic sound of bare feet as Jonah joined her; and when she turned to look at him, she suddenly knew exactly why she was thinking what she was thinking.

Jonah, who'd come to tell her she could go ashore now, found the words drying up on his tongue. She was watching him from the middle of his living room, still dressed in the skimpy white bikini, and she was looking at him in a way that broke his heart. And made him want to sing for joy at the same time. It was a look he'd never dared hoped to see on her lovely, unconventional face. In fact, he wasn't sure that he was only dreaming it.

He took a step towards her, watching her, waiting to see if that look would change — to see if she'd turn away from him, or break the spell.

But she didn't.

He took another step, and still she looked at him mutely from those big violet eyes, and when he reached for her, the look was still there.

For a long, unfathomable moment, they looked at each other, communing in that pagan, age-old way that men and women had, and then his head slowly bent. Her chin angled up in reciprocal conspiracy and their lips touched. Clung. A co-mingled taste of sea-salt and sun-warmed padded flesh. Her tongue flickered into his mouth, making him shudder, and her heart kicked viciously against her ribs.

She moved closer against him, her arms sliding around his waist, her hands reaching underneath the loose shirt to touch tanned, warm, hard flesh. Her fingers smoothed around the curve of his ribs, then dipped into the indent that was his spine.

Under her lips, he sighed, filling her lungs with the air from his own, and he lifted his head briefly, just briefly, before he bent and scooped his hands behind the backs of her knees. He lifted her easily, still holding her eyes with his own, ready and willing to put her down again at her signal, but her eyes only glowed more heavily, her lips curving into a faint smile.

'You're sure?' he said, because he wanted to be sure himself.

'Yes,' she whispered huskily.

And still he hesitated. He wanted this moment to be perfect, simply because he knew he was going to remember it for the rest of his life. And that it might have to last him the rest of his life.

'There was a time,' he said softly, 'when you didn't trust me.' It wasn't a question. He'd known it. He'd felt it, deep in his soul — like razor blades dragged across a raw burn.

'Not now,' Tahnee said simply.

It was all he needed to hear. Carefully he carried her back to the boat's sleeping cabin, letting her legs slowly slip out of his arms, his fingers running over her smooth calves, then the tenderness of her thighs, as she slid down the length of his body, her feet reluctantly touching the floor.

She felt tiny against him, the top of her head not even reaching his chin, and he slowly sank to his knees, kissing the length of her as he went — tiny kisses that began at her forehead, traversed the length of her nose, her lips, chin, throat and between her tender breasts, before finally coming to rest in her navel.

Tahnee threw her head back and moaned.

Her waist was so small his big, brown hands covered it as he spread his fingers around her, then lifted one hand up and behind her to unhook her bikini bra. With a slightly damp whisper, the two white triangular scraps of material fell forward and on to the ground, revealing pale mounds, pink-tipped and puckered with the damp.

Jonah gently kissed first one, then the other, then sucked the quivering flesh deeply into his mouth, his tongue warm against her slightly chilled flesh. He felt her shudder and fall even harder against him, and his hands firmed around her waist, steadying her. Slowly, gently, he began to push her backwards, and then she was lying across his bed, her high cheekbones flushed with colour. He stood and shucked off his shirt, revealing a bronzed, hairless chest that quickly covered her as he bent his head to kiss her once more.

He felt her nails raking his back and his loins hardened painfully in response. Slowly he kissed his way across her belly, nipping, nearly-biting, playful kisses. When his lips reached the waistband of her white bikini briefs, he twanged them playfully with his teeth, then glanced up at her. His hazel eyes seemed to darken as she watched him, and then he was slithering backwards off the bed, coming to rest on the floor on his knees.

Looking down the length of her own body to his flushed, hard and tight face, she saw him reach up with his two index fingers and loop them around the bikini bottoms at her hips. He pulled them down slowly, inch by inch, then tossed them over his shoulder. She saw his hands on her calves, lifting them, and separating her legs. He kissed the inside of one knee, then the other, kissing his way higher and higher, up first one tender inner thigh, and then the other, until he was thrusting his hot, clever tongue deep into the heart of her.

She gasped, arching high off the bed, but his strong hands held her captive as she thrashed her head from side to side on the pillow; his tongue, having found the hard button of flesh, teased it mercilessly.

Tahnee felt her thigh muscles contract and moaned hard and low in her throat, her hands reaching out either side of her to bunch the sheet into her fists. Her heels began to drum on the side of the bed as the sensations deep in the heart of her femininity began to burn and spasm. She cried out, a long, low, helpless moan, then watched him through half-lowered lids as he quickly stepped out of his shorts. Then he moved up over her, bare skin against bare skin, his hands appearing beside hers to hold them, his hard, bare thighs nudging hers imperiously, appeasingly, pleadingly apart.

Eagerly she answered his unspoken proposition and opened herself to him by scissoring her legs around him, crying out in triumph as he entered her in a single, careful, powerful thrust. She cried out again, helplessly, as her body erupted, then gasped, quietened, and began to gasp again, when he began to stroke within her, slow, deep movements, almost withdrawing altogether before starting again.

She clenched her muscles around him and saw his eyes deepen in shocked satisfaction. Then they were dancing together, faster, harder, each kiss, each caress, each thrust and corresponding surrender taking them higher and further, until it left them both gasping and crying out together, lips locked, bodies straining, mingling and then, finally, melting.

Tahnee closed her eyes and slept. For the first time in a long time she felt safe. And happy. And home.

★ ★ ★

Flloyd had gone straight to his office from the marina, and now he sat at his desk, listening to the voice on the other end of the line. He hadn't known anyone in Florida, Tahnee Sawyer's home state, but luckily Fritz had,

289

and had passed on his name.

Now he listened as Detective Third Grade Sam Dubowsky talked.

When he was finished, Flloyd thanked him, and told him that if he ever fancied a cheap holiday, he was to get on a plane to Barbados and he could crash at his place for a fortnight. He doubted the cop would ever come, but even if he did, it would be well worth it.

Tahnee Sawyer's father — who was no less a personage than the billionaire owner of a famous manufacturing empire — was currently in hospital having undergone surgery for serious ulcers. The old man seemed to be doing well and was due out soon, and there were no rumours that his illness had done his giant corporation any harm. Dubowsky knew of nothing against Sawyer, and although no huge billion-dollar empire could be totally legit, in Flloyd's cynical opinion, Calvin Sawyer sounded as if he was more or less on the up and up. Certainly, no-one in Florida law enforcement had anything against him. His daughter, likewise, was squeaky clean, with no hints of a turbulent drugs-and-alcohol past that tended to plague the children of the very wealthy.

In fact, the only hint of anything being amiss was the absence of the second Mrs

Sawyer from the scene. Dubowsky seemed to think an imminent divorce was in the offing, but social scandal wasn't something Flloyd was particularly interested in. Dubowsky had promised to send some stuff over by fax, and sure enough, a minute or so later, the printer began to hum.

Flloyd stood beside it and patiently peeled off the pages as they came — most of it coming from newspaper archives, showing Calvin, Cordelia and Tahnee Sawyer at various functions, charity bashes and so forth.

Flloyd read it through dutifully, but without much interest, until he came to take a closer look at one of the colour shots of the stepmother, Cordelia. The caption underneath cited the former fashion model's not-quite-so-glittering career, making it obvious that the gossip editor was not a fan. But it was the description of Cordelia's 'famous' Titian hair that caught his attention. Earlier, he'd gone back to the shops that Tahnee Sawyer had visited, interviewing the people she'd shown her photograph to, and asking what she'd wanted.

All of them had said much the same thing. The beautiful blonde with the unusual hairstyle had showed them a picture of a pretty redhead, and asked if they'd seen her. Their descriptions of the woman in the photograph matched very closely that of Cordelia Sawyer.

Now, the policeman mused, according to Dubowsky, Cordelia Sawyer hadn't been seen by her ailing hubby's bedside. But Calvin Sawyer's daughter was running around unprotected on Barbados, trying to find her stepmother, and, what's more, dragging his old friend Jonah Rodgers into something distinctly iffy.

Flloyd nodded. Oh yes. Yes, indeedy, things were beginning to come together. And he might just have the beginnings of an idea of how a certain Marcus Bolton could fit into this picture too.

Quickly, he reached for his computer and switched it on. Normally he wasn't much of a computer geek, but he had to admit they sometimes had their uses. Like now, for instance, when he wanted to find out if Cordelia Sawyer, one-time wannabe model, had ever crossed paths with Marcus Bolton before.

As he typed in key words for his chosen search engine, Flloyd leaned back in his chair, content to let the mechanical monster do all his legwork and paper-chasing for him. When it had finally trawled all its databases, what it finally spat out didn't surprise him at all.

* * *

The following afternoon, Delphine was reclining by the pool at her inn, when a shadow fell across her. She lowered the book she was reading eagerly, but when she glanced up, it wasn't Dylan. Nevertheless, the smile which had come to her face stayed there as she recognized the friendly face of James Miller.

She was wearing a one-piece modest swimming suit of a rich deep chocolate brown, and over it she was wearing a see-through coffee-coloured beach robe. Instantly, she swung her legs over the sun-lounger and touched the terracotta tiles with her bare feet.

'Mr Miller, how nice to see you again,' she said, reaching out her hand. Quickly, the old man took it. 'Please sit down.' She indicated another sun lounger, and watched, smiling slightly, as the retired solicitor pulled one over and sat down on it rather gingerly.

Catching her look, he smiled sheepishly. 'I always expect these things to collapse under me.'

'Let me get you a drink from the bar,' she said, indicating a thatched beach hut on the opposite side of the pool, where the inn's bartender spent his days serving up fruit-and-rum concoctions and keeping a wary eye out on the pool.

'Oh, well,' James said doubtfully. 'I can

never get used to the idea of beautiful ladies buying me drinks,' he demurred.

Delphine laughed. 'I'm flattered. But you must want something cold and long? It's really hot today.'

'A fruit juice then, please,' he capitulated, and Delphine got up to fetch the drinks. James Miller's glance fell to the book she'd put down on the glass table beside her lounger, and raised an eyebrow as he recognized a volume of poetry by Dr John Donne. Cerebral stuff!

Delphine came back with two long glasses chiming with ice and pieces of fruit, and, without being asked, raised the parasol that was fixed in the middle of the table, giving them both shade and the semblance of privacy.

James Miller took a long sip, then opened the old-fashioned briefcase he'd brought with him. 'I went through my father's papers, as I promised,' he said quietly. 'And found some interesting notes.'

He handed them over, not looking particularly happy, and watched pensively as Delphine read them. The paper was yellowed and old and dated from the 1930s. The handwriting was small, but very neat and perfectly legible.

'I think you'll find this the most interesting,' James said, spreading out the pages, then selecting four or five pieces. Delphine recognized them almost at once.

'It looks like a rough draught of the will I found in my attic.'

'Yes,' James Miller agreed unhappily. 'And from my father's private notes, it seems that Moorcroft Mowbray was indeed determined to write his nephew by marriage out of his will.'

Delphine looked at the old man gently. 'Have you told Dylan about this?' she asked quietly, and wasn't surprised when he nodded.

'I felt I owed it to him, you understand,' he said, without apology. 'And I had to tell him that I'd be handing the documents over to your lawyer before the case tomorrow.'

'I'd rather you didn't,' Delphine said quickly, then bit her lip. She didn't really want to go into the whole Bolton situation, and besides, the last thing she wanted was to drag this nice old man into her troubles. 'Can't you just hand them to the judge yourself, when the time comes? I take it you'll be called to testify?'

The old man sighed. 'Most irregular. But then, if I may say so, the speed with which this case was docketed seems most . . . unusual too.'

Delphine blushed, sensing censure, and

shrugged helplessly. 'Things are getting out of hand,' she admitted miserably. 'I wish Dylan would just promise me not to turn the house into a hotel. I'd rather we settle this whole matter out of court.'

James Miller, who'd been looking unhappy until now, suddenly smiled. 'You like him, don't you? Young Dylan?' And as Delphine blushed even deeper, he nodded. 'Known him since he was a boy. Strong-willed, and sometimes hot-headed, I know. But he's a good man. A very good man. You won't do better, you know.'

Delphine laughed hopelessly. The chance would be a fine thing!

'I'm not looking forward to tomorrow,' she said sadly. Once the court case was over, then, no matter which way it went, she'd have no more excuses to see Dylan Gale again. To talk to him, or have him near her. Already she could feel the wrenching sense of loss.

Impulsively James Miller, who was a kindly soul and something of a romantic at heart, reached across and patted her hand. 'Chin up, my dear. It was about time Dylan took a tumble. He can't always have things his own way, you know. I've a feeling you'll be good for him.'

Delphine felt her throat ache as she realized that the old man was taking it for

296

granted that Dylan was as smitten with her as she so obviously was with him, and didn't have the heart to disillusion him. But when he was gone, she gathered her things together and returned to her room, no longer in the mood to lounge in the sun.

Tomorrow might be the last day she'd ever see the man she loved. If she won the case, he'd never want to speak to her again. And if she lost, she'd have no reason to stay on the island and would have to go back to England at the end of next weekend.

Either way, she was going to have to learn to live with a broken heart. And all her lost dreams.

12

The courtroom was surprisingly small and light. Delphine, who'd expected something darker and grander, had to smile at herself for her naiveté. Modern-day law, especially as practised on sunny Barbados, was not a case of dark pews and be-wigged and be-gowned advocates any more! All the officers of the court wore lightweight suits, and when the judge who was to hear their case came into the room, Delphine was not particularly surprised to see a young-looking forty-something woman, with a beautiful Afro-Caribbean profile and wearing a smart Prada suit.

'Be upstanding for her honour, Judge Rosalie Poe,' a voice called, and Delphine hastily got to her feet.

The room was practically empty of spectators, but that, Delphine mused, was hardly surprising. This was hardly a sensational murder case, but a run-of-the-mill dry-as-dust probate wrangle. Besides herself and her advocate Frederick Cramer, and on the opposite side, Dylan Gale and his lawyer, there was only an old lady sitting in the public benches, placidly eating a banana, and a bored-looking young man lounging a few seats behind her. Presumably a journalist, hopeful for a titbit of news. If so, he was hardly likely to get it here, Delphine thought wryly.

'Mr Cramer?' The judge glanced at Frederick Cramer, an unreadable look on her face, and Delphine felt her stomach tighten as the man rose to his feet. Although he was representing her, Delphine felt no pleasure as he succinctly and cleverly put her case before the court, producing document after document to back it up, and finally, producing James Miller as a witness on her behalf.

The retired solicitor took the stand, testified to the finding of his father's notes, and handed them over to the court bailiff who passed them on to the judge. Rosalie Poe inspected them quickly, while the court waited. Although she had no knowledge of law at all, Delphine couldn't help but feel as if the whole case was being handled in an extraordinarily brisk manner, a conclusion that was obviously shared by Dylan's advocate, who more than once during the proceedings frowned in either anger or bewilderment.

James Miller somewhat apologetically confirmed that his father's notes did indeed seem to add credence to the fact that Moorcroft Mowbray had intended to make a second will, disinheriting his nephew by marriage, Christopher Allinson.

Dylan's advocate, who Delphine heard addressed by the court as Mr Browning, cross-examined immediately, sensing a sympathetic witness, and Miller readily admitted that he himself had no knowledge of a second will being drawn up by his father.

Frederick Cramer next called several technical witnesses, who'd been at work on the original will found in Delphine's attic, and who attested to the authenticity of such things as the date of the paper and the ink used, while a calligrapher and handwriting expert confirmed that the signature matched that of other, authenticated Moorcroft Mowbray signatures. By the time they were finished, it was apparent that nobody doubted the will's pedigree. At that point, it being lunchtime, the judge called for a recess.

Delphine glanced across at Dylan, who was just rising from his seat. He was wearing a dark blue, lightweight suit and a white shirt with a pale lilac stripe; his tie was silver and lilac, and his light blond hair gleamed in the sunlight, loaning him an almost angelic air. He glanced at a slim watch on his wrist, and, in turning, spotted her watching him. He smiled grimly and gave an ironic bow.

Delphine felt tears leap to her eyes and quickly turned away, but from the way he gave a quick double take and frowned, she rather feared he'd seen them. Before he could cross over the few feet separating them, she turned and all but ran for the door.

★ ★ ★

Jonah Rodgers stared at Flloyd Turnbull as if he'd grown another head.

'Pick your jaw up off the table and drink your beer,' Flloyd advised dryly, and Jonah, numbly, did just that. They were sitting at a table at Lazy Joe's, a tumble-down beach bar of the old school, situated not far from The Crane in the parish of St Phillip. It was dark and smoky inside, the two men having discovered it some years ago after a successful fishing trip. The original Lazy Joe had long since gone to his reward in the big resort in the sky, but his widow still ran the place with a surprisingly iron fist. There was never any brawling at Joe's. Now, Jonah lifted his bottle of Banks beer and took a hearty swallow.

'You're serious,' he finally said, and Flloyd grinned widely.

'No, I just said it to see the look on your face. Of course I'm serious. Her father owns half of the retail market in the Mid-west. Or some such thing,' Flloyd added casually, took a pull on his own beer, and eyed his friend with a knowing look. 'I thought you'd be pleased her daddy's a billionaire. Most men I know would be dancing a jig. So why do you look as if I've just run over your dog?'

'Sawyer,' Jonah said, ignoring his friend's pique. He still felt as if he'd been poleaxed. 'You know, now you come to mention it, I think the washing machine back in Mum's apartment in Chicago was a Sawyer.'

'And her electric iron, cooker, and fridge too probably,' Flloyd said, remembering that his own father's lawnmower bore the familiar Sawyer logo. 'Good ol' US manufacturing know how,' the policeman drawled. 'Nice to hear there's still some companies actually producing stuff instead of just moving money around. Right?'

Jonah took another long pull of beer. 'Yeah, right,' he said flatly.

Flloyd sighed heavily. 'Look, what's with you? I thought you'd be pleased about this. It means your little lady is no drug-runner's moll after all. In fact, I'm almost certain she's the victim in all of this. I thought, in light of the fact that you've obviously fallen for her like a ton of bricks, that you'd be happy.'

Jonah put his bottle of beer down on the

table top with a hard bang. He closed his eyes for a moment, feeling sick to his stomach, then shook his head.

When his friend had first told him who Tahnee was, he'd gone numb. Now that feeling was wearing off, and was being replaced by sheer despair.

Flloyd, all humour draining from his face as he realized his friend was really upset, leaned forward on his chair. Someone chose a golden oldie on the jukebox, and the haunting strains of someone singing about going through the desert on a horse with no name filled the air. 'What?' Flloyd asked softly.

Jonah looked at his old friend, and laughed painfully. 'Oh dammit Flloyd, use your head. I'm a beach bum, basically. I got a boat mortgaged to her gunwales, a motorbike to get me from A to B, the few ragged clothes that I stand up in, and my charm. And now you tell me the girl I love has a daddy worth billions. No doubt she's got a trust fund of millions herself. Owns — what was it — a fancy art gallery in Florida?'

Flloyd slowly leaned back in his chair, frowning. 'Oh yeah,' he finally said. 'Since you put it that way.' He'd been so sure he was giving his friend good news that he hadn't really thought it through.

'Let's face it, no woman like that is going to seriously look at me, right?' Jonah said, swallowing down a hard, painfully tight ball that was lodged in his throat. 'What could I give her?' he asked despairingly. 'She only turned to me in the first place because she's in trouble.'

Flloyd sighed heavily. His pal was right, of course. It was only in fairy tales, or Hollywood romantic comedies that rich girls ended up with guys like them. It never happened in real life.

'Yeah, well, speaking of trouble,' the policeman said. 'Not that I want to add to your woes, but I think I might know what's going on.' And so saying, he began to lay it all out for him.

When he was finished, Jonah gazed at him from wide eyes set in a pale face. 'You think her stepmother's been kidnapped, and she's here to pay the ransom?' He summed it up neatly. 'Well, that fits in with the diamonds and all this cloak-and-dagger stuff. The kidnappers are obviously running her ragged around town trying to pick up on any tails she's got.' Suddenly he leaned forward. 'Hey, you're not tailing her still, are you? What if you're seen?' he demanded sharply.

Flloyd's eyes narrowed. 'What diamonds?' he grated.

Jonah told him about the face of pot cream, while Flloyd shook his head, a sardonic smile on his face as he listened. 'And you were gonna tell me about all of this when exactly?' Flloyd challenged.

Jonah reached for his now warm and flat beer and took a swig, a shrug of his shoulders being the only answer.

Flloyd too shook his head. 'I'm gonna let that slide,' he said at last. 'Seeing as you're in love and all, and not thinking straight.'

'So what do we do now?' Jonah said, then, before his friend could speak, pointed a warning finger at him. 'And don't tell me that *I* do nothing, or any B.S. like that. I'm not backing off. I'm sticking with her right to the end of this thing.'

Flloyd regarded his friend's angry flashing eyes and tight, dark jaw, and smiled wearily. 'OK, bro, OK. No need to get heavy. I wasn't going to suggest you abandon the lady. If what I suspect is true, she's gonna need you soon anyway.'

Jonah frowned. 'What do you mean?'

Flloyd glanced around. 'It's lunchtime. Want something to eat? Do you think they still do that killer pepperpot stew here?'

'Quit stalling,' Jonah said. 'What's going on?'

Flloyd sighed heavily. 'This may sound

crazy, but I don't think Mrs Cordelia Sawyer has been kidnapped at all, that's all,' he said. And ignoring his friend's falling jaw for the second time that morning, raised his hand to catch the eye of a pretty barmaid and order two rounds of stew.

★ ★ ★

The court reconvened promptly at two o'clock, it now being Dylan's turn to set his case before the judge. This was done surprisingly quickly, because he called only one witness, the solicitor that he'd used when buying Mowbray House.

He confirmed that a thorough background check had been done on the house that met all legal requirements, and that everything had been in order. Gordon Forboys had been the legal owner, and payment had subsequently gone through. Skilfully, Wade Browning, Dylan's advocate, placed evidence in front of the judge that his client had paid good money for a property that he had every reason to believe was legally available to be sold.

Afterwards, there followed some complicated legal and technical wrangling on the issues of probate and statute of limitations that frankly Delphine couldn't follow. She knew only that Dylan's lawyer argued fiercely that the will she'd found in her attic was null and void due to never being probated, and that because of the time elapsed since its being written it couldn't now be relevant. Frederick Cramer made his own case that a dying man's wish should be honoured, especially one that had been legally set out, according to the laws of the land. Obviously something had gone wrong, for the second will had not been acknowledged, but that didn't change the fact that Moorcroft Mowbray, owner of Mowbray House, had willed said house to his business partner, Matthew Godalming. And that Delphine Phillips, as the only living relative of Matthew Godalming, was legally and morally entitled to claim her rightful inheritance.

After that, the judge retired to consider the legal arguments, and Delphine rose shakily to her feet. In her heart of hearts she was sure that Dylan had the better case. After all, he'd given Gordon Forboys a fair price for the house, and would be considerably out of pocket should the case go against him. What's more, Dylan was a well-known member of the Barbados business community, and surely it would send shock-waves through the business world if a judge should rule that a man could pay good money for a property, and then have it snatched away from him. On those rather pragmatic and practical reasons alone, Delphine was sure that she would lose the case.

And, in fact, didn't much care at this point. The whole day had been a nightmare for her. Her love of Mowbray House, the romance of the circumstances surrounding it, the legitimacy of her feelings for both Dylan Gale and the old house, had been reduced to hard, dry, legal wrangling, and it made her feel sick at heart.

She left the court on leaden feet, sure that the judge would take days, if not weeks, in her deliberations. Surely the complex technical questions alone that had been raised would take weeks of careful research? She doubted that her own case could be the only one in existence where a will had turned up unexpectedly, so there was bound to be precedents, but even so, she expected she'd have to come back to the island later in the year to hear the verdict.

Outside, she glanced at her watch, surprised to see that it wasn't yet five o'clock. Behind her, she heard two male voices talking low, and, turning around, was not surprised to see Dylan and Wade Browning conversing quietly.

Dylan, spotting her, said something to his lawyer, who glanced at her, nodded, and set off down the steps, nodding at her pleasantly in passing. Of Cramer there was no sign, for which Delphine was glad. She didn't think she could cope with him just now.

'Well, it went faster than I expected,' Dylan said dryly, as he walked towards her. Delphine watched his approach with a dry and aching throat.

'It was horrible,' she said flatly. 'I wish I'd never found that damned will in the first place.' And then she realized that, if she hadn't, she would never have come to Barbados, and never have met Dylan Gale. 'No, that's not true,' she said at once. It felt superstitiously wrong to deny the very thing that had brought them together, even if it was going to be responsible for her inevitable heartbreak.

'Now *that* I believe,' Dylan said drolly. 'You took one look at that place and fell for it, didn't you?' he said, almost accusingly.

Delphine smiled. 'I did. And you? Do you really see nothing special about it at all?' And held her breath as she waited for the answer.

Dylan shrugged uncomfortably. The truth was, he'd wanted to buy the house from the moment he'd seen it. He glanced at her, saw the tension and strain in her face, and something longing, something vulnerable in her eyes, that caught at his heart and squeezed tight.

It was time they got this sorted out, once and for all. He took a long, slow breath.

'Let's go out there and see, shall we?' he said, and taking her arm, manoeuvred her determinedly down the steps. She let him lead her to his car without demur, and slipped into the lush interior of the Jaguar XJS without a word.

Her heart was beating so hard she could almost hear it. So sure was she that something momentous was going to happen that she simply sat there like a mannequin, unable to do or say anything.

When he climbed in beside her she was still motionless, so he reached across to pull her safety belt across and secure it in the slot. As he did so, she felt his knuckles brush gently across her right breast, and pulled in a sharp breath, very much aware that his head was so close to hers that she could reach out and push a silvery-blond lock behind his neatly shaped ear.

She could see a small patch, just under his chin, that his razor had missed that morning, and felt a giddying need to lean forward and plant a kiss right there. Then he was straightening up, not even meeting her eyes, and reaching for his car keys. He turned them viciously in the ignition.

His knuckles gleamed pale as they clasped

the steering wheel far too tightly. He'd heard her small indrawn breath at the intimacy of his touch, and the truth was, he was barely in control of himself.

He drove out to Bathsheba very, very carefully.

★ ★ ★

As Dylan and Delphine drove north towards Bathsheba, flying in from the east, a medium-sized airliner was just touching down at Grantley Adams Airport.

Marcus White had worked there as a customs officer for many years, eyeing passengers as they came and went with knowing, alert eyes. Occasionally he would call one of them over to him as they streamed through towards passport control, dragging heavy suitcases with them, their weary faces nearly all smiling now that they'd finally reached their destinations, their hopes for a much-needed holiday clearly showing on their faces.

The majority of them he let go past. The pale-skinned family with clamouring, over-tired children. The groups of giggling women, usually office workers, out for their statutory two weeks of sun, sand and sex. The regular island-hoppers and business men and women.

But some caught his eye. Like the man who was coming now.

He was not particularly pale, but had an average tan, that told Marcus he probably worked in a warm climate. He was alone, but dressed casually. Not young, not old, mousy-haired and slight in build, his clothes were good quality but not expensive, designer gear. He didn't keep his face averted, nor his eyes cast down, two sure signs of somebody with something to hide, but let his gaze roam casually past. In short, there was nothing obvious to alert Marcus White's inner radar, but something 'pinged' deep in his chest the moment he saw him.

Smoothly, Marcus stepped forward, a small, black man wearing an airport uniform, and intercepted the passenger with a welcoming smile. 'Hello, sir, sorry to inconvenience you. Would you just step this way for a moment?'

The debarking passenger showed no surprise or impatience, nor did he say anything. He merely followed where Marcus led, to a small room off the main corridor, that contained nothing but a table.

Catching the eye of a colleague to follow him — for airport regulations insisted there must be two personnel present when a spotcheck was carried out — Marcus lifted the passenger's suitcase on to the table.

His colleague, a tall, thin man with curly ginger hair, asked for the passport, and, with half an ear, Marcus listened to their conversation as he searched the case.

His colleague, Peter Phelps, spoke first. 'Mr William Moore?' he asked, quoting the name in the passport.

'That's me,' the man replied. Midwestern US accent, Marcus thought automatically. A twang of bluegrass in there somewhere.

'Here on business or pleasure, Mr Moore?'

'Oh, purely pleasure. I do love the islands. Went to Mystique last year. The US Virgins before that. Plan on doing Trinidad sometime next year. Or maybe St Lucia.'

A little too much information, Marcus thought, but there was nothing suspicious in that. Most passengers singled out for extra attention tended to get nervous whether they had reason to or not — and spoke too much as a consequence.

He opened Mr Moore's toiletries, and found nothing more ominous than toothpaste and floss, shaving lotion and sun cream.

'And the length of your stay, sir?'

'Ten days.'

Package tour, Marcus thought, somewhat surprised. He didn't look the type. Finding nothing in the case, Marcus repacked it

313

neatly and carefully, caught his colleague's eye and gave an almost invisible shake of his head.

'Well, thank you for your time, sir,' Peter Phelps said, as Marcus handed back the case.

'Sure, no problem,' Mr William Moore said.

Back in the corridor outside, the two airport employees watched him walk down to the passport check-in point. 'OK, Marcus?' Peter asked curiously. Everyone knew that Marcus White had a good nose for the wrong ones. 'Want me to alert the dogs?'

'No,' Marcus said shortly. Sniffer dogs could spot drugs instantly, of course, but there had been nothing about the man or his luggage to warrant that kind of attention.

Even so, as the nondescript Mr Moore exited the terminal, he felt a vague sense of unease. There was something about the man that he just didn't like.

Outside, instead of joining the queue for taxis, Mr William Moore waited at the kerb, glanced at his watch once, counted to ten, lifted his wrist to glance at his watch again, counted to ten, then did so for a third time. At which point, a small, rusty hatchback pulled out of a rare parking space, and drew up beside him.

Mr Moore opened the passenger door and

slid in, regarding the driver carefully.

'Hello, mate,' the driver, a big man, said in a hearty Australian accent. 'Welcome to the island. I've got something for you.' And so saying, handed over a black briefcase that had been sitting on his lap.

Once the car had hit the open road, and there was nothing but verdant countryside all around, Mr Moore briefly opened it, and checked the rifle within. He said nothing, but grunted approval at the state-of-the-art telescopic sight, and long, tapering bullets.

★ ★ ★

Dylan pulled up outside the house and turned off the ignition. Then he climbed out and walked around to the passenger-side door, opening it for her. 'Come on, I think we need to talk,' he said softly, hand out-stretched.

Delphine, her heart thundering in her chest, gave him her hand, and felt her elbows go weak as his fingers curled around her wrist.

They walked to the porch in silence, Dylan reaching into his pocket to retrieve a single Yale key. He opened the front door and stood back to let her go in first.

She was dressed in a simple pale blue

sleeveless dress, with a V-neck and an attractive, handkerchief hem. Low-heeled dark blue sandals completed the outfit, showing off superbly shaped legs and a neat pair of ankles.

'I just want to check on the kitchen,' Dylan said, heading off that way. 'I called the fire brigade out after the fire, just to make sure that everything was safe. I just want to check everything's still OK.'

Delphine nodded, and moved off to the front room. There she wandered over to a grimy window, which looked out over a breathtaking view. Sinking down on to the dust-sheeted sofa beneath the window, she sneezed as the dust motes tickled her nose.

'Everything's fine,' he said, coming in through the door, and then hesitating as his eyes found her. She looked so forlorn sitting on that ridiculous dust-sheet, her mass of dark hair a stark contrast against the hessian, her pale limbs just turning now to the colour of honey. And when she looked up at him with those dark pansy eyes, he felt his world once again lurch dangerously on its axis.

'Dylan, can't we do something about all this?' Delphine begged, gesturing around her. 'What if we agree that neither of us should have it?'

Dylan had to smile. What a solution. Only

a woman would ever think of it! 'And that's the thinking of an Oxford academic, is it?' he teased.

Delphine had to laugh. 'No, seriously. I mean, we could turn it into a museum or something.'

'A museum?' Dylan raised one eyebrow in surprise. Now where had that idea come from? 'Do you really want to fill this house with exhibits and glass showcases and have disgruntled tourists traipsing through it only when it rains, wishing they were on the beach instead?' he demanded scornfully.

Delphine flushed, something inside her finally snapping. She'd been miserable all day, and this was the final straw. How could a man as clever as this one be so dense?

'No, I don't want that,' she snapped, scrambling to her feet. 'I don't want tourists of any kind in here at all, you stupid man,' she all but yelled. 'I want you and me in here, and our children and some dogs, and I want to potter about in the garden and transform it myself, and I want — '

She stopped abruptly. Had she really said all that out loud? And then she saw the stunned look on his face and she realized that yes, she had.

Slowly she raised an appalled hand to her mouth. 'Forget I said all that,' she mumbled, but he was already striding towards her, shaking his head.

'Not on your life,' he said, his voice shaken but with just a trace of laughter in it. 'Say it again.'

Delphine tried to turn away from him, but he was already there beside her, his hands holding the tops of her arms in a firm grip.

'Sweetheart, just talk to me,' Dylan pleaded, seeing her big eyes begin to shimmer. 'I won't laugh at you, I promise. I need to know.'

And something in his tone of voice made her heart stop cringing. Instead of feeling embarrassment and heartache, she felt surprise instead.

'You sound as if you really mean that,' she blurted.

Dylan slowly smiled. 'I'm not in the habit of saying things I don't mean,' he chided gently. 'For instance . . . ' he took a deep breath. 'When we first met, I thought you were a cheat, a liar and a damned fine actress. I thought you were a heartless hussy, with the most fiendishly clever disguise I'd ever seen.' And he touched her chin with his forefinger. 'This beautiful, innocent face.'

Delphine swallowed hard. 'And now?' she whispered.

'Now, I think you're everything you seem to be. A lonely girl who found a will in her attic, and came to the islands looking for a dream. A little adventure, maybe. And found a hostile, pig-headed hotelier instead,' he laughed shakily.

Delphine, a sense of bewildered delight growing inside her, smiled tremulously. 'You weren't that bad,' she insisted, not quite truthfully. 'Besides, you stirred me up. Shook me out of my complacent little world. You probably did me a lot of good.'

Dylan wasn't to be distracted. 'You said you wanted us to live in this house,' he reminded her. 'That you wanted to fill it with our children and, I believe, dogs were mentioned.'

Delphine blinked, instinctively trying to draw back, but there was no mockery in his eyes, only an intense green gaze that demanded the truth.

'I did say that,' she admitted. 'And I meant it,' she added firmly. After all, what did she have to lose? She was a woman in love.

Dylan let out his breath in a long, slow exhale. 'I'm so glad,' he admitted. 'It's been driving me crazy.'

Delphine felt her heart leap. Could this really be true? Could it be happening to her of all people? Was he really saying what she thought he was?

'What do you mean? What's been driving

you crazy?' she whispered.

'I thought you only loved this house,' he said, and laughed as she stared at him in amazement. 'I know. Stupid, isn't it, but all this time, I've been jealous of Mowbray House. You seemed to covet it so. Want it, desire it. And from the moment we first met, I've wanted you. Desired you. Coveted *you*.'

Delphine swayed in his arms. 'You really want me?' she whispered.

'Right from the start,' he admitted huskily. 'I told you. I always mean what I say.' His green eyes darkened to the colour of a stormy sea. 'Let me show you how much,' he purred. And with that, he pushed her backwards, on to the sofa.

The dust-sheet let out a great puff of dust, and Delphine sneezed again. Dylan, chuckling, rolled her off the sofa and on to the floor, twisting around so that he landed first, on his back, and took her slight weight on to his chest and stomach.

Then, rolling again, he was on top of her, his lips on hers, loving and demanding. He ran his splayed hands over her ribs, his separated fingers moving either side of her nipples, making them burgeon into tight, hard buds.

She gasped as he ran his fingers over her shoulders then up into her glorious dark locks, spreading them around her head on the dusty carpet, where it gleamed like ebony. Her eyes were impossibly big and round, their obsidian depths melting as he pushed the pale material of her dress off her shoulders.

He sent his lips across the delicate contours of her shoulder-blades to kiss and nibble the tender indents at the side of her neck, before rising to tug gently on her ear lobes, first one, then the other.

Delphine, feeling slightly anxious, watched his face as he pulled the loose dress down, revealing her breasts. But then his green eyes narrowed with pleasure and possessiveness at the sight, and she knew she'd been foolish to be afraid. Then she could see only the top of his golden head as he dipped to suck on first one nubbin of flesh and then the other.

Delphine moaned helplessly, closing her eyes, leaving her in gentle darkness, where all she could do was hear and feel. Hear his breathing, harsh with mounting passion, and feel his fingertips, smoothing across her skin, making her naked. His lips, kissing, exploring, rousing, wickedly knowing.

He was a lover of great experience, and seemed to know instinctively that she was as ignorant as he was knowing. And so he was gentle, patient, instructive, wise. He showed her where he liked to be kissed, touched, kneaded, held. He helped her strip the clothes from his body, and guided her carefully when they at last joined.

And Delphine cried out, tears of joy seeping from beneath her long dark lashes as she held him in her arms.

Finally, when it was over and they lay naked and welded together, a soft breeze sprang up and whispered around Mowbray House, for all the world sounding like a sigh of approbation.

13

Tahnee woke to the sound of a maid rattling her trolley down the corridor, and rolled over in bed. Yawning, she lifted herself on to one elbow and gazed at the clock. Nearly eight.

She showered slowly, then dressed in amber shorts and a scoop-necked, amber, lemon, black and white patterned blouse, which she tied in a knot at her midrift, leaving her navel exposed. Her short cap of hair dried quickly, and a few brush strokes had it shining like a silver cap. She didn't bother with make-up, but made her way to breakfast, smiling and not at all surprised to see Jonah seated at one of the tables, waiting for her.

As she approached the table, she felt her heart lift at the look of longing and welcome in his eyes. He brought with him the scent of the sea. He was dressed in his usual uniform of ragged, cut-off jeans and disreputable T-shirt. His hair was curly from a recent shower, and for once his jaw was cleanly shaved.

'Hungry?' he asked, as she drew out a chair and sat down beside him.

Tahnee shot him a smouldering look.

'Ravenous,' she said, and heard him draw in a quick breath as he caught her double entendre. She smiled mischievously.

'Well, we can always go back to the *Whale* to eat. I caught a fresh — ' He stopped as a waitress appeared beside them, and handed Tahnee a note.

'Sorry to interrupt, madam,' the young girl said. 'But this was delivered by hand this morning, and he was most insistent that I give it to you the moment you came down.'

Tahnee opened her mouth to ask the waitress what the man had looked like, then quickly closed it again. Her meddling might already have cost Cordelia her life. Or a finger. Instead, she swallowed her curiosity, and said tamely, 'Thank you.'

She didn't want to open it in front of Jonah, but on the other hand, she could hardly ask him to leave. So she rose to her feet, mumbled something about the ladies room, and moved away.

The moment she was out of sight, Jonah got out his mobile phone and called Flloyd, who said he'd be right there.

In the ladies room, Tahnee leant against a cold basin, and with shaking hands, opened the envelope. Inside was a tiny tape recorder. She inserted the cassette she'd retrieved from the bouy and listened to the mechanical voice.

THIS IS IT. TAKE DIAMONDS TO MAYCOCK'S BAY RIGHT AWAY. ON WATERFRONT YOU'LL SEE RUBBISH BIN PAINTED BLUE. ALL OTHERS ARE WHITE. PUT DIAMONDS IN BLUE BIN AND WALK AWAY. STEPMOTHER WILL BE RELEASED ONCE DIAMONDS ARE AUTHENTICATED. DON'T LEAVE HOTEL ROOM UNTIL YOU HEAR FROM US HERE TO PICK HER UP. NO COPS, OR YOU'RE BOTH DEAD.

Tahnee felt her knees sag, and put her hand over her mouth as a loud sob escaped her. At last, the nightmare was coming to an end.

★   ★   ★

Delphine Phillips looked down at their joined hands, then up to the face of the man walking beside her. He had the profile of an Adonis, she thought wistfully, and wondered, yet again, if she was really awake. She wouldn't be surprised to find she was dreaming. After all, the events of yesterday were already taking on a surreal feel, as if they'd happened long ago to a fairytale princess who was only on nodding acquaintance with the real woman. Then he looked down at her, and his dark green eyes smiled, and all doubts fled, like wimpering cowards. 'Nervous?' he asked cheerfully.

Delphine licked her dry lips. 'No,' she lied. 'Why should I be nervous? I'm only going to meet your parents. Right?'

'Right,' Dylan confirmed. 'And neither one of them were ogres, last time I checked.'

Delphine smoothed down the midi-length white skirt she was wearing. 'I wish I had something more formal to wear,' she said plaintively. The coffee-coloured blouse she was wearing frothed with lace at collar and cuff, but to make up for that, she'd piled her mass of dark hair on to her head and tamed it with a tortoiseshell comb. With a shimmering of gold eyeshadow and the bare attentions of a pale plum lipstick, she hoped that she at least managed to look respectable. She didn't realize that a few strands of dark hair had escaped, and clung damply to her skin, or that her dark brown eyes were aglow with happiness. She was heart-stoppingly beautiful, and he felt proud to be walking down the street with her.

'What if your mother doesn't like me?'

Delphine whispered, and Dylan glanced at her and laughed.

'What? Not like the woman who wants to fill Mowbray House with her grandchildren? A smart Oxford-educated woman, who captured her son's heart and made him the happiest man on the islands? You're right — she's going to hate you.'

Delphine squeezed his hand hard. 'You're rotten to me,' she said, and grinned widely.

Dylan stopped as he reached a pair of double gates that guarded a large, plantation-style house in one of the most exclusive suburbs of Bridgetown. 'After you,' he murmured. 'And don't worry. I won't let them eat you.'

Delphine shot him a chiding look, and took a deep breath. Then he leant down and whispered, 'You're the only woman I've ever brought home. Or ever will.'

And suddenly, all her fear was gone.

Neither one of them noticed the car that had idled behind them for the last few hundred yards or so. Inside, William Moore pulled to a halt by the kerb, and reached for a camera. He zoomed the lens in close, and took several head-shots, then noted the time and location in a notebook. In it were several other meticulous entries, that began at 7.30 the previous evening.

Usually he liked to tail his marks for a few days, but in this case he didn't think it would be necessary. There was no way he could make the hit at Gale's offices, or his home, or this place. They were all far too residential or busy. And the woman's holiday inn was out of the question. But that big empty house on the cliffs, where he'd first picked them up — that would be ideal. Isolated, and with ideal vantage points from the dense foliage, it would be a doddle.

All he had to do was stay on their tail until they went back and that would be that.

★   ★   ★

Jonah watched Tahnee walk back towards him from the ladies room, instantly aware of how tense she had become. There was a tight, almost excited look in her eyes, and when she told him that she was going to skip breakfast and do a little shopping, he wasn't at all surprised. She looked as if she was about to jump out of her own skin, the way she fumbled nervously for her bag, took a quick swallow of the fruit juice she'd ordered, and fiddled with her watch.

'OK, woman's stuff,' Jonah said lightly. 'You can count me out. I'll go back to the *Whale* and scrub her decks. She likes that.'

'Lucky *Whale*,' Tahnee said, with a shaky smile, feeling nothing but vast relief that he was making this so easy for her. Jonah nodded then reached out and kissed her, long and slow, on the lips. Trying to tell her without words that she could rely on him. A little sigh feathered past her lips as he drew back, then with a bright smile he was gone.

As far as the next corner, where he'd parked his bike. There he swung his leg over the pillion, reached for his helmet, and glanced around. A little hatchback parked on the opposite side of the road flashed its lights, and Jonah nodded. He couldn't see his friend inside, but he knew that Flloyd, as well as other plain clothes officers, must be spread out, ready to follow.

When Tahnee came out a few moments later and hailed a cab, Jonah waited a while before drawing out and following. He was well aware that Flloyd would prefer it if he wasn't here at all, but there was no way he was going to let her out of his sight. So he wasn't going to blow it by letting himself get spotted — either by Tahnee, or any other watching eyes. But after what Flloyd had told him about Marcus Bolton's possible involvement, he wasn't going to let her do this alone either.

'See, told you,' Dylan teased, as he watched her swing her beautiful legs into the passenger seat of his Jag. 'They adore you.'

He closed the door and sprinted around to the driver's side. Delphine watched him, her face aglow.

It *had* seemed to go well. Dylan's father had been, physically, very much like his son, and seemed amused at the way Dylan fussed around her, while his mother, a smaller, brown-haired woman with a placid personality and wise smile, had chatted to her as if they were old friends. Two hours had gone by in a flash, during which time Mr and Mrs Gale had learned her whole life history.

'It was a subtle interrogation, I'll give them that,' Dylan said dryly as he fastened his seatbelt.

'Well, that part was never going to be a problem,' Delphine said easily. 'A more respectable upbringing than mine is hard to imagine. But do you think they thought we were right for each other?' she asked anxiously. It was the one question girlfriends had agonized over since time began. Will my mother-in-law be a help or a hindrance?

'Are you kidding? Mum took one look at the way you look at me, and she was won over, just like that,' Dylan said — accurately, as it turned out — and snapped his fingers. 'I'll bet they're in there now, discussing the wedding.'

Delphine held her breath. 'Wedding?' she repeated.

Dylan looked across at her, and smiled gently. 'Let's go to Mowbray House,' he said softly. 'I've packed a picnic, and there's something I want to ask you.' And give you, he thought, thinking of the diamond ring he'd bought that morning before picking her up. It was an unusual antique ring, with a central diamond surrounded by dark, smoky topaz stones that reminded him of her lovely eyes.

He felt in his heart that she was going to love it.

* * *

Tahnee got out of the taxi and asked the driver to wait. He nodded, instantly reaching for that day's paper and turning to the sports page. She stepped on to the narrow pavement and glanced around. There were a few scattered dwellings, visible mostly as roofs in the trees, and on the roadside of the railings that ran along the sea-front, a few mobile stores were set up — sellers of ice cream and watermelons mostly, pandering to the tourist trade who liked to wander off the beaten track in search of unpopular beaches.

It was a blustery day, however, and the esplanade was largely deserted. She walked to the railings, looking left and right. She could see two rubbish bins — both painted white. Unsure which way to go, she turned left and began to walk.

The time was 11.32.

★　★　★

William Moore saw the Jag indicate right, and smiled briefly to himself. Things were looking good. Gale seemed to be heading for Bathsheba. And the woman was with him. He'd be able to take them both out together, which was what he'd been hoping for. When the client wanted a couple taken out, it sometimes presented problems to have to do them one at a time. It meant the remaining partner was alerted, and could go into hiding, which made his job all that much more difficult.

But today, even the weather was on his side, for a stiffening breeze would mean there probably wouldn't be many people walking the cliffs.

Tuning the radio on to a local reggae station, William Moore tapped his hands on the steering wheel in time with the beat, and smiled at the thought that, all being well, he'd probably be on the midnight plane home. His little daughter had a birthday party coming up in two days time — she'd be eleven — and this was one he might not have to miss.

He glanced at the briefcase on the passenger seat beside him. It was a good rifle. It wouldn't take long to assemble.

★　★　★

Tahnee bit her lip as she saw, in the distance, the next rubbish bin was also white. It looked, too, as if the railings didn't go on for much longer. Making the decision, she turned abruptly, and began to walk back the way she'd came.

Below her, on the beach, a man walked a dog — a large Alsatian. Leaning on the railings some way away were a pair of lovers — teenagers, by the looks of them. If she'd looked closer as she passed them, however, she'd have seen that they were older than they looked. And both wore earpieces, through which they could hear a voice, giving them instructions.

Tahnee saw her taxi, still waiting patiently, and the driver looked up as she approached, then shrugged and went on reading his paper as she simply walked by him with a bare smile.

She glanced at her watch again. It was nearly five to twelve.

* * *

Dylan pulled the wicker picnic hamper from the boot of the Jag, and put it on the ground. Then he reached for a blue and white check blanket, which he draped over his arm, then glanced behind him, sure that he'd heard a car door close. But there was nothing on the drive, or the road beyond, and since the nearest house was nearly a quarter of a mile away, he supposed it was someone heading for the beach below.

He turned and saw Delphine watching him, her big eyes sombre and expectant, and he felt his entire being flood with warmth. It was not just physical either. His mind felt free and clear, his heart full, his soul content. He was about to ask the woman he loved to marry him, and she watched him, knowing he was going to ask, longing to hear the words.

It was the ultimate, perfect moment. One that would last a whole lifetime.

In the bushes far to the right, William Moore knelt and opened his briefcase, and began to assemble his rifle.

Tahnee's heart fluttered as, in the distance, she saw a dark blue square. A rubbish bin, but this one not the ubiquitous white. She glanced around, but could see no-one paying any attention to it at all. Then she supposed that whoever was watching her might just as easily be doing so from out at sea. A powerful boat could be quickly run ashore, a strong pair of sprinting legs could climb the steps and claim the prize, once her taxi had left the scene.

Whatever, it was none of her business now.

She was only glad, in the end, that she hadn't had to involve Jonah Rodgers. She'd have hated it if anything had happened to him, or his beloved boat.

Her pace quickened as she approached the bin. Once there, she reached into her bag and pulled out the pot of face cream and hesitated. Should she take the diamonds from the pot? What if the kidnappers, when they got here, didn't recognize the pot of face cream as the prize?

Then she saw the bin was totally empty, so whatever she left, they'd have to know it had been delivered by her. Quickly, she put the pot inside, dead in the middle, then turned and walked away.

The middle of her back felt itchy. As if she could imagine someone staring at her, two eyes drilling into her back. Or maybe a gun sight. She shuddered, telling herself she'd watched too many late-night thrillers. Why would someone shoot her, for heaven's sake?

* * *

William Moore lifted the rifle to his eyes, and checked the range. Then he reached for a small screwdriver, and made a fine-tune adjustment to the positioning of the rifle sight. He checked it again, and again, made a tiny adjustment. Assembling a rifle wasn't as easy as most people thought. It took skill, and practise, and many years of experience.

After all, it wouldn't do to miss.

* * *

Tahnee breathed a huge sigh of relief as she felt the handle of the taxi's door beneath her fingers and, opening it, she almost fell inside. The driver glanced up, slightly concerned by his fare's pale face.

'You OK, young miss?'

Tahnee swallowed back a hysterical urge to laugh. 'Fine. Back to Bridgetown, please.'

Jonah Rodgers, from his position offroad

on a small bluff overlooking the bay, breathed a huge sigh of relief, and followed the taxi back to the city. He had no interest in what might be happening back at the drop site. His girl was safe, that was all he cared about. From now on, it was Flloyd's show. And that was fine with him.

He had his own worries now.

Namely, telling Tahnee everything. And knowing that he was almost sure to lose her when he did. No girl liked to be lied to, and one as independent and feisty as Tahnee was bound to feel as if she'd been taken for a fool. But he owed her the truth. She deserved no less.

★   ★   ★

'Champagne?' Delphine said, sitting on the blanket and watching Dylan pull things from the hamper one by one, as a magician might pull things from a hat. Instead of the white rabbit, or dove, or bunch of paper flowers, however, there was Dom Perignon and fluted glasses, rich French cheese and paté, grapes and buljol salad.

They were on the grassy clifftop between the house and the set of steps leading down to the beach, and the sight of the steps reminded Dylan of his PI's report, which had been delivered yesterday. Gabby had come through all right, telling Dylan all about the secret passageway that was thought to exist between Mowbray House and the beach. No wonder a crook like Bolton wanted to get his hands on the house, Dylan mused now. The egress was probably in the cellar somewhere. But he didn't want to spoil the moment by talking about that now.

Instead, he poured the wine, and handed her a glass. Delphine's eyes widened as he leaned forward, and gently clinked his glass to hers. 'To us,' he murmured.

She sipped the cold, delicious liquid, and felt her heart flutter as he reached two fingers into the top pocket of his shirt and drew out a small, black box. She put her glass down on the blanket, eyes riveted to the jeweller's box as he opened it. And gasped at the black and white gem inside. It was perfect — unusual, exquisite. All that she could ever have imagined in an engagement ring. She lifted her hand and watched, wordlessly, as he slid the gem on to her long, tapering, pale finger.

'Will you marry me, Delphine Phillips?' Dylan Gale whispered, and Delphine raised dark brimming eyes to his.

They shone like obsidian, lovely and happy.

William Moore, seeing them through the sights of his telescopic rifle, thought they were probably the most beautiful eyes he'd ever seen.

Such a pity.

His finger began to move towards the trigger.

★ ★ ★

Flloyd Turnbull watched the blue bin from the back of the hatchback, the man beside him equally glued to his pair of binoculars.

'Suspect approaching,' a voice crackled in his earpiece, the voice young and female, and belonging to Constable Mavis Withnall, one half of the 'teenage' couple, mooning about by the railings. 'Male, early thirties, black, wearing an orange shirt and khaki slacks.'

Flloyd responded, telling all units to hold back. When the suspect reached the bin, glanced around, then reached inside, Flloyd smiled gently. 'Yes, that's it,' he muttered, making the sergeant beside him grin in response. 'A nice little present for you. Now take it back to your master like a good little minion.'

He'd already recognized the courier as one of Marcus Bolton's gang of thugs. He could have ordered the arrest then and there, but he wanted to get the big chief himself. And to do that, he had to catch Bolton red-handed, with no squirming room. This time, he was going down.

★   ★   ★

William Moore turned the rifle from the face of the woman on to the man. Whenever he had to do two hits simultaneously, if one was male, the other female, he always took out the male first. They were the more dangerous target.

Gale was turned away from him, giving him a perfect view of the back of his head. It couldn't be better. By the time the girl had a chance to react, he'd have the second round chambered and ready to fire. Even if shock didn't hold her immobile, even if she got to her feet and tried to run, he'd be able to take her down easy.

He was kneeling behind a large flowering shrub, with the barrel of the rifle resting across a fairly thick branch. He could, of course, hold the gun steady free and clear, but it was always nice to have something to rest it on. The extra stability made the shot that extra bit more certain.

Positioning his head carefully, he sighted down the barrel, and took the first of three long breaths. It was always important to get the breathing right, as his old army instructor had drilled into him.

Always fire on the exhale.

Slowly, carefully, he let the first of his deep breaths slip through his thin lips.

And froze as something cold and hard was pressed into the back of his neck.

'Don't move,' Inspector Brian Quincy said softly.

★ ★ ★

Tahnee walked into her room and collapsed on to the bed. She was shaking and, although she knew it was far too early yet, stared at the telephone, willing it to ring. She jumped when a soft knock sounded at the door, but smiled with relief when, a moment later, it opened and Jonah put his head around.

Tahnee scrambled up to sit, cross-legged in the middle of the bed. 'Am I glad to see you,' she said. Then frowned, as she saw the look on his face. He looked serious. No, more than that. He looked downright grim.

'You might not be so glad in a minute,' Jonah said heavily. And walking to the bed, sank heavily down beside her. 'Just believe me, when I tell you, I love you.'

Tahnee opened her mouth, then closed it again, as the brief flash of euphoria she felt at his words suddenly chilled inside her.

Normally when a man said he loved you, it didn't fill you with a deep sense of foreboding.

Especially when you were beginning to suspect that you were head over heels in love with that same man.

'What's going on?' she said flatly.

*   *   *

Delphine felt tears on her face as she leaned forward into his embrace. Dylan, gathering her closer against him, kissed her deeply, their glasses of champagne forgotten as they fell over, their contents seeping into the blanket.

Delphine was lost in the moment, eyes closed, savouring the warmth and safety of his arms, and everything that this moment foretold — the promise of passion to come, the stretch of years ahead, full of laughter and tears, triumph and disaster, the creation of precious moments that would turn into precious memories to last into old age. The merry-go-round that was marriage, children — a lifetime.

When she opened her eyes, she could see the same realization in his own green gaze.

'I love you so much,' Dylan whispered. 'Don't ever leave me.'

'I won't,' Delphine promised.

And then gasped, as someone coughed, loudly and clearly, right beside them. Dylan sprang around and up, coming to his feet in one lithe movement, just like a cat.

He stared, nonplussed, at the man in front of him. He was in his late forties, dressed in black slacks and white shirt, with dark hair just going grey at the temples. He wore a neat moustache.

'Mr Gale? Dylan Gale?'

Dylan nodded warily. 'Yes. What's going on?'

'Detective Inspector Quincy, sir. I think it would be best if you and the young lady sat back down,' Brian Quincy said, and it was only then that Dylan realized that Delphine had got up to join him.

'What's the matter?' Delphine said quietly, slipping her hand through Dylan's. Something was obviously dreadfully wrong, but she felt no fear. Not with Dylan by her side. Together, she knew they could cope with anything.

Brian Quincy looked back over his shoulder, where two uniformed constables were leading a man down the drive. One of them was carrying, in a large plastic evidence bag, what was obviously a rifle.

'I'm afraid, sir, that you and your companion were in considerable danger. For that I would like to sincerely apologize.'

But Dylan was hardly listening to him. Instead, his face was flooding with a dark, ugly colour.

'Bolton!' he said explosively, and Brian Quincy nodded.

'Yes, sir. It seems you have some inkling of what's going on and why. Care to share it with me?'

Dylan nodded vaguely, but he was no longer looking at the policeman. Instead, he pulled Delphine closer and hugged her so tight she could hardly breathe. Not that she minded.

'I nearly lost you,' Dylan muttered, raining feverish kisses across her face. 'I nearly lost you,' he repeated, hugging her closer, as if he could absorb her into his very being.

Coughing discreetly again, Brian Quincy turned and walked a few paces away. He was smiling, even as his mind raced. Things had certainly happened fast, since that phone call yesterday from a customs officer at Grantley Adams.

On receiving news that this experienced officer was unhappy about a new arrival, he'd sent a constable to the airport to get a picture of the 'suspect' from airport security tapes. This he'd quickly run through Interpol, getting a red-notice notification almost immediately.

Mr William Moore had more aliases than the actors' guild, and was suspected of being a freelance hitman operating chiefly in the US. Brian Quincy had instantly alerted his superior, who'd authorized overtime for nearly the entire island's constabulary. Consequently, Moore had quickly been traced to a nondescript motel in Speightstown, and from then on had been closely monitored.

It had quickly become obvious that the hitman was stalking Dylan Gale, one of the island's most successful businessmen, and it hadn't taken long for another inspector, one Flloyd Turnbull, currently engaged on another hot case, to get in touch. His information consisted of rumours from the street which confirmed that Dylan Gale had earned the animosity of no less a personage than Marcus Bolton.

So when William Moore had been observed to extract a rifle from his case, with his quarry in plain sight, Quincy had wasted no time in taking the initiative. His only bad moment had come when he'd started to creep up on the gunman, dreading the snapping of a twig, or the flight of some alarmed bird or animal to give the game away. Luckily, however, the hitman had been too engrossed in what he was doing to ever suspect that he himself was being stalked.

Now, Brian walked a little way down the driveway, giving the lovers some time together, and contemplated the glowing congratulations of his chief. Who knows, with an internationally wanted hitman behind bars, surely a promotion was in the offing?

When he returned to the handsome young couple a few minutes later, he found them waiting for him patiently. The young English woman looked composed and calm, and Brian felt a brief surge of admiration for her. Not only beautiful, but full of grace, too. Dylan Gale was a lucky man.

'Now sir. Can you tell me why someone would hire an assassin in order to be rid of you?'

Dylan Gale smiled. 'Oh yes, Inspector,' he said softly. 'I can indeed.'

But as Brian Quincy listened, with growing excitement, to a prominent businessman handing him Marcus Bolton's head on a platter, he wasn't aware that it would be Flloyd Turnbull who'd have the pleasure — finally — of slipping the handcuffs on to one of the biggest crooks on the island.

★ ★ ★

'You told this policeman pal of yours all about me?' Tahnee repeated carefully, when Jonah finally finished talking. 'Days ago? All this time, you knew what was going on, but you didn't tell me?'

Jonah winced. He'd known it was going to be like this. How could it ever have gone any other way?

'I didn't know what was going on at all,' he denied flatly. 'I was hired by this beautiful blonde, who was obviously up to something shady. I told my policeman friend — and that was where it should have ended. But it didn't. You got under my skin. I found myself following you, wanting to help you. Even when you pulled a gun on me. And then we made love, and I knew I didn't care what was going on. You could have been a younger version of Ma Baker for all I cared. But by then it was too late — Flloyd was following you, and figuring things out. By the time he told me about your stepmother, and the fake kidnapping, things were getting way out of control. All I could do was follow you and be there if you needed me.'

Tahnee still couldn't take it all in. But she was aware that the growing anger inside her died a sudden death, as his final words sank in. 'You were out there just now?' she whispered.

'At Maycock's Bay? I sure as hell was,' he confirmed. 'And if anyone had tried to hurt you I was on the bike, ready to pick you up. We could have gone cross-country if they'd been in a car — that bike of mine is a tough old girl, and she's got a good turn of speed. I could have got myself between you and any trouble in a matter of seconds.'

Tahnee went hot, then cold. Hot, because the fact that he was prepared to risk so much for her made her feel so special she could burst. And cold, when she remembered that feeling of being watched — maybe by someone with a gun.

'And supposing they shot you?' she suddenly raged. 'At least I had a gun in my bag. Oh Jonah, you could have died,' she wailed, throwing herself into his arms.

Jonah laughed, surprised by her unexpected reaction, and hugged her close. 'Well, we're here, and we're fine. And, with a bit of luck, Flloyd is picking up the bad guys even as we speak,' he reassured her.

Tahnee lifted her head and looked at him. 'And he really thinks the kidnapping was a ploy too? Just like I did?' Briefly, she told him about thinking that she'd spotted her stepmother, and then what the note had said later, about cutting off one of Cordelia's fingers.

Jonah swore softly. 'No wonder you fainted that time,' he said softly. 'Poor baby.' He kissed the tip of her nose tenderly. 'But yes, Flloyd is pretty sure this Marcus Bolton character is in on it with her. He's a big crook around these parts — and she'd have needed a partner to help. Apparently they knew each other from way back in your stepmother's not so lily-white past.'

Tahnee shrugged. 'You know what? I don't care any more. It's over.' And she hugged him again, and kissed him, hard. Then laughed wildly, and kissed him again.

Jonah kissed her back, but reminded himself that this meant nothing. She was just euphoric and at the end of her tether, in need of a shoulder to lean on. Soon, soon she'd be gone, back to her fancy life in Florida.

And he'd be left alone.

★　★　★

Flloyd Turnbull had no idea where the courier was taking him as he turned off down a lonely road. But when the dip in the landscape revealed a single bungalow dwelling, its remote location alone told him it would be a good place to keep someone out of sight.

He and his team pulled off the road well

before they could be spotted, and were hunkered down flat on the ground, watching through binoculars, when the courier parked his jeep by the front door.

When the door opened it wasn't Bolton who answered, but a woman with red hair. Flloyd smiled. 'Well, hello, Cordelia,' he said softly. Then, into his walkie-talkie: 'OK, Tech. I want directional microphones on now. I want you to pick up and record every word.'

Cautiously, his team made their way down into the dell and surrounded the bungalow. And a minute later, a co-ordinated attack from front and rear brought all six members of the team into the bungalow's main living area.

Where Marcus Bolton sat rooted to the spot, his hand full of face cream and diamonds, his face darkening with anger and fear.

★ ★ ★

Delphine and Dylan left the station house later that evening, knowing that Marcus Bolton would no longer be a threat to them, and after having made sure that Inspector Brian Quincy would dance at their wedding.

As they walked out on to the teeming streets of the capital, holding hands and with their whole lives together stretching out ahead of them in glittering promise, Tahnee Sawyer closed her eyes wearily as the airliner she was on lifted into the dark night sky.

Below, Jonah Rodgers saw it take off, and watched it until even its winking lights were lost to the stars. Then, his heart like a stone in his chest, he turned his bike towards the marina.

★ ★ ★

A week later, Jonah was heading for port, a talkative and obsessive fisherman from Milwaukee needlessly guiding him towards his berth at the dock. The man, who'd had a good catch and was riding high, tipped him fifty bucks, and Jonah was just stuffing it gratefully into his back pocket when he glanced up to watch a very trim yacht surge into the harbour.

Ten million, he thought automatically, if not more, and grinned without envy. He never gave it another thought until he saw it getting closer and closer, and even closer. Strange, craft like that usually moored at the other end, in millionaires' row. He stopped washing down the deck, where the Milwaukee fisherman had cleaned his catch, and began to grin in delight as he realized the craft was actually going to berth right next to the *Whale*.

She was called the *Shooting Star* and Jonah tapped the side of the *Whale*'s wheelhouse as she docked. 'She might look flash, but she's not as beautiful as you, girl,' Jonah murmured encouragingly. He watched as an obviously professional crew set about securing the boat, then froze as a familiar figure appeared on her deck.

Tahnee looked down at him from the upper deck of the ritzy yacht and grinned. 'Hey down there. What's the weather like?'

Jonah swallowed hard, and grinned. 'Warmer than it is up there. I hear the air is thinner.'

Tahnee laughed delightedly, then turned, and smiled as a man joined her. For a moment, Jonah felt his heart plummet. But then he saw that the man was old, small, almost ill-looking. Then Tahnee reached across and kissed the top of his forehead before running lithely down the deck and disappearing from view.

The man on the *Shooting Star* leaned on the railing and looked down thoughtfully at Jonah Rodgers.

'This your boat, then?' Calvin Sawyer called down, looking over the vessel carefully. 'She seaworthy?'

Jonah patted his boat again, whispering to

her not to take offence. Landlubbers were notoriously ill-informed.

'She is,' he said firmly.

Calvin saw both the gesture and heard the note of pride in the young man's voice, and smiled. Tahnee had been right. He was in love with his boat. He only hoped he loved his daughter more — or there'd be trouble.

Just then, Jonah heard pounding feet, and turned to look as Tahnee ran towards him. She was dressed in a wrap-around pink skirt and silver lamé top. She was barefoot, her eyes sparkling. It made him catch his breath.

He wasn't sure he could cope with this. When she'd left, he'd actually heard his heart break. Now here she was, back again and mending it with just one dazzling smile. But when it broke again . . .

Then she threw herself into his arms, laughing. 'It's all right,' she said, into his ear, her breath warm against his skin. 'Dad's on the mend, and didn't even mind too much about Cordelia. I told him he needed a holiday to escape the hoo-hah back in Florida, and that I knew just where to come.'

Tahnee pulled away and grinned down into his beloved, rugged face. 'I had to rush to catch the plane that night, it was all a bit frantic. But I wanted to get back to break the news to Dad before he read it in the papers.'

Jonah sighed, dragging the air back into his lungs. 'Of course you did,' he said softly. So that's why she'd left so fast, with barely a word. But what happened when their holiday was over this time? When the press attention died down, and it was back to business as usual? Then he gave a mental headshake. What did it matter when she left again? For however long she stayed this time, he'd live for every moment.

Tahnee, unaware of his fatalistic thoughts, pulled out of his arms a little, but only so that she could twist around and look up at the yacht. 'Well, what do you think, Dad?' she called up to the man on the boat.

'About what? The boat or her captain?' Calvin called back teasingly, and Tahnee laughed.

'Both. Because I'll be spending all my time with both of them from now on.'

At this, Jonah made a small sound, one that saw her turn back to look at him quickly, a small worried frown drawing her pretty brows together. She said humbly, 'That is all right, isn't it? I haven't got it wrong? You do want me?'

And Jonah, unable to speak, simply folded her into his arms and held her tight.